SWEET

LISA HAHN

CONTENTS

Acknowledgements

Thanks to Don, Jonas, Cassie, Blueberry, Jackie, Mom, Megan, family, friends, and readers.

CHAPTER ONE

The tinkling of piano keys filtered through the humid air as every dancer in the high-ceilinged room dipped into his final curtsy or bow. When the last chord died down and all the dancers were again standing upright, the sounds of the piano were replaced with a respectful round of applause. The custom of a formal bow or curtsy followed by the clapping of hands at the end of class was known as reverence, and it was always one of Cat's favorite parts. Traditionally, reverence was an opportunity for dancers to show their gratitude toward their instructor and the pianist but Cat saw it as more than just that. It was a time for her to celebrate her hard work and reflect upon what she needed to improve.

It had been a good class. Cat felt strong and ready for the upcoming season, certain she was dancing better than ever due to the unusually long break they'd had over the summer. Bretton Falls Ballet was starting late that year because of the resignation of their former artistic director, Lillian Smith. Her husband's health was failing, and she'd begrudgingly left the company she loved to care for him. It had taken her months to find someone she thought would be a suitable replacement for herself, and the rumors floating around the studio were that the person she'd chosen would start soon.

Simon Clarke, the current assistant artistic director, and one of Cat's biggest supporters, swept into the room just as the applause began to wane.

"Listen up, everyone." He lifted his arm overhead in a willowy gesture that hinted at what a brilliant dancer he'd been. "*Nutcracker* rehearsals start tomorrow. The schedule and your roles are posted outside the locker room."

The studio fell eerily silent at his announcement.

Phoebe Braxton, one of the most talented dancers in the small company, and one who often got the most coveted roles, spoke up first.

"How can we put together a ballet without an artistic director? Are you assuming the position?"

The thought of Simon directing made Cat's heart sing. He'd wanted her to be promoted to a soloist position after her first year, but Lillian had always been adamant about Cat's place in the corps. So Cat continued to do her time as a backdrop for the soloists, and dreamed about progressing on her path from the corps to soloist to prestige, as a principal dancer.

"No." Simon shook his head, a few wisps of black hair falling into his eyes. He delicately brushed them aside before clasping his hands behind his back. "The new director starts today. His name is Dmitri Fedorov." He paused, smiling smugly as if he enjoyed dropping this bomb so unexpectedly. "You may know him from his illustrious career with American Ballet Theatre."

Cat's mouth fell agape. Dmitri Fedorov was considered one of the greatest dancers of their generation. Unfortunately, his career had been cut short in the middle of the previous season after a disastrous car accident mangled his left knee when the cab he'd been riding in collided with another vehicle. Dmitri disappeared after it had been revealed that he would never dance again, never so much as attending another ABT performance.

To top things off, Dmitri was widely considered to be one of the most gorgeous men on the face of the planet, even outside of the ballet world. He'd made his mark on the New York social scene, attracting beautiful and successful women other men coveted. And how could he not? Years of ballet had toned and sculpted his lean body to perfection. With his fair skin, piercing blue eyes, inky hair, and immaculate bone structure, Dmitri Fedorov looked like he'd walked right off a billboard.

"How were we cast if Mr. Fedorov has never watched us dance?" Phoebe crossed her arms over her slight chest.

"On the contrary, Miss Braxton. Dmitri has been poring over last year's rehearsal and performance footage." He adjusted the purple silk scarf around his neck. "Any other questions?"

A few people shook their heads but no one responded. Cat assumed that after the initial shock died down, everyone was champing at the bit to see the cast list. At least, that was how she felt. *The Nutcracker* wasn't the most exciting ballet to perform, especially since they did it every year. However, a new artistic director might breathe new life into the old classic.

"Very well, then." Simon held up a hand in farewell. "Be ready for rehearsals tomorrow. I'll be in my office if you need me."

Once he exited the room, the dancers came alive with buzzing whispers and the exchange of gossip. Surely they wanted to share some story they'd heard about Dmitri Fedorov's infamous womanizing, and some were trying to predict who'd landed what role.

Abby, Cat's closest friend and a soloist in the company, rushed over to where Cat stretched out her right leg on the barre. "Can you believe it?" Her cute, round cheeks were pink from exertion. "Dmitri Fedorov is our new director. It's crazy."

"Almost too crazy." Cat pinched the skin on her thigh before sliding into a split with her left leg still on the polished wood barre. "It feels like I'm dreaming."

Abby sank to the floor, hiked up her pink leg warmers, and started untying her pointe shoe ribbons. "Well, you're just glad Lillian is finally gone."

"Abby!" Cat planted both feet on the ground and playfully swatted at her friend's shoulder. "That's awful."

"I didn't say you're happy her husband got sick." Abby shrugged with one shoe in her hand. "But we both know how much she held you back."

Even though she'd been with the company for six years, Cat hadn't advanced past the corps. Lillian preferred taller, sylphlike dancers. At five-foot-two, Cat was not her cup of tea. However, Lillian's personal preferences never deterred Cat from trying her hardest during every class, rehearsal, and performance, certain her work would eventually pay off. She didn't always have a go-getter attitude, though. After high school and a round of disappointing rejections from the bigger companies around the country, Cat had slinked off to the Bretton Falls Ballet, a company she'd performed with as an apprentice during her youth, hoping to hone her skills for her auditions the following season. Unfortunately, Lillian's immediate and constant criticism of her work had done a number on her confidence. It had taken Cat a few years to believe in herself again. By then, she was too old to be considered by the major companies she'd always dreamed of dancing for.

"It's true." Cat reached out a hand for Abby, pulling her much taller friend to stand. "Let's go see what we got."

By that point, everyone had filtered out to view the cast listing.

"It feels good to be out of these shoes," Abby said, smoothing a hand over her pale blond hair. "I swear, sometimes my tolerance is higher for this stuff on other days."

Cat wrapped her arm around Abby's waist as they walked. "Nothing feels better than the first few seconds your feet are free from your pointe shoes. It's total nirvana."

"If that isn't the truth." Abby slung her arm over her Cat's shoulders as they entered the hall.

Cat instantly sensed something was awry. The usual excitement that followed a casting announcement had been replaced with a weird energy. No one rejoiced over the part they'd been assigned, and no one wept for the role that had slipped through their fingers. Instead, everyone had broken off into their little cliques and were whispering among themselves.

Almost all of them gathered in the crowded, yet oddly hushed white-walled hallway shot darting glances in Cat's and Abby's direction as they approached.

Abby leaned in and whispered in Cat's ear. "Did we do something wrong?"

"Not that I know of." Since Bretton Falls Ballet was a relatively small company, there weren't many dancers from around the world clamoring to join its underpaid and overworked ranks. Instead, the company was comprised mostly of former students of the Bretton Falls School of Ballet and other local studios. Occasionally, dancers from other states and even other countries would show up at auditions, but they were a rarity. Because of this, many of the company's members had grown up training together and many of the cliques they'd formed in adolescence remained. Cat and Abby stuck together, but for the most part they were friendly with everyone. None of the other dancers had any reason to feel threatened by either of them. Under Lillian's direction, Cat was never going to get a big role, and Lillian considered Abby far too immature to make it past her rank as a soloist despite her undeniable talent.

"Seriously." Abby tugged on Cat's arm and brought her to a stop. "Something's up."

"It's probably nothing," Cat said to convince herself as much as Abby that everything was fine. "Plus, I want to see if I've been upgraded from the role of party guest." With Lillian gone, Cat genuinely hoped there was a chance Simon had sung her praises to the new director, who'd then give her a better role.

She grabbed Abby by the hand and weaved in and out of small groups of dancers to the list pinned on the wall. Cat started searching for her name at the bottom and worked her way up, the same way she always did. Pleased to see she wasn't listed as a party guest, she continued to scan the list. She went through the pas de deux parts, the duets that were performed in the Land of Sweets segment of the second act, and didn't see her name there, either. Dejected, she scanned up, feeling more and more worried that she might not have even made the cut. Maybe the new director was even more prejudiced against short dancers than Lillian.

"Oh my god," Abby squealed beside her. "Cat, you're Clara!"

"What?" Cat immediately looked to the top of the cast list to the lead role. Sure enough, her name was written right beside it.

Clara: Catherine Brown

"Holy shit."

The hallway had gone silent somewhere between her stepping up to the cast list and the moment she'd realized she was no longer being relegated to the periphery.

Every company staged *The Nutcracker* differently. Some cast children in the roles of Clara and the Prince, not once suggesting an inkling of romantic interest between them. Other companies used their adult performers to fill the lead roles, playing on the attraction between the two. Lillian always gravitated toward the romantic and produced a *Nutcracker* that one notable reviewer had sarcastically referred to as "the greatest love story ever told."

Because of the ambiguity surrounding Clara's age and the minimal time she spent dancing during the two-act ballet, it wasn't a coveted role.

But it was a lead role and it was Cat's first.

She felt a hand on her right shoulder. At thirty-two, Marcy Gray was one of the oldest members of the company and a highly-regarded principal dancer.

"Good luck." Her deadpan delivery and lifted chin told Cat Marcy didn't mean what she said. "You're going to need it. Dmitri Fedorov is notoriously hard to please. Just ask anyone he partnered with at ABT."

"Thanks," Cat said sharply with a fake smile. She might have only been a member of the corps, but that didn't mean she was going to let mean girls like Marcy get into her head and mess up this opportunity for her.

Turning her back to Marcy, Cat faced Abby. "I'm going to talk to Simon."

"Call me later, okay?" Abby was too excited for her hardworking friend to pick up on Marcy's icy and insincere regards. "We need to plan what you'll wear to the first day of rehearsal."

"Talk then." Cat gave Abby a quick hug then started off in the direction of Simon's office, fighting the urge to break into a light jog. It probably wouldn't have been a wise choice, being that she was still wearing her pointe shoes. Cat knew she knocked too loudly at his office door, but her enthusiasm for her new role was proving to be difficult to contain.

"Come on in," Simon said in the floating, sing-song voice.

She burst through the door but then gently shut it behind her, not wanting to cause a scene. For all she knew, everyone could have been watching her rush down the hallway.

"You knew about this, didn't you?" She pressed her hands to her heated cheeks, smiling wide.

Simon sat back in his rolling chair, crossed his ankle over his knee, and grinned. "You're a beautiful dancer, Catherine. It was only a matter of time until the right person noticed."

"Did you have anything to do with this?" Simon had been insisting Lillian pay more attention to Cat for years, so she shouldn't be surprised that he had put in a good word for her with the new director.

"Not at all." Simon held up his hands defensively. "Dmitri is quite taken with you. If *The Nutcracker* goes well, I except you'll be promoted to soloist next season."

Cat began to pace the small room, unable to stand still. "I can't believe this is finally happening." She held her pointer finger and thumb together like she was squishing something tiny between them. "I was this close to giving up hope."

"It won't be easy. I've spent several hours watching tape with Dmitri and he has an eagle's eye for form and technique. He'll be expecting a lot from you." Cat stopped pacing and turned to him with a frown between her eyebrows. "But I'm certain you're up to the task," he continued quickly, noticing her nervous look. You're a woman with something to prove. If I know you, you'll work your tail off to be the best damn Clara Bretton Falls Ballet has ever seen."

Feeling invigorated by the opportunity and Simon's faith in her, Cat wished rehearsal would be starting that afternoon. She had such a burning desire to dance that it was making it hard to stand in one place.

"I'm going to nail this shit," she quipped, nodding confidently.

A sharp knock sounded and before Simon could respond, Dmitri Fedorov stepped into the room with a commanding presence. He walked right past Cat as if she wasn't even there. Normally, she'd be worried if the artistic director entered a room and didn't acknowledge her. But this time, she wasn't so concerned. It gave her the perfect opportunity to gawk at his tight ass in his worn jeans.

"How did everything go?" he asked in a deep, gravelly voice, forgoing a formal greeting or pleasantries.

"Well enough." Simon sat up straighter in his chair. A ballet god like Dmitri Fedorov wasn't someone to be casual with, even if you were an assistant artistic director with a decent career of your own. "They're pleased to have you on board, and they're anxious to start their season."

Dmitri rested his cane against his leg and rubbed his palms together. "Hopefully they're as eager to start as I am."

"I'm sure they are." Simon motioned to where Cat stood behind him. "In fact, Catherine came by to tell me how excited she is to tackle the role of Clara."

At the mention of her name, Cat pried her eyes away from her new boss's derrière just in time for him to turn around and face her. While she was careful to hide her appraisal of his body, Dmitri was not as shy. His gaze raked over Cat, examining her from the blunt tips of her pointe shoes to her brown hair wound into a neat bun. Self-consciously, she tugged at her powder blue wrap sweater.

She swallowed hard, feeling faint under his intense perusal.

"This *Nutcracker* is a very important show for me. It's the start of my new career and my chance to prove myself." He took a few steps toward her, stopping only a few inches from where she stood. "I'm counting on you."

She wasn't sure why Dmitri sized her up and remarked the way he did. The only thing about Dmitri Fedorov she was sure about was how handsome the man was in person. She'd seen him before in photographs and videos, and naturally she'd found him attractive. With his shoulder-length dark hair, intense blue eyes, and lean physique, how could she not? The way he carried himself was riveting. He was all confidence and impeccable posture. She looked to Simon. He'd already reclined back in his chair and brought his faded San Francisco Ballet coffee mug to his lips.

Rather than reveal that Dmitri had caught her off guard, she decided to play it cool. "He's a little intense, huh?" she asked, hooking her thumb toward the door.

"His parents were both dancers, so he grew up in this world." Simon waved a hand over his head, gesturing toward the playbills and photographs crowding the walls. "I hardly expected him to be normal," he said, chuckling.

Cat lifted one shoulder. "I guess."

"Don't let him intimidate you." She should have known Simon would figure out she was trying to hide the dizzying effect Dmitri had had on her. Simon had been with the company since she started dancing at its school, and he'd quickly become an honorary uncle. "He wouldn't have cast you in the role if he didn't think you could handle it. Like he said, it's an important moment in his career. He wouldn't have risked it."

She gave him a firm nod. "You're right."

"Besides," he added as got up and rounded his desk, placing a hand on her shoulder. "It's not like you were cast in the leading role of *Swan Lake*. Clara should be a piece of cake."

Lisa Hahn

CHAPTER TWO

When Cat opened the back door into the kitchen of the Land of Sweets, her mother was standing at the stainless-steel commercial stove, stirring in the top of a double boiler. She had a hot-pink, chocolate-splattered apron tied at her waist and her short brown hair was pulled off her face with a wide black headband. She tapped her foot on the blue laminate floor while she stirred, likely thinking of the next ten things she had to do. As the owner of the candy shop, she always had a growing to-do list. Cat had learned everything she knew about hard work from Louise; she just happened to have a tad more patience than her mother did.

"Hi, Mom," Cat sang out as she shut the door and hung her purse and scarf up on a hook, giving her mom a big grin.

Louise glanced up at the old, analog clock on the wall. "You're late. I started to worry."

"I'm sorry. I stayed a little late to talk to Simon," she shivered, glad that she made the decision to keep her red hoodie on. Her mom always kept the place cool to prevent the chocolates from melting. "I actually have some exciting news."

"So do I." With a nod of her head, she motioned toward a pile of leaf-shaped molds laying on a nearby countertop. "Grab those for me and we'll talk while I pour this mint chocolate."

Cat retrieved the molds and set them on the large table in the center of the room. "So, who's going to go first?" She plopped down on a stool.

"You first." Louise smiled in the loving, motherly way that made Cat feel safe and supported even at twenty-four years old. "Judging from the grin that's on your face, I'm guessing you have very, very good news."

"Okay. Backstory first." Cat slapped her hands onto the cool steel surface of the table. "We have a new director. It's Dmitri Fedorov."

In the middle of painstakingly pouring the chocolate into one of leaf shapes, Louise stopped and snapped her head up to look at her daughter with wide eyes. "*The* Dmitri Fedorov?"

Louise was familiar with all things ballet. Though she'd never even as

11

much as slid her own feet into a pair of pink slippers, she knew all the French terminology and the names of the best dancers, past and present. Dmitri Fedorov was one of those dancers.

"The one and only. And he's diving right in. We start *Nutcracker* rehearsals tomorrow." Cat paused for dramatic effect, her smile growing so wide she thought her cheeks might split. "And he picked me to play Clara."

Louise unceremoniously dropped the pot of chocolate so close to the molds it nearly landed on them, then rounded the table and threw her arms around her daughter's neck. "I'm so proud of you, Catherine. I knew this day would come."

"Thanks, Mom." Cat nestled in her mother's embrace, feeling her support, and enjoying the hug for a few seconds. "Now what's your good news?"

Louise pulled away and waved off her daughter's question as she returned to the task of pouring chocolate. "It's nothing." Her eyes avoided direct contact.

Cat dropped her head to the side, amusement twinkling in her eyes. *Louise has always downplayed her own triumphs.* "No way. Tell me."

"Now's not a good time."

"Please," Cat begged. "C'mon. Tell me."

"Oh, all right." Louise picked up a rag and dabbed it along the edge of her candy molds. "An old bakery in Saratoga is closing its doors. I've had my eye on the property for years, and I've always adored the location. It's right in the center of town on Main Street."

"You're moving the shop there?" Saratoga Springs was only a thirty-minute drive from Bretton Falls, but it would still mean a lot of changes for their little family. It would be harder for Cat to make it to her shifts after rehearsals, and it would mean her sisters wouldn't be able walk to the store from school anymore.

"Not exactly." Louise returned to the task of pouring chocolate, peeking up occasionally to make eye contact with her daughter. "Saratoga would be my second location, so I would need to find a second-in-command to help me out up there." She paused, stopping to wipe another drip. "I thought you might consider the job, before I heard all about your good news, that is."

If things had continued going the way they were, it probably would have been a perfect opportunity for Cat to retire from dance and start a new career. As a member of the small company's corps, Cat barely made enough money to cover her bills. As a store manager, she could finally start paying her mom back for all the money she'd put into her dancing.

Louise reached over and patted Cat's hand. "Don't worry. I'm not telling you to quit the company and take this job. Just know that it's available if you want it. If you can really wow Dmitri Fedorov, maybe he can promote you within the company. That would be my preference, and I know it would be yours too."

For Cat, landing this role was just the beginning. Soon she'd dance the roles she'd always dreamed off, climb the ladder at the company, and impress the directors of even larger companies. She never once considered this production of *The Nutcracker* would be her swan song, even when she'd thought she would merely be a party guest in the first act, as always.

Still, she had to weigh the benefits of continuing with Bretton Falls Ballet. Her dancing had been a source of financial hardship for the Brown family for years. A second Land of Sweets shop would pull in money Louise could put into her younger daughters' college funds. As things stood, Grace and Elise hoped loans and scholarships would finance their higher educations. After all the sacrifices Cat's family made for her, shouldn't she be willing to make one for them? She'd spent six years as one of the lowest ranked dancers in one of the country's lesser-known ballet companies. Maybe if this production didn't lead to bigger and better things, Cat should take the managerial position.

Shuffling toward the fridge with the plastic molds in hand, Louise said, "Just consider it, Catherine, but don't let my offer distract you from your new role. Dancing is what's most important until you decide it isn't anymore." She tipped her chin toward the row of crisp, white aprons by the door into the shop and winked. "In the meantime, I need you out front. Store opens in five."

Cat pulled an apron off its peg and slid the top loop over her neck, looking toward her mom as she knotted two strings at her lower back. "I'll think about it, Mom. I promise."

Louise, who had been kneeling to slide her mint chocolates into the fridge, stood, and gave Cat a supportive nod. "You're a smart woman. I know you'll do what's best."

Cat pushed through the swinging door and entered the storefront. Other than the studio, the Land of Sweets was her happy place. Bright colors lined the walls in uneven, candy-cane stripes. Scents of chocolate and caramel filled the air. Since she was either on stage or in the studio every day wearing skintight clothing, Cat rarely ate any of her mom's candy, but that didn't mean she couldn't enjoy the aroma. Louise had made it a point to hire dancers from the company and the school to work in the store, so Cat was always surrounded by her people. A food reviewer once commented that the Land of Sweets felt like Bretton Falls Ballet's satellite location, what with all the waif-like girls working behind the counter. Perhaps managing another candy shop would be a natural progression for her. After all, she'd been helping her mother in the kitchen since middle school. Ensuring the day-to-day operations of the store went smoothly would be second-nature.

The caveat was that she wasn't passionate about the Land of Sweets like she was about dancing. She'd dreamed of being a ballerina for as long as she could remember. So many people grieved the loss of unrealized dreams that it seemed like a waste to throw hers away, especially right after Dmitri Fedorov waltzed into her life and handed her a part that should have gone to a principal member of the company. She owed it to herself, and her mother, to see this opportunity through before she made any decisions about the second Land of Sweets.

It meant everything to her that a dancer of Dmitri's caliber had plucked her from a sea of ambitious corps ballerinas and inserted her in the starring role in his very first ballet as artistic director. She recalled the way his gaze had roamed over her body earlier. Initially, she'd assumed he was sizing her up as a ballerina, admiring her thin limbs, swan-like neck, and narrow waist. But he would have already noted those things from the video he'd watched. Otherwise, he wouldn't have cast her as Clara in the first place. Now that she was away from the studio, her initial excitement fading over *The Nutcracker* casting, she was free to daydream as much as she liked. And in her daydreams, Dmitri Fedorov *wanted* her.

The idea wasn't farfetched. Dmitri was well-known in the ballet community for his flirtatious interactions and post-performance dalliances with other dancers or hangers-on. Due to his appearance on several high-fashion magazine covers, his reach spanned beyond the American Ballet Theatre community and into New York City's social scene. He'd only been a few hook-ups with the rich and famous away from becoming a household name before his accident.

Maybe after their last *Nutcracker* performance, Dmitri would sweep her into a vacant changing room and make love to her in a way that was far more meaningful than it had been with any of his amours in the past. He'd coo her name in her ear, promising to give her the world.

If she did decide to take her mom up on her offer, *that* would be one hell of a way to go out.

CHAPTER THREE

Dmitri's phone buzzed as soon as he walked through the front door of his apartment. To avoid his parents' calls, he'd taken to turning the damn thing off when he was at work. He didn't want to deal with their nagging while he was on the job, but he couldn't ignore them altogether. Even though most of their conversations were about the city and the company he'd left behind, he knew they were worried about him. How could they not be? He'd left NYC a broken man. No matter how hard he tried to go without it, he walked with a cane now, and he had the disposition of a hornet whose nest just got knocked down.

He shut the door behind him and then leaned his weight into the cane as he reached back to pull his phone from his pocket. There was no need to check the caller ID. His parents were the only ones who called him anymore. He'd scared everyone else away.

"Hello."

"Dmitri, why don't you answer the phone for your mother? I've been calling you all day," Constance Fedorov complained in her scratchy used-to-smoke-too-many-cigarettes voice.

Dmitri never understood how she had the lung capacity to perform some of the most intricate and challenging roles the American Ballet Theatre had ever seen, all while smoking a pack or two a day.

"I turn my phone off at work."

"Why?"

He squeezed the rounded top of his cane so hard that his knuckles turned white. "Because I need to get things done while I'm there."

Much needed to be done to ensure a successful *Nutcracker*. In the interest of time, Dmitri would keep many of the props, sets, and orchestral arrangements Lillian had used in her holiday productions over the years. However, he didn't want his first foray into direction to come across as a step-by-step carbon copy of Lillian's work. He wanted to do something fresh. Something that was his.

"I wish you'd call more often. Your father and I miss you." He could hear the sadness in her voice, softening her old Bostonian accent.

Dmitri walked into his living room and sank down into his favorite plush brown recliner; it was one of the few things he hadn't left behind in New York. He'd wanted to throw out his dance memorabilia and the expensive things he'd bought, but his parents wouldn't hear it. They'd had everything put in a storage unit a few blocks from their apartment.

"I've only been gone a couple of weeks, and we talk almost every day."

She sighed. "I know. I just don't understand why you left. I know you can't dance anymore, but there was still so much for you to do with ABT."

Dmitri winced when she mentioned his disability. The throbbing in his knee was a constant reminder he'd never step on stage again, but it was still difficult to hear. He'd eaten, slept, and breathed ballet ever since he was old enough for his parents to enroll him in class. As the only child of two highly regarded professional dancers, it had been his destiny to continue his family's legacy. He had for over a decade, and he was sure they were the best years of his life. Until that life got stripped away.

"I don't want to be in New York." Being there reminded him of what had happened. He couldn't get in a cab anymore without watching the driver with the diligence of a standardized test proctor. Was he driving safe? Yielding when necessary? Stopping at red lights? It also didn't help that the site of the accident was only a block from the ABT rehearsal space.

"But why not? Your family and your friends are here. You could have a job, too. You know the company will take you on as an instructor and possibly as a choreographer later if you demonstrate a capacity for it."

It was his turn to sigh into the receiver. "I have a job here."

Dmitri knew he could have stayed in the city and worked alongside his parents at ABT. His family had been involved with the company for decades. As soon as the people in charge learned of his forced retirement from performance, they'd offered him a teaching position at the school.

But he didn't want that. Dmitri had spent his whole life up until his accident following in his parents' footsteps, living the life they'd wanted for him. And he'd been perfectly content. Dmitri loved his craft and his family. But something inside him changed the day he'd found out that his dance career was over. Now he despised the spotlight. If he stayed at ABT, his and his parents' legacies would follow him around everywhere he went. In Bretton Falls, he could have a fresh start. Or as fresh of a start as he could possibly hope for.

"You could have a better job here," she argued.

"I have complete creative control over an entire company. That would never be the case if I stayed in the city." It was true. ABT would pay him well, but there would always be people vying for the coveted artistic director position.

"Is it even worth it? How good could the dancers there be?"

Immediately, Catherine Brown came to mind. Despite having performed with the greatest dancers of his time, there was something about the way she moved that made it impossible to peel his eyes away from her. With her short stature and athletic style, she was a firecracker on stage. He had no idea how Lillian Smith had managed to hide her in the corps for so many years. Especially with that smile. When her lips curled up and her pretty green eyes shone, it was like a spotlight illuminated her. Cat was undeniably gorgeous, a characteristic that would make it difficult for Dmitri to work with her. Even though he hadn't been with a woman since his accident, he found himself drawn to the pint-size woman with the killer smile and the unquestionable talent.

According to Simon, who'd known Cat since she was a girl, she'd auditioned for other companies right after high school but never had any luck. After a few disappointments, she'd opted to stay with Bretton Falls, hoping to advance there. Now, at age twenty-four, she was just as good as many of the ballerinas at ABT. He wasn't going to tell her that, though. He needed her in Bretton Falls.

"There are many good dancers here. Of course, most of them aren't the caliber we're used to working with, but they're all competent." He cringed as soon as the word came out of his mouth. It wasn't the most flattering way to describe his company, and he knew his mom was looking for every opportunity to dissuade him from staying.

"Competent? How about ethereal, inspiring, dynamic, passionate? Dancers with those qualities are who you should be working with."

"We have plenty of ethereal, inspiring, dynamic, and passionate dancers here. Come out and see for yourself sometime."

Dmitri made the offer only because he knew she would never take it. ABT's season was in full swing, and his parents were far too dedicated to the company to travel upstate for a few days. Also, it had been years since they'd left the city. Before now, they'd had no reason to. Their whole life was there.

"You know I can't right now. Your father and I are always at the studio."

"I'll be sure to send you a recording of the final production, then."

She blew out a heavy breath, and Dmitri knew that now she was pressing her skinny fingers to her temples. It was what she always did when he frustrated her. He nearly smiled at the mental picture, almost missing the way things used to be.

"I'm sorry, but I have to go. My landlord is stopping over with a document for me to sign." It was a lie, but Dmitri didn't want to continue the conversation. He was tired of talking in circles, unsuccessfully defending his choices.

"Okay, dear." Her tone grew softer and sentimental, like it did every time he ended one of their calls. "Please give me a call tomorrow. I want to know you're okay."

He was fine. Different, irritable, and likely a bit depressed, but fine.

"Everything is okay. I promise."

"Say you'll call tomorrow."

"I'll call tomorrow."

"You're a good boy, Dmitri. I know you'll come to your senses."

Boy. She'd always thought of him as her little boy, even when the halls at ABT were abuzz with his latest conquests and late-night adventures. It was why she was having such a difficult time with his departure. She needed to let go and accept that at thirty-two years old he could make his own decisions.

"Talk to you tomorrow," he said in the nicest tone he could muster before ending the call. He dropped the phone in his lap before scrubbing his hands over his face, trying not to let his temper boil over. While he had been known to get a little bit testy when things weren't going the way he wanted them to during a rehearsal, Dmitri was much easier to set off after the accident. He couldn't help but live in the permanent state of residual anger.

Slowly, he extended and bent his knee a few times, hoping to relieve some of the stiffness. He cursed himself for the times he'd left his cane propped up against his desk when he refilled his coffee mug or retrieved something from the printer. He'd refused to be dependent on the varnished piece of wood, to the point where he'd aggravated the injury since he'd arrived in Bretton Falls. A quiet burn throbbed in his knee, imploring him to always favor his bum leg.

Heeding the warning, Dmitri braced his cane on the hardwood floor and pushed to stand. He limped to the kitchen, where he pulled a tumbler from the cabinet. He turned it over in his hand a few times, considering its size before swapping it out for a larger glass. He filled it with ice before pouring in several shots of vodka, and then he took a sip of his dinner.

He'd probably order food at some point, but he wasn't hungry quite yet. Ever since regular performance and long days at the studio had become a thing of Dmitri's past, he'd spent most nights camped out on the couch watching whatever he could find on TV. A lifetime of dedication to ballet had made it impossible for him to follow the sitcoms, movies, and TV dramas. He justified his nightly veg fests as an opportunity to make up for his deficit in pop culture knowledge, not a way of shutting out the world that once consumed him.

Dmitri had different plans for that night. *Nutcracker* rehearsals were to start the next day, and he wanted to make sure that he was ready to officially assume the role of artistic director. He'd already been working there for a few weeks, but he hadn't yet interacted with his dancers. He needed them to respect, trust, and fear him all at once, a feat all his previous directors at ABT had achieved with gusto. He sat down at a small desk tucked away in the corner of his dark living room and flicked on a small, red-shaded lamp. He put his glass down and lifted his laptop cover, clicking on the media player. After pressing play on the opening overture, Dmitri closed his eyes and visualized the choreography he'd teach tomorrow.

Lisa Hahn

CHAPTER FOUR

After their daily technique class, the cast to stayed in the main studio to work on the opening choreography. Everyone involved stretched their muscles, sipped water, and whispered among themselves about what they thought it would be like to work with Dmitri Fedorov.

As they all soon found out, it wasn't an entirely pleasant experience. Dmitri was a hard taskmaster. His choreography was more nuanced than Lillian's and everyone struggled to pick it up. The pianist hadn't played more than six straight bars of music in a full hour and a half. Someone would falter or forget a step, and with a sweep of his arm, Dmitri would bang his cane against the floor before yelling, "Again!"

Cat was exhausted. And parched. There were times in the final hours before a show where Lillian would work her dancers harder than usual if she had a bad feeling about a scene or string of choreography, and Cat had hated it. The over-rehearsal only amped up the dancers' nerves and Lillian's frustration. This was different. While she was tired and thirsty, she didn't mind putting in the hard work for Dmitri. Maybe it was because she wanted to impress him, or maybe it was because of the way his eyes flared with passion as he tried to impart his vision to the group.

She shook the thought of Dmitri's passion from her head. If she let herself cross that line, if she let herself see him as anything more than the new artistic director, she could mess up the opportunity he'd given her. She needed to focus on her dancing, not on how much she wanted her new boss.

"One more time." Dmitri waved his arm overhead in a circular motion, signaling for everyone to take their places.

Cat quickly made her way to her starting point. She certainly felt more pressure now than during rehearsals last season, but she also felt more motivated. It was her opportunity to prove that she deserved a place at the top of the company. And, now that she'd talked to her mom, she knew it that it might be her last chance to do so.

Taking a deep breath as the pianist played the opening bars of the overture, she prepared to move flawlessly through the next few minutes of choreography. She was determined to not be the reason Dmitri stopped the group and made everyone start over. With a group of dancers around her, she gestured animatedly like they were playing a game and enjoying the Christmas Eve festivities. It would be one of the few instances in the first act where she would not be the center of attention.

Out of the corner of her eye, she glanced at Dmitri and her heartbeat increased. He'd tugged a hand through his hair, pulling it off his face and revealing his impeccable bone structure. Cat knew from photos and footage she'd seen of his dancing that his body was just as beautifully etched. Or at least it had been before his accident. Currently, he had on a loose-fitting black tee that exposed his still-powerful arms.

Dammit. She turned her focus fiercely on the task at hand: pretending to play make-believe with a slew of other grown-up women. When the pianist stopped, the dancers waited with bated breath, looking to their director to see if he was pleased by their performance.

It was difficult to tell. Dmitri's expression was stoic, his features hard. He glanced up at the raised ceiling like he was gathering his thoughts, waiting a few beats to speak.

"Very well. Break for twenty minutes and then reconvene here. Simon will run through everything with you and work to clean it up. Clara and Prince, we'll be in Studio B."

With that, he turned and left the room. No insight on what needed work. No praise for moves executed well. Just cool indifference.

Cat straightened her shoulders even though she desperately wanted to slump from exhaustion. It had been several months since any of the dancers had taken part in a day-long rehearsal, and it showed. Everyone's chests heaved more than normal, and they all raced to gulp down the water years of training had taught them only to sip, to avoid upset stomachs. But Cat refused to let her fatigue show. If she and Nick, the dancer playing the Prince, had to work with Dmitri alone, she planned to reinforce his decision in casting her as his lead.

After retrieving her things from along the front mirror, Cat walked back to the pale yellow-tiled locker room. There Abby was resting on a bench, a pair of baggy gray sweatpants pulled up over her royal blue leotard.

"Thank god you're finally here," she moaned, pressing a hand to her taut stomach. "I'm starving. We haven't done this in a while."

"Tell me about it." Cat sat alongside Abby and began unlacing her pointe shoes to give her aching feet a break. "I'm going to need to sit in an ice bath tonight. How was your Arabian rehearsal?"

Abby had been chosen to perform one of the many partnered dances at the beginning of the second act. In honor to celebrate their heroism in her triumph the Mouse King, the Sugar Plum Fairy arranges for Clara and the Prince to indulge in sweets on a throne while enjoying a show put on by everyone in the court. The Arabian was less than three minutes long, but the slow, languid, and unusual music was a pleasant contrast to the rest of the arrangements. That, along with eye-catching blue and gold costumes, helped the pas de deux stand out. It had long been one of Cat's favorites. If she hadn't been cast in the lead role, she'd be jealous of her friend.

Abby reclined on the bench and pressed the back of her hand to her forehead in a display of mock weariness. "Draining. I've never seen so much pointe work in an Arabian, and Simon only gave us a half of the choreography."

"I'm definitely going to stop at the pharmacy on my way home to pick up some Epsom salt." Cat sighed, placing a pointe shoe on her bag instead of inside of it. It was best to let them air out.

Abby sat up onto her elbows, her face brightening. "A bath sounds awesome right now."

"Just a few more hours." Cat slid on a pair of unattractively large and bulky slippers. A lot of the dancers wore them between rehearsals to keep their feet warm. "Nick and I have a private session with Dmitri next."

"Really?" Abby raised an eyebrow. "It's your chance to impress him," she added, with a suggestive lilt in her voice.

"I plan to." Throughout the earlier rehearsal, Dmitri had nitpicked every little thing the dancers did, but offered no direct criticism for Cat, like he had for so many of the others. She felt confident in her abilities and excited to show off in front of the new man in charge. The prospect of having his full attention was daunting, but she was more than willing to take on the challenge.

The two friends split a banana and chatted about the choreography they'd learned so far. Cat filled Abby in on her mom's new business venture and the opportunity she had to manage the second Land of Sweets. As always, Abby was nothing but optimistic, claiming Cat would do so well as Clara that she wouldn't even have to think about hanging up her pointe shoes again after the opening night performance.

After their break, many of the other dancers came back into the locker room to lace up their shoes for round two of rehearsal. Before she headed out, Cat traded her sweater knit black shorts for a floral wraparound chiffon skirt she'd made herself. In what little spare time she had, she designed skirts and leotards for her and Abby to wear in class. Cat always thought the fact that she chose to spend her time away from the studio designing outfits to wear the next time she went back was proof of her love for her discipline.

Skirts often made it easier for the director to observe the lines of the body, hence her switch from shorts. She also knew, by the way she often caught the male members of the company checking out her out when she wore the black and pink floral wraparound, that it had a flattering fit. As Cat tied the ribbons into a bow behind her back, she told herself that didn't matter. She didn't hope to impress anyone. At least not with her body.

When she walked into Studio B, Dmitri was already there. Sitting in a folding chair, he had one ankle crossed over his opposite knee and his cane resting on top of his legs. He looked up as soon as the wooden door clicked shut behind her, shaking his head with apparent frustration.

"Where's the Prince?" he asked in a monotone voice.

Cat glanced at the door and then back at Dmitri. "I don't know. He's probably in the men's locker room getting ready. I didn't see him out in the hall."

His gaze shifted up to the clock on the wall. "It's two o'clock. Time to start." Dmitri's mouth formed a firm, impassive line as Cat wondered what exactly he wanted her to do about Nick's lateness. The two dancers had never been especially close. Nick had joined the company when Cat was in middle school and had long been one of the high-ranking dancers that refused to fraternize with the underlings in the corps. Part of her wondered if his lateness was a silent protest over having to partner her.

"Sorry." There was a hint of a question in her tone. "I'm sure he'll be here soon."

Cat placed her bag against the wall and approached her director. "I just wanted to say how excited I am to work with you. I always enjoyed what you did with ABT."

Dmitri looked up at her, seeming disinterested in her opinion. Several seconds passed before he spoke, making her want to squirm.

"Thank you."

As soon as Dmitri's curt reply rolled off his tongue, Nick causally entered the room with a black bag slung over his slender shoulder. "Sorry I'm late. I left to run a couple of errands and lost track of time."

He dropped his stuff beside Cat's and she could have sworn his upper lip curled as soon as he saw her. Tilting her chin up defiantly, she ignored his silent scorn. She wasn't going to let him or anyone else make her feel unworthy.

Dmitri switched the cross of his legs and leaned back into his chair. "I don't know how Lillian used to run things, but lateness is unacceptable as far as I'm concerned." He swept his arm toward Cat. "She was here on time."

Cat bit back a smile as Nick's brown eyes widened with remorse.

"I'm sorry, sir. I promise it won't happen again."

"It better not." Dmitri stood, motioning for the two dancers to meet him in the center of the room. He spent the next several minutes showing them the first bit of choreography for their pas de deux in the opening act. There were a lot of lifts, which excited Cat. She'd trained in partner work but never had a chance to exercise those abilities in the corps. Due to her small size, Nick could lift her with ease. She thought they were executing everything well, given they were only learning the choreography, but Dmitri was displeased. He slammed the end of his cane to the ground every time they did something he did not like, which meant they heard the beating of wood on wood every few seconds.

Near the end of the day, the two dancers were performing a difficult lift, which required Nick to lift Cat up overhead in a picture-perfect arabesque. While in the air, Cat's chest pitched forward as she struggled to clench the muscles in her back that would help her stay upright. She faltered and squirmed, nearly losing control of her position altogether when Dmitri threw his cane to the floor, startling Nick. His hands slipped from Cat's torso, but he recovered in time to catch her around the waist before she tumbled to the ground.

Dmitri retrieved his cane and stomped over to them with an obvious limp. Even with his uneven cadence, he walked in a purposeful, masculine way that made Cat forget that she'd nearly fallen.

"Have either of you ever done an arabesque lift before?" His voice was tepid and laced with disappointment.

Cat kept her gaze glued to Dmitri and her mouth shut, assuming he'd asked a rhetorical question.

Nick chose a different approach. "Sorry, sir. As a member of the corps, Catherine didn't practice lifts very often. I had a difficult time holding her because she was squirming." He cast a dismissive look in her direction. "It will probably take some practice to get it right."

Dmitri pursed his lips. "So you're saying it was her fault?"

"I mean, sort of." Nick brushed a hand over his close-cropped dark hair, looking uncomfortable. "Like I said, she just isn't used to doing arabesque lifts. I'm sure she'll get it, though."

Dmitri stepped toward Nick, closing the distance between them and leaving Cat on the periphery of their conversation, a place she was perfectly content to be. Judging by his narrowed eyes and bared teeth, she did not want to be on the receiving end of whatever Dmitri was about to say. "It looked to me like your partner struggled with the position and you weren't doing everything you could to support her. Since you're such an *expert* on arabesque lifts, tell me what the man is supposed to do when his partner falters and leans forward."

Nick blinked a few times, looking scared. While Lillian had always been hard on Cat, she had a select group of favorite dancers she rarely criticized and Nick was one of them.

"You should adjust the location of your hand on their rib cage." Nick dropped his gaze to the floor.

"And did you do that?" Dmitri asked

"No." Nick's voice had fallen to a whisper.

"So, are you partially at fault?" Dmitri wrapped one arm around the front of his torso and brought the other to his chin, looking every bit as smug as Cat imagined he felt. Nick had screwed up, in more ways than one, and Dmitri was forcing him to admit it.

He nodded. "Yes."

Dmitri motioned toward Cat. She was impressed by the way he easily intimidated a man with an ego the size of planet Jupiter. It said a lot about his own self-assurance and knowledge about their discipline.

It was also incredibly hot.

"Don't you think you should apologize?" It was clear from the tone in Dmitri's voice that Nick didn't have a choice.

He looked to Cat. "I'm sorry."

Even though he sounded sincere, she wasn't sure he meant it. She would be willing to bet Nick would head back to the men's locker room at the end of the day with nothing but unkind things to say about Dmitri and Cat. He was that kind of guy.

Still, it felt good to hear him say it. He had tried to blame the entire arabesque fiasco on her. Even though she was mostly at fault, Dmitri was right: Nick could have helped her out. If the whole incident had gone by without Dmitri making Nick admit his fault, it would have set an unpleasant precedent for the rest of the time they partnered each other. Nick would act like the know-it-all veteran, all the while treating her like a lowly member of the corps who didn't deserve the role she'd been awarded. And possibly sabotaging her.

A restrained smile crinkled the corners of her eyes. "Thanks."

Spinning on his heels, Dmitri turned to face her. "Don't look so pleased with yourself, Miss Brown. If you don't perfect your lift technique, I'll replace you without a second thought." He looked back and forth between the two dancers. "I suggest you both spend some time practicing before we meet tomorrow with your understudies. If they outperform you, they'll be my new leads."

With that, he brushed between the two dumbstruck dancers and exited the room.

CHAPTER FIVE

Dmitri drove along Main Street in Bretton Falls, observing the various Thanksgiving decorations spotting the storefronts. A cornucopia filled with boots at the shoe store. A paper mache turkey at the toy store. A display of ceramic pumpkins at a pharmacy. He suspected this street would be even more extravagantly decorated when Christmas rolled around.

Though Dmitri had lived in Bretton Falls for a few weeks, he hadn't taken the opportunity to explore the area. He didn't like to venture from his apartment or the studio often, even in a town where he only knew a few people and likely wouldn't be recognized. However, he'd grown tired of the limited choice of pizza or Chinese from the strip mall across the street from his apartment complex. One person could only eat so much greasy food before it began to have ill effects. Rather than wait for his body to start rejecting his new, unhealthy diet, Dmitri decided to drive around and seek out other places to order his meals from.

There was a Thai food restaurant that caught his eye, as well as a café boasting its many healthy options on a folding board out front on the sidewalk. His dinner for the evening would likely come from one of those two places. The lack of choices made him miss the city for a fleeting second. There, he could get whatever type of food he wanted in thirty minutes' flat. The convenience wasn't worth facing his demons, though, which was why he weighed his minimal mealtime options as he approached the Land of Sweets.

The candy shop immediately caught his attention. Its brightly colored façade and *Nutcracker*-inspired name drew him in. As a former dancer, Dmitri hadn't often indulged in candy or cake. The habit of avoidance was one Dmitri intended to break now that it no longer mattered what he looked like in tights.

After snagging a parking space right in front of the store, he climbed out of his car and took note of the festive interior. Through the front windows, he could see a winged figure decked out in pinks and purples on the back wall and assumed she was the famed Sugar Plum Fairy. The other walls

27

were painted in multicolored candy stripes and lined with display cases filled with dozens of various sweets. White painted tables and chairs lined the big storefront windows.

As he swung the shop door open, the mouthwatering scent of chocolate immediately met Dmitri's nose. The aroma itself was enough to make him want to buy one of everything. If it all looked as good as it smelled, he thought he might.

As he approached the nearest display case to look over the shop's selection, a door from behind the counter opened. Catherine Brown walked out, stopping dead in her tracks and looking like she'd seen a ghost. Her doe eyes were even wider than normal, and her lush, pink lips parted.

"Hello, Catherine." He tipped his head. While he was just as surprised to see her as she must be to see him, he had years of experience running into exes, old hook-ups, and dancers whose contracts ABT hadn't renewed, which gave him the ability to keep his cool in situations like these.

"Hi." Her voice had a breathless quality as she stayed rooted to her place by the door.

Even though she wore an apron a size too big on her petite frame and had a smudge of chocolate on her cheek, Catherine looked every bit as beautiful as she had at rehearsal. She had the grace and posture of a ballerina that even non-dancers could recognize. He wondered why she'd never made it into any of the more prominent companies.

"I didn't know you worked here." Dmitri tried to keep his reaction casual, even though it felt as if fate had brought him here…if he believed in fate. Ever since his blow-up at rehearsal over the arabesque lift, he hadn't been able to stop thinking about Cat. He might have been too harsh on both of them, but he had to be. Nick had gotten too comfortable as one of the previous director's favorites and was used to resting on his laurels. That attitude would not work under Dmitri's direction, especially during this period of trial and error during his first ballet with the company. Everything needed to go smoothly. Dmitri needed to prove to himself, his parents, and the entire ballet community that he'd made the right choice in choosing to run a lesser known company.

Cat, on the other hand, had been trying too hard. Based upon her strength and spunk, he imagined she could perform an arabesque lift with ease if she stopped overthinking it.

She stood before him, looking equal parts adorable and drop-dead gorgeous, and he knew he'd been right to cast her as his lead. With her long, brown hair twisted into a braid over her shoulder, the youthful exuberance in her features was on full display. The audience would fall in love with her as Clara, he was sure of it.

He just had to make sure he didn't fall in love with her, too.

She twisted the end of her braid around her fingers. "This is my mom's store. I'm here almost every day after rehearsal when there aren't any performances."

"That explains the name." Pressing his weight into his cane, he stooped down to check out a tray of macarons that looked just like the ones he'd always drooled over at the French bakery on his old block. "Has your mother always been supportive of your dancing?"

"She has." Cat leaned against the sparkling clean counter and rested her chin in her hand. "In fact, she almost lost it when I told her you were our new director. She thinks you're cute."

Dmitri couldn't help but grin at her remark and the very casual way she said it. All the other dancers at Bretton Falls barely spoke to him, as if they were afraid to say the wrong thing. He appreciated that Cat was bold enough to address him like a normal person and not some kind of unapproachable ballet deity...even if he had been intentionally aloof since he's been here.

He gestured toward the case. "I'll take a half dozen macarons."

"Coming right up." She grabbed a box off a counter behind her and met him by the display case. "What flavors would you like?"

"What's your favorite?" He regretted his flirtatious tone as soon as the question slipped past his lips. Not only was he her boss, but Dmitri didn't want to crush her spirit with his perpetually sour attitude. She'd never climb the ranks of Bretton Falls Ballet if the dark cloud that hung over him shadowed her as well. Also, if he did indulge in his baser instincts and took her to bed like he wanted to, everyone in the company would cry nepotism and foul play. She needed to succeed based on her own merit, much like he wanted to prove he could succeed in the dance world away from his parents and ABT.

"Red velvet," she answered without hesitation. "Easily."

"Make it two red velvet, two raspberry cream, and two pistachio."

Cat carefully put each little cake in the pink box, taking care to ensure she didn't scrape them along the sides. Dmitri studied her face, smiling to himself each time her pink tongue poked through her lips while she concentrated on boxing his dessert.

She placed the last macaron inside. "Would you like anything else?"

"That'll be it." He reached into the back pocket of his jeans and pulled out his wallet. For a moment, he thought her gaze followed his hand but she looked away before he could confirm that she'd checked out his ass.

They walked over to the register, where Cat rung him up. Dmitri studiously looked around the shop the entire time to keep from staring at her. Now that he'd gotten a glimpse into what she was like outside of the studio, he was even more intrigued by her. Cat was cute, playful, and entirely unlike the uptight ballerinas and socialites he was used to.

It was refreshing.

"Here you go." She handed him the box, flinching when his fingers brushed hers during the exchange. "Hope you enjoy the macarons. They're one of my favorite things Mom makes."

He gestured over his shoulder to the storefront rows of tables. "Will you join me for one?"

CHAPTER SIX

Cat's cheeks heated at his request, and she knew exactly why. Over the years, Simon had stopped by multiple times and asked her to sit with him while he enjoyed whatever treat her mother had recommended that day. But Simon was like an uncle to her. Dmitri was her intimidating and attractive new boss.

She scanned the shop, looking for an excuse to turn him down. "Sorry, but I'm working."

Dmitri glanced over both his shoulders, likely noting the empty shop and the equally empty parking spaces out front. "You don't look too busy."

If rehearsal had been any indication, when Dmitri wanted something, he got it. He'd made demands of the dancers all day that they'd eagerly worked to fulfill.

In the current moment, away from the studio, he had her pinned in place with his unrelenting stare.

"Why don't you grab a table and I'll be right over," she conceded before slipping into the back. After shutting the door, she pressed her forehead against the cool metal and closed her eyes. "Holy shit," she muttered.

"Language," Louise chirped in a sing-song voice. "Your sisters are here."

Sure enough, when Cat opened her eyes and spun around, Grace and Elise sat at the table in the center of the room with open notebooks and textbooks laid out before them.

"You know we've heard worse, right?" Grace, the fifteen-year-old, tossed her sleek brown ponytail over her shoulder before motioning toward Cat to wipe the chocolate off her cheek.

Cat wiped at the spot with the back of her hand, wondering if Dmitri had noticed the smear.

"I've *said* worse," Elise, the seventeen-year-old, muttered under her breath. Her remark made Grace and Cat smile. Elise was the most daring of the Brown girls. Her purple-streaked hair and all-black wardrobe served as proof.

"I heard that." Louise shook a wooden spoon, dripping chocolate onto the floor. When she noticed the spatters, she scowled and brought the utensil back over the double boiler. "Look what you made me do. Elise, please clean this."

Adjusting her black-rimmed, cat-eyed glasses, Elise let out a dramatic sigh. "Yes, Mother." Moving at a leisurely pace, she slithered off her stool, pulled a rag off an oven handle, and began wiping up the mess.

Once Elise crouched down to take care of the spilled chocolate, Louise, still stirring her sweet-smelling concoction, turned her attention to Cat. "Shouldn't you be out front? I heard you ring up a customer but I didn't hear the bell on the door."

Cat smoothed an errant strand of hair off her face, wondering if she should reveal who was out front. Louise would make a big to-do over a dance celebrity patronizing her establishment, which Cat imagined could be quite embarrassing. On the other hand, maybe she needed her mom out there to help dial back the sexual tension. Her skin had already flushed with enough heat to melt chocolate.

"Dmitri Fedorov is out there." She pushed away from the door and headed toward the beverage station. "I came back to get us some coffee."

A thud sounded, and Cat spun around.

Louise had dropped the spoon to the blue linoleum.

"What?" She gripped the edge of the stove like her knees were going to buckle. "In my shop? What an honor! Did he know we own it?"

Cat poured coffee into two disposable paper cups. "No. He just ended up here, I guess. I don't know. He's not much of a talker. Bought a half dozen macarons, though. He wants me to sit down and eat one with him. I know I'm on the clock, but you don't mind, right?"

"Of course not!" Louise wiped her hands on her apron before hurriedly pulling it over her head. "I have to meet him."

Grace tapped the eraser end of her pencil against her glossy lips. "First he makes you the star of his debut show and then he invites you to share dessert. Sounds like he's aiming to make you the new star of Bretton Falls Ballet."

"Or he's aiming to make her the new star in his bedroom," Elise quipped, still kneeling on the floor, now cleaning where Louise had dropped the spoon.

"Elise!" Louise playfully whipped her daughter with her apron. "Don't say that about your sister."

Cat sipped her coffee and foolishly hoped it would wash away her nerves. After all, everything she felt for Dmitri had to be one-sided. He had a reputation as a womanizer, but she also knew that ballet came first for him. There was no way he would risk his new career for her, would he?

Cat spun on her heels, with a piping hot cup of coffee in each hand.

"Let's go." She nodded to the door. "I'm sure Dmitri will be happy to meet you." Cat suspected that wasn't necessarily true. Dmitri had been cold and guarded at the studio, but she needed her mom out there as a buffer—someone to make sure she didn't leap across the table to maul him.

Louise pulled her headband off and ruffled her chin-length bob with her fingers. "Do I look okay?"

"You look perfect. Come on."

When Cat pushed open the door, Dmitri immediately looked up. His blue eyes softened at the corners, losing the hard-edged stare. A flicker of a smile twitched on his mouth, and she felt a tug on her heart. She'd just realized that deep down beneath uncompromising façade, the detached man had a warmth she suspected she could bring out.

However, it would be something she could never dare to find out. *Dmitri is my boss.* She silently vowed to repeat that mantra anytime she felt anything for him that didn't mirror her respect for him as the new director.

She felt yet another tug at her heart when Dmitri's expression dropped after Louise appeared behind her.

"Mr. Fedorov." Louise clasped her hands beneath her chin, beaming. "It is truly an honor to have you here."

"Mrs. Brown, I presume." Dmitri braced himself on the table and his chair, wincing as he stood.

The flash of pain across his face marked another tug at Cat's heart. She couldn't imagine having her dance career ripped away, only to be left with a painful reminder of what used to be and could never be again.

Louise must have noticed his discomfort, because she rushed around the counter to greet him.

She accepted his outstretched hand and shook it vigorously. "Thank you so much for stopping by. You must have thought it was quite a coincidence when you saw Cat behind the counter."

Dmitri's gaze flickered to hers briefly. "I did."

Undeterred by his icy demeanor, Louise turned to Cat with her hands on her hips. "You didn't charge Mr. Fedorov for his macarons, did you?"

Cat ground her lips together, second-guessing her impulse to invite her mother out there after all. "Yes, Mom." She held up the two cups before placing one down on the table near where Dmitri had been sitting. "Coffee's free, though."

Just as Louise's eyebrows began to furrow, Dmitri waved off her concern with a flick of his wrist. "I would have insisted I pay. I don't want any special treatment."

"Very well, then." Louise's bright smile returned as Cat and Dmitri sat down. "I'll leave you two. I'm sure you must have boatloads of things to discuss." She rounded the counter and stopped at the door to wiggle her fingers in a playful goodbye. "Hope to see you back real soon, Mr.

Fedorov."

He lifted his coffee in acknowledgement before taking a sip.

"I took a guess and left it black." Cat held her own cup up, letting the steam hit her face. "We have milk and sugar on the counter if you need it."

Dmitri set the cup down, swallowing hard. "You were right. I prefer it black."

Again, his gaze tangled with Cat's. Trails of heat blazed everywhere his eyes raked over her.

"So." *Dmitri is my boss. Dmitri is my boss.* Nonchalantly, she pushed the macarons toward him. "Which one do you want?"

He waited a beat before answering, watching Cat as she pulled back the top of the box. "Red velvet." He reached in and took one of the small treats. "And you?"

"The other red velvet, of course." Cat lifted it out and nibbled on the edge. Her diet didn't allow for high amounts of sugar. She'd have a stomachache if she ate her macaron as fast as Dmitri did. His was gone in two bites. "What do you think?"

He nodded. "It's very sweet, which I'm not used to. I'm sure you understand."

"When you live your whole life in tights, it's difficult not to think of those things." Cat bit off another small morsel. When Lillian had headed Bretton Falls Ballet, she'd often met with Phoebe and Nick in private. They were her confidantes, and she took their concerns and critiques seriously. Maybe this was an opportunity for her to be that person for Dmitri. After all, everyone else in the company was too afraid to even look at him, let alone engage him in conversation. "So, how do you think the first day of rehearsals went?"

He tilted his head from one side to the other as he sipped his coffee. "It went all right."

Cat placed her barely touched macaron on a napkin and began spinning her cup. Dmitri might have been one of the most talented dancers and handsomest men to ever grace the planet Earth, but he certainly lacked skills in the conversation arena.

"Is there anything you think I can do better?" She braced herself, ready for a litany of things she should work on. After hearing him voice nothing but complaints throughout the rehearsal, it seemed natural to assume as much.

"Arabesque lift," he answered, leaning back in his chair and crossing his ankle over his good knee.

Truly a man of few words.

Cat nodded in agreement. "I know, but I promise I'll get it down next time we work on it. I've been watching videos on my phone all night, and I know what I have to fix to do it perfectly."

When Cat had asked Nick to stay and work on the arabesque lift after rehearsal, he'd answered with a terse "no" before grabbing his things and storming out of the studio. She'd chalked his reaction up to his unfamiliarity with being put in his place by the director. She'd had no choice but to turn to videos.

"Good." One corner of Dmitri's mouth curled into a devilish smile that made something deep in her abdomen clench.

"Anything else?" she asked, inching closer to the edge of her seat.

"Nothing right now. We'll talk again. I'm sure I'll have something for you to work on then."

Cat bit down on the inside of her bottom lip to stop herself from beaming. She knew she was doing a good job as Clara, but Dmitri confirming it made things even sweeter.

"Are you going to finish that?" he asked, tipping his chin toward her forgotten macaron.

"I've had enough." She pushed it toward him. "You can finish it."

Leaving the napkin on the table, Dmitri scooped up the macaron and bit into it. A trace of frosting lingered on his lip as he chewed, and Cat struggled not to reach across the table and wipe it off. They'd touched earlier in the day as Dmitri gave alignment corrections during rehearsal, but Cat knew swiping her thumb over his full, red lips would feel far more intimate.

Dmitri is my boss. Dmitri is my boss.

The two sat in amiable silence as Dmitri ate the cake and Cat sipped her coffee. When he finished, Dmitri closed the to-go box and stood.

"It was a pleasure running into you this evening."

Cat bit back another smile. "Same here." She hooked her thumb toward her station behind the counter. "I'm here most evenings after rehearsal if you ever want to stop by and talk shop."

It might have been a forward for her to offer, but Cat didn't care. Whether it was physical attraction or a genuine desire to shape her into the prima ballerina she was meant to be, Dmitri had taken an interest in her, and Cat didn't want to squander an opportunity to get on his good side.

"I'll keep that in mind." Dmitri grabbed his cane, bowed his head in farewell, and made his way out the door.

Lisa Hahn

CHAPTER SEVEN

Cat unfurled a few feet of silky navy blue ribbon from its spool before laying it flat on the kitchen table. With her mom still at the store and Grace studying with a friend, it was the perfect place for her to set up shop. She had a small desk tucked away in the corner of her bedroom, but she always felt too cramped for space when she worked there.

Once she'd measured and cut the ribbon, Cat brought out the chiffon she'd use to make the skirt. The fabric featured big, floppy sunflowers on a blue backdrop. The moment Cat had seen it in the store, she knew she had to have material to make a skirt for Abby. It was bright and upbeat, just like her best friend. Once Cat had the fabric cut and hemmed, Elise came into the kitchen.

"Hey, sis." She held up a handful of balled-up lilac chiffon. "I picked this up for Violet."

Violet was Elise's best friend and a first-year member of Bretton Falls Ballet. While Elise dedicated herself to whatever visual art she preferred at the time, Violet lived for long hours spent at the studio. While the two seemed like an odd pair, the bond they'd forged in early childhood had more strength than their differences.

"Let's have a look at it." Cat abandoned her task and began to unfold the material her sister bought. The pretty purple material was dotted with small white rosettes. Cat had seen it in the fabric store before, but never picked it up. It didn't suit her's or Abby's style, but it would be perfect for a classic beauty like Violet. The blond-haired, blue-eyed eighteen-year-old girl would turn a lot of heads in her new skirt.

"It's beautiful." Cat draped it over the back of a chair and stood back to admire it. "Violet will love it."

"Cool." Elise patted her sister on the back. "And you're sure you can have it done by her birthday in two weeks? I know you're busy with *The*

Nutcracker now."

Elise spoke the truth. The first week of rehearsals had been grueling. Practices ran late every day, which meant Cat had arrived late to her shifts at the Land of Sweets. It helped that she and Dmitri had developed a bit of a rapport after his unexpected visit to the shop. He'd pull her off to the side to share his corrections, rather than shout them out for all to hear like he did with everyone else.

"I still have the weekends. Well, most of them, anyway." Dmitri had announced on Friday that he would be instituting all-day Saturday rehearsals instead of the half days they were all used to.

"Awesome." Elise paused, gripping the back of a chair as she scraped at a chip in the white paint with one of her nails. "So, I was thinking, maybe you could start selling these skirts. Make some money, you know? It might be a good career for you after dance is over, too."

Cat lifted a single eyebrow. "Have you been talking to Mom?"

"No." With a thud, Elise plopped down in the chair. "But I did overhear her on the phone with Grandma, and I know you might quit dancing to manage her new store."

"And you think I'd be better off starting my own line of dancewear?" Cat asked as she pinned the ribbon to the chiffon she'd hemmed earlier.

"Yeah, I guess." Elise propped her elbows up on the table and rested her chin in her hands. "I mean, you love ballet but you don't love making candy. Mom loves making candy."

Elise's concern was sweet. However, Cat wished she didn't know about their mother's offer. If she gave up dancing to run a second Land of Sweets, both of her sisters were smart enough to figure out she was doing it for them and neither girl would forgive her easily for it. Cat hadn't given much thought to her potential career change. Instead, she'd focused on excelling as Clara in hopes her efforts would lead to a promotion within the company. Then she'd be making enough money to help her mom out a little bit.

"Well, I don't know what I'm going to do yet, but I'm certain that whatever choice I make will be what's best for me and the rest of our family."

"You can deny it all you want, but I know you feel guilty about Mom spending every last dime she had on you. None of the rest of us feel badly about it. Especially Grace and me. You're the talented one. Always have been. Mom was right to put all of her stock in you."

"Don't worry about me, Elise." Cat lifted the skirt and lined it up with the needle on the sewing machine. "I have a good feeling this *Nutcracker* won't be the last ballet I dance. Things are going really well."

"Really?" Elise's heavily lined eyes brightened.

"Yes, really. I think the new artistic director likes me."

Before she could go into any detail, the doorbell rang.

"Abby?" Elise asked with a knowing smile. Cat and Abby spent every Saturday night together. They were just as close as Elise and Violet but had far more in common.

Cat nodded as she leaned in closer to the sewing machine, making sure she'd lined everything up perfectly. "Can you stall her at the door? I want to sew the ribbon to the chiffon and surprise her with the finished product."

Elise stood, propping a hand up on her slender hip. "How will I know when I've stalled her long enough?"

"The buzzing sound coming from this will have stopped." Cat patted the top of her machine. "After that I just need to clip the thread and tie it off."

"I'll do my best," Elise said, before turning and leaving the kitchen.

Before the words left her sister's mouth, Cat had already begun stitching the skirt. When she finished, she could hear Abby and Elise talking in the hall, their voices growing louder as they approached.

"Why is Elise asking me a million questions about your neighbor's Christmas decorations?" Abby asked as she entered the kitchen wearing a pair of jeans and a mint green sweater that brought out the highlights in her naturally blond hair. A textured purple coat hung over her arm. "Yeah, I know it's a little early to have them out, but's only a few twinkle lights and an inflatable snowman." She hid her mouth her hand like she wanted to tell Cat something in confidence, even though Elise would hear her clearly from where she stood in the doorway. "I'm worried about her, Cat. She gets stranger by the day."

"She gets stranger by the day," Elise repeated in a high-pitched voice that sounded nothing like Abby. Sometimes the two of them fought like they were sisters.

Ignoring their banter, Cat turned and held up the skirt. "What do you think?"

"Oh, Cat. It's so pretty." Abby ran her fingers over the fabric admiringly. "And soft."

"And it's yours." Cat handed it over. "You better wear it on Monday. I want to see how it looks in class."

"No need to wait." Abby put her coat and handbag down on the counter beside a brand new stand mixer. The floral border around the ceiling might have been peeling in places and the kitchen table wobbled, but they always had the best appliances. An experienced baker like Louise wouldn't have it any other way. "I'm putting this bad boy on right now." She tied the blue ribbon around her slender waist and stood back for Cat and Elise to see. "How does it look?"

"Great." Cat gave her two thumbs up.

"I think you should wear it to dinner," Elise mumbled as she leaned against the moulding and chewed on her black-painted nails.

"Ha ha," Abby said dryly as she untied the skirt and wound it up to whip at Elise, who easily batted it away.

Cat started gathering her supplies and tidying up, a wry smile on her face. "Let me put everything away and then we'll go. Okay?"

"No problem." Abby plopped in the seat Elise previously occupied. "I take any excuse I get to sit down." She massaged her thigh. "I've never been so sore."

"Tell me about it." Cat dragged over the garbage can and brushed in the stray scraps and trimmings. "My back hurts from doing more lifts in a week than I've done in my entire career."

"You and Dmitri seem to be getting along well," Abby said, dragging out the words suggestively.

The implication in Abby's tone made Cat falter. She swept a few scraps of fabric off the table with so much force they blew right past the trash and landed on the floor. "Oops." She knelt to pick up the snippets, giving herself an opportunity to calm her nerves. She took a soothing, deep breath and stood. "What makes you say that?"

"I see the way you two are always huddled together between run-throughs." Abby narrowed her gaze on Cat in an accusatory fashion. "And so does everyone else. I heard Phoebe and Marcy speculating in the locker room today about why Dmitri seems to go easier on you than he does on everyone else. I was in a bathroom stall, so they didn't know I was there. You better watch out. If they think you've slept your way to the lead role, those girls will tear your throat out."

Phoebe and Marcy, the two top female dancers in the company, had always been nice to Cat but she'd never been a threat to them before. Knowing they would accuse her of sleeping her way to the top made Cat furious. She balled up a scrap of chiffon and spiked it into the trash. She might have wanted to sleep with Dmitri, but she wouldn't. She couldn't risk an opportunity to advance within the company and help her family out financially for a chance with a guy who'd likely slept with so many ballerinas she couldn't count them on all her fingers and toes.

"Hold up." Elise pushed off the wall with her foot. "Is this the same guy that came into the shop the other night?"

Cat nodded in confirmation, unplugging her sewing machine and wrapping the cord around its body. While she hadn't overtly flirted with Dmitri in class, she also hadn't been able to keep her eyes off him. It felt like there was a magnetic force pulling her gaze to him. She was also hyperaware of how often he looked at her. More than half of those stolen glances had occurred in the breaks between run-throughs, when everyone wasn't occupied with choreography and physical exertion.

"Mom kept going on and on about how cute she thought he was," Elise continued. "Grace and I tried to get a peek at him, but Mom kept pushing us away from the door."

"Your mom's right," Abby confirmed with a nod of her head. "But cute is kind of a tame word to use to describe Dmitri Fedorov. Gorgeous is more like it."

"Oh, I know." Elise smiled devilishly. "I searched him on my phone the second Mom made us go sit down." She pulled out a chair and sat. "So, what's the deal? Is my sister into the hot director or is he into her?"

"Neither." Cat knew Elise wasn't asking her, but she jumped in to supply an answer anyway. "I'm more like a teacher's pet, if anything."

"I know it's nothing." Abby ran her fingers through the ends of her long hair as she spoke. "But I also see the way he looks at you. Sometimes when we run through a section, I swear, you're the only person he's watching."

"I'm his lead and I've never had a lead role before. Of course he's keeping an eye on me." Cat sat down in the seat catty-cornered to Abby's, her brow furrowed. "I really hope people don't make more out of this than there is."

"Unfortunately, my friend, they already are." Abby patted Cat on the shoulder, pouting sympathetically. "But it's easy to find the up side of this situation. Everyone's just jealous. You're the lead in the new director's first ballet. Obviously, he works with you the most."

"So you don't think they actually believe it?"

She shook her head. "Probably not. It's just an easy way to explain away why you're the lead and they're not. It keeps them from having to admit that you're going to be a better Clara than either of them ever were."

Phoebe had danced the part the previous year. With her deep red hair and blue eyes, she had been ethereal and effervescent in the role. The whole production felt like a meshing together of the traditional classic with something unusual, like *A Midsummer Night's Dream*. Cat considered it one of the best show runs she'd ever been a part of.

Before that, Marcy had danced as Clara for several years in a row. Though Phoebe outshone her, Marcy had received very high praise for her spirited performances. This year, Phoebe had been cast in another coveted role: the Sugar Plum Fairy. Marcy, on the other hand, was Cat's understudy. She had every reason to want Cat to fail.

Cat slammed her fist down on the white tile-topped table, feeling more determined than ever to prove to her fellow dancers that she was just as good as they were, if not better. "You're damn right I will be. Plus, I'm working with Dmitri Fedorov." She flicked her wrist dismissively. "They had Lillian the witch directing them."

"That's the spirit. Now come on." Abby stood, motioning for Cat to do the same. "Let's eat. I'm starving."

"Let me guess. You're going to the Main Street Café." Elise crossed her arms over her chest, looking smug.

"Yeah. So?" Abby asked as she carefully draped her new dance skirt over her arm to carry it out.

Shaking her head, Elise rolled her eyes. "You two are so predictable."

CHAPTER EIGHT

By the time Dmitri barged into Studio A, his dancers had already gathered. They hushed upon his entrance, something that had become habitual among them. Cat was the only one who ever dared to catch his eye. While the others were adjusting their posture or putting one last emergency stitch to ensure their ribbons would stay attached to their pointe shoe, she would flash a smile that made his already weak knee feel even weaker.

With every day of rehearsal that passed, he became more sure she was not only the most beautiful woman on the planet, but the most beautiful dancer as well. Her Clara was youthful and vivacious, a welcome contrast to so many of the mousy and polite versions of the character Dmitri despised. She fit his vision for the role perfectly; the problem came in the other ways he'd been envisioning her.

He'd driven past the Land of Sweets every day of the past week, fighting the desire to stop off for a macaron and an opportunity to be in Cat's company. But he knew that would make things worse. The more she endeared herself to him, the harder it would be to keep an appropriate amount of distance between them.

That Monday, she sat sprawled out on the floor beside the fair-haired dancer she was always with. Both girls were deep in a wide-legged straddle stretch, their stomachs resting on the floor. They were facing each other with their chins propped up on their hands. Dmitri watched Cat, hoping to elicit the same smile she'd gifted him every morning after their brief tête-à-tête the week before.

Her eyes flickered in his direction, her angelic smile faltering briefly. The whole exchange lasted for a fraction of a second before Cat went back to talking to her friend as if he hadn't just entered the room. Dmitri clenched his jaw and tightened his grip on his cane, feeling cross, not just over the rejection, but the way it stung. Why should he care if one of his dancers

43

greeted him or not? In fact, he preferred the way the others allowed him his space and decided to forgo unnecessary pleasantries.

With a solid thud, he rapped his cane to wood floor and captured the attention of his dancers. They all snapped their heads up to look at him. Except for Cat. She slowly pushed up from her stretch with her eyes averted to the ground in front of her.

"I want to start off from where the Sugar Plum Fairy leads Clara and the Prince to the throne to watch the performances." He waved an arm overhead. "Everyone to their places."

The dancers quickly pushed their belongings off to the sides before scurrying into position. Cat made quick work of tightening her canary yellow wrap skirt before linking her arm with a reluctant Nick. Dmitri had noticed the cool indifference Nick treated Cat with during the first week of rehearsal, and he'd wanted to kick himself for casting Nick as the Prince. Unfortunately, he was the strongest male dancer they had and Dmitri needed him to play the part. Based upon what he'd seen from the ranks of the Bretton Falls men, they weren't getting a lot of talent auditioning from other schools in the country. Most of the dancers Dmitri had to work with wouldn't be company members, if not for lack of interest from better-qualified individuals.

Luckily, Nick's poor attitude didn't seem to deter Cat. In fact, it seemed to fuel her. Her fiery determination was one of the many things Dmitri found sexy about her.

He ran a hand through his hair and blew out a heavy breath, trying to cleanse her from his system and focus on his work.

He tapped the top of the piano, signaling for the music to start. The cheerful melody filled the room and the dancers sprang into action. Cat joyfully fluttered across the stage as Nick guided her. For a moment, Dmitri imagined himself as Cat's Prince. After all, he'd played the role several times, many of them with partners less able than Cat. He was certainly a more austere Prince than Nick, who seemed more boyish than what Dmitri had envisioned.

Resting his cane against the front mirror, Dmitri clapped his hands, signaling the dancers and the pianist to stop.

"From the top, and this time, Prince, don't smile so goddamn much. You look like a child who'd just been promised ice cream after dinner, not a prince who's proudly showing off his kingdom to the woman he's fallen in love with."

A few snickers arose from the group, but they were stifled before Dmitri could figure out where they'd come from.

"Let's try to be professional here, people. Save your laughter for the locker room." He pulled a metal folding chair away from the wall. It wasn't comfortable, but it was better than bearing weight on his bad knee for too long. "Again," he said as if everyone already should have reset in their places. When the dancers returned to their positions, Dmitri thumped his cane to the ground. "Begin."

The pianist started again, playing a few cheerful bars of introduction so the dancers could prepare. Dmitri focused on Cat. She replicated her gestures and movements from before, looking positively breathtaking in the process. The late morning sunlight caught in the flow of her yellow skirt and made her glow. The sight was positively breathtaking, so much so that Dmitri didn't glance at any of the other dancers. He let them continue to the end of the scene, too taken with Cat to interrupt with corrections.

However, he did notice that she had tilted her head too gravely to the side when she gestured to Nick. The posturing made her look more like a caricature than a character.

The dancers glanced up at their director as they finished, hopeful they'd made it through to the end because he'd had no scathing criticisms to share.

"Take a minute for a water break and then return to position." As the dancers began to disperse, Dmitri stood and waved Cat over.

Smoothing a hand over her chestnut-hued bun, Cat looked over her shoulder at the others, seeming unusually self-conscious. With her thin arms crossed over her chest, she hurried over to him.

"What's up?" she asked, stopping nearly two feet away and glancing quickly over her shoulder again.

Dmitri stepped toward her, halting when he noticed her recoil. He tried to make sense of her strange behavior, wondering what he could have done to offend.

He certainly wasn't used to women drawing away from him, especially when they'd been so receptive to the attention he paid them before.

Dmitri tugged at the hem of his basic, white T-shirt as he attempted to get himself in check. He shouldn't have been upset over the way Cat distanced herself from him. After all, not only was she one of his dancers, she was his lead. They both needed to stay focused on *The Nutcracker* if his first production with the company were to be a success. The fewer distractions they both had, the better.

"Be careful you don't dip your head too far to the side when pantomiming. It looks unnatural."

She nodded. "Anything else?"

"That's all."

He watched as Cat headed toward her peers, the tapered back of her lush yellow skirt swaying behind her as she moved, and practically hypnotizing him. Dmitri was sure that given a chance, he could study her body for hours. If it weren't for the way her skirt stilled just then as she approached Phoebe and Marcy, he probably wouldn't have noticed the exchange between them.

In childlike fashion, Marcy leaned in to her friend and cupped a hand over her mouth before whispering something. The two dancers erupted into a fit of giggles while Cat bristled. Digging her heels in the floor, she stopped and threw her hands onto her slender hips.

"What did you just say?" she asked, her tone bitingly fierce.

Marcy looked Cat up and down, doing her best to look unimpressed. "I'm sorry, but I wasn't talking to you."

The dancers in their immediate area stopped what they were doing to listen in.

"But you were talking about me, and I think that gives me the right to butt in."

Dmitri had a feeling he knew what this display was about. He'd seen it before in the decade he'd spent working at ABT, as well as during the years he'd danced in preparatory studio company for promising young performers. Every time someone new got an exciting opportunity to showcase her talent, the veterans who were used to dancing the best roles would get territorial and jealous. The world of ballet was competitive, and situations like these were difficult to prevent.

But as artistic director, Dmitri felt compelled to step in. If he didn't want his prima ballerina getting distracted, he would have to put a stop to their bullying before they got to her.

"Marcy, now I'm curious." As soon as Dmitri spoke, the room fell silent. The dancers nearby scurried away as he approached, trying to shield themselves from the wrath of their director. "What did you say?"

Amusement vanished from Marcy's face as her eyes grew wide. At this point, even Phoebe had disappeared into the crowd.

But before she could answer, Cat stepped in. "It was nothing. I overreacted. She doesn't need to say it in front of everyone."

Yet that was what Dmitri had asked of her. His temper flared at Cat's blatant disregard of his authority in front of the cast. He couldn't let this slide.

"Marcy, I ask you again: what did you say?" He enunciated each syllable slowly, every one sounding like a threat. Marcy's eyes had filled with tears that looked like they would spill over onto her rosy cheeks if he made her repeat the deplorable thing she'd said.

"She doesn't need to. It was nothing." Cat looked to Marcy, hoping to find camaraderie. "Right? It was nothing."

Marcy only blinked in response. Dmitri got the impression she'd never been called out on her bullshit before and didn't quite know how to take it. *Good*, he thought. This would be an important lesson to her: don't start what you don't intend to finish.

He wasn't sure what to do about Cat. Up until now, she'd seemed like a mild-mannered dancer focused on progressing her stagnant career. Openly defying the new director wasn't any way to accomplish that goal. He looked at her with narrowed eyes. She stood with her hands balled up into fists at her sides, her jaw visibly tight with tension.

"Was I talking to you?" Dmitri spoke slowly, struggling to keep his composure.

"No." Cat looked around the room curiously, noticing everyone's attention on her for the first time. Pulling her bottom lip between her teeth, she took a step toward him. "But I really think you should listen to me."

Even though she'd dropped her voice to a whisper, the studio had grown so quiet she felt like she was shouting.

Dmitri stewed, furious over her defiance and turned on by her tenacity. Only the fieriest of dancers dared go toe-to-toe with their directors.

"My office. Now," he seethed through gritted teeth, pointing to the door.

Cat blinked in surprise, her eyes growing as round as saucers. She glanced over her shoulder at her friend, who looked just as shocked as she did.

Dmitri addressed the room in a booming voice. "The rest of you take a break while you, over there," he pointed at Cat's friend, "go find Simon and tell him to he needs to run rehearsal."

"Me?" the blond girl croaked nervously, pressing a hand to her chest.

Dmitri looked around the room mockingly. "Does it look like I'm talking to anyone else?"

Before she could stammer out a pathetic response, Dmitri turned and limped to the exit as quickly as he could. When he got there, he threw the old door open so it slammed against the wall with a crash. He could tell by the shuffling of pointe shoes on the carpeted floor that Cat had followed him out into the hallway, which pleased him.

Dmitri flung open his own office door just as before, entering the room and walking straight toward the window opposite. It looked out at the woods behind the building, a scene filled with greenery and majestic trees. It's been only a few weeks since he'd arrived here, but he gazed out at it often when he needed to feel grounded. It reminded him of where he was and how his life had changed. A year ago, he had skyscraper views and the adoration of the entire ballet community. Today, he had a view of resplendent nature and the curious interest of the community.

When he heard Cat pad into the office behind him, he leaned his cane against the blandly painted beige wall and gripped either side of the window frame. "Shut the door," he growled.

"I'm sorry for what happened back there," Cat said as the door clicked shut. She'd apologized, yet there wasn't a hint of remorse in her voice.

"And what exactly are you sorry for?" he asked, aware it was the type of question parents asked their children. But, in a way, Cat had been acting like a child. She had no place interrupting his conversation with Marcy, especially since he'd only been trying to help her.

"I challenged your authority, but you should know I did it for a good reason."

Dmitri barked out a laugh as he turned to face her. He wasn't surprised to see there wasn't an inkling of guilt in her expression or her stance. Her toned arms were crossed over her chest, her head cocked to the side. With her mouth in a firm line and her humorless eyes, she didn't look afraid, like Marcy or any of the other dancers did when he called them out.

His blood boiled at her continued defiance, and he wondered if she understood just how angry she'd made him. Even when Marcy had stepped out of line earlier, he'd viewed her indiscretions as a mild annoyance. But Cat brought out a fury in him he hadn't felt since he'd found out his on-stage career was over.

"There is never a good reason to challenge my authority. I run this company, so I decide who should have to face consequences for their actions." The volume of his voice hovered just below a shout, but even so, he knew that Simon would be able to hear him from the office next door if the blond dancer hadn't fetched him yet. He had a feeling that poor girl might still be frozen with fear.

Dmitri was pleased to know he at least had that effect on some of his underlings.

Cat's cheeks turned red, making her look every bit as angry as Dmitri felt.

"I couldn't let Marcy repeat what she said." She glanced down at her shoes, seeming uneasy. "Not in front of everyone."

"What did she say?" Dmitri wasn't merely asking her to share; his demand to know what catty thing Marcy had said was clear in his stern voice.

"It doesn't matter," she muttered, looking over her shoulder at nothing in particular. He suspected she merely hoped to avoid his glare.

Without his cane, Dmitri rounded his desk, eliminating the barrier between them. "It most certainly does matter, especially after the scene you caused."

"I was trying to protect one of us," she argued, her aggravation clear in her voice.

"Tell me," he sneered, deep and gravelly.

Cat unwound her arms and threw them wide out to her sides. "Marcy wondered when we're going to start going at it during rehearsal. According to her, everyone already knows we're fucking."

"What?" Dmitri snapped as a blast of white-hot anger surged through his veins.

Cat faltered for a second, swallowing hard, likely taken aback by the enraged man before her. "Abby heard Marcy and Phoebe talking about it in the locker room during rehearsal on Saturday. Apparently, it's a rumor they're starting."

Moving the quickest he had since the accident, Dmitri lunged at Cat and pinned her back against the door. He felt the slightest inkling of pain in his knee at the fast movements, but the sensation was dull compared to the overwhelming lust he felt for the woman before him.

He seized her behind her neck with one hand, pressing the other against the wall beside her head and effectively trapping her. There was enough space separating their bodies for a wisp of air to squeeze through, but nothing else. Dmitri could feel the heat radiating off her, spurring him on.

"Wh-what are you doing?" she stuttered through panted breaths.

"I'm not going to have everyone accusing me of sleeping with one of my dancers if I'm not going to reap the benefits of it."

Before she could react, Dmitri crushed his mouth against Cat's. The intimate contact lit sparks deep in his belly, exploding into a warm feeling of pleasure that flooded his entire body. Cat must have felt something similar. She moaned too, parting her lips and allowing Dmitri to lap his tongue over hers. Cat swiftly reciprocated, bringing her hands up to fist the front of his tee.

The kiss felt so good, Dmitri instantly forgot what he'd been angry about, and focused only on how breathtakingly exquisite it felt to be close to her. It felt better than his most highly acclaimed performances had, all rolled into one colossal, emotional experience.

And therein lay the problem. Dmitri didn't usually connect with women this deeply. They were a source of pleasure to be enjoyed so he could go back to focusing on what mattered: ballet. To make matters worse, Cat danced for the company he ran. He didn't know if she was the kind of girl who could brush the kiss off as a one-time release of tension.

Dmitri pulled away, his gaze dropping to Cat's heaving chest as the sound of heavy breath filled his ears. Her breasts looked beautiful, lush, and perky in her skin-tight black leotard, so much so that he had to step away. He'd already lost control with her once, and he couldn't let it happen again.

With his palms, he flattened down the places on his shirt she'd wrinkled with her grip, before motioning to the door. "Go back to rehearsal. I'll be there in a few minutes." Noting her still flushed skin and swollen lips he added, "Stop off at the locker room to collect yourself before returning."

Dmitri would do the same, though he wasn't sure what would calm him down. He considered having a punching bag installed in his office for times like these. He was going to need a way to release his pent-up frustration, especially now that he knew how incredible it felt to get lost in Cat. And they'd only kissed. Imagining what anything else might feel like would be torture.

For someone who didn't have a difficult time expressing herself, Dmitri expected Cat to have a sassy parting remark for him. Instead, she merely nodded and left the room.

CHAPTER NINE

Cat's heart still pounded in her chest when she re-entered the studio. Dmitri, who seemed completely unbothered by their argument and subsequent kiss, ignored her as she walked by and instead focused on the Spanish pas de deux being performed before him. Simon, however, pressed a hand her back in that reassuring way he often did when Lillian blamed Cat for a choreographic error made by other members of the corps.

But Cat didn't need consolation in that moment. What she needed was a glass of wine and someone to vent to. She looked to Abby, who flashed her a sympathetic grimace, complete with a protruding lower lip. The two would talk during the break, but first Abby had to focus on her Arabian pas de deux, which directly followed the Spanish. Through a complicated array of hand gestures only her best friend would understand, Cat silently told Abby to focus and to meet her outside after the break. A late autumn chill had crept into the air, driving most of the dancers to hang out in the locker rooms or mill about the hallways during the breaks. She knew she and Abby would find privacy outside, by the two old wooden picnic tables.

Abby nodded in confirmation and offered a weak smile. *If only she knew*, Cat thought.

Dmitri had kissed her. But it was more than that. The second their lips met, Cat felt a wave of heat wash her body, leaving her hyperaware of Dmitri's touch in its wake. Kissing him was a full-body experience; every part of her hummed with the vibrations of her rapid heartbeat.

And then it had ended, far too quickly for her liking. Before she could get a good sense of why Dmitri had kissed her, he'd practically kicked her out of his office. The quick dismissal hurt more than Cat would ever let him know.

As the two Spanish pas de deux dancers scurried off the side, Cat made her way around everyone gathered by her place on the throne beside Nick.

He smirked at her as she sat, clearly amused by her altercation with their director. He probably hoped she'd pissed Dmitri off so badly he'd be ready to promote Marcy up from her role as understudy.

Cat worried about that too, although it was one of her more minor concerns. Though she was a beautiful dancer, Marcy could not perform the role like Cat could. Dmitri had tailored the choreography to her strengths, adding in lots of high-energy pirouettes and jumps she excelled at. Knowing what a perfectionist Dmitri was, she had a good feeling he wouldn't swap her out for someone who rotated in their pirouettes a fraction of a second slower than she did. Not yet, at least.

For the time being, Cat was more worried about her body's reaction to Dmitri's kiss. Never before had a kiss made her feel her pulse all the way down in her toes. She was addicted to that feeling now, even though she knew it would be an addiction she could never feed.

Dmitri is my boss.

Dmitri was her boss, and he'd seemed eager to be done with her as soon as his lips left hers.

Bent on not letting what had happened with Dmitri interfere with her performance, Cat focused determinedly on her role for the next hour. Dancing and learning new choreography provided ample material to occupy her mind, though it proved to be difficult to forget about Dmitri when he was the one teaching her said choreography.

When rehearsal let out for lunch break, which was far too short for any of them to eat anything of substance before returning to rotating and jumping, Cat made a beeline to the locker room. She threw on a baggy, black pair of sweatpants and then made her way over to the picnic tables.

A few minutes later, Abby rushed out of the side doors, looking like she was fighting the urge to sprint over. A black scarf with white polka dots fluttered in the breeze behind her, and she'd donned a pair of sweatpants that were four times her size. Bulky clothes were essential to keeping warm between rehearsals.

Giving in, Abby ran the last twenty feet over to the picnic tables. "What happened?" she asked before she even stopped moving. After plopping down on the splintered bench across from Cat, she continued, "That was crazy. You made Dmitri so mad. I can't believe you talked back to him like that. And in front of everyone. So much for being the teacher's pet. What on earth—?"

"He kissed me," Cat cut in, needing to get it off her chest.

Abby's jaw dropped as she blinked in surprise. "He what?" She jumped up from her seat and rounded the picnic table to sit right next to Cat. "He kissed you?"

Cat nodded, looking over each of her shoulders to make sure no one was around. "He yelled a bunch first, but next thing I knew he was kissing me."

Abby clutched each of Cat's hands between her own. "I'm scared to ask for more details."

Unaccustomed to sharing these sorts of details with anyone, Cat felt her cheeks heat. But she couldn't blame Abby for inquiring. If she'd found her out best friend had just kissed their new boss, who also happened to unearthly attractive, she'd be curious too.

"There's really not much to tell. We argued for a few minutes, and then, before I knew it, he was against me."

Abby pulled her hands away to cover her face as she erupted into a fit of giggles. "Oh my god, Cat. That's so wild. Ballerinas all over the world would die from jealousy if word got out about this."

Cat shook a finger at her. "But word can't get out about this. It's bad enough Marcy won't stop running her mouth about Dmitri and me." She dragged her hands over her face and sighed. "And now the rumors she's been spreading are basically true."

"No way." Abby wound her arm around Cat's shoulders. "You guys only kissed and it just happened. In Marcy's version of the story, you two have been sleeping together since Dmitri arrived in Bretton Falls. According to her, you sank your conniving little claws into him before he began contemplating *Nutcracker* casting."

"Now what am I going to do?" Cat asked, dabbing at the corners of her eyes with the sleeve of her black wrap sweater to make sure she didn't have any makeup smudged on her face when she went back in. "There are awful, bitchy women spreading rumors about me, and I just kissed our new boss."

"First of all, Dmitri kissed you. He was out of line, not you. And—" Abby paused to reach deep into the pockets of her enormous sweatpants and pulled out a bag of carrot and celery sticks. "Secondly, you need to eat something unless you want to pass out during rehearsal and give everyone something else to talk about. Thirdly, I know you're freaked out because our boss just kissed you, but you need to shake off all this craziness and focus on your dancing. That's what's important."

Nodding, Cat pried open the zipper seal on the bag of veggies and pulled out a carrot. Abby was right. If she let everything get to her, she might be a sub-par Clara, which would mean another year in the corps, which would mean her mom would likely start pressing her to consider the managerial position at the new Land of Sweets.

Cat snapped her carrot stick in half and popped part of it into her mouth. "I guess this is the kind of bullshit you have to deal with at the top, huh?"

Abby smiled, jovially patting Cat on the back. "You wanted to be there."

"And I still do." Cat sat up a little straighter as resolve set in. "I just need to prove that I belong there."

The pair noshed on veggies while Abby filled Cat in on what she'd missed during practice: Simon seemed to enjoy Dmitri's choreography and Marcy had turned right back into her usually catty self almost immediately. The two of them headed back to the locker room a little late, having gotten caught up in their conversation. By the time they'd laced up their pointe shoes, most of the other dancers had gone into their rehearsal spaces.

Feeling better after her chat with Abby, Cat held her head high as she entered Studio B for a session with Nick, their understudies, and Dmitri. When she opened the door to the studio, Marcy, Nick, and Nick's understudy Jerimiah were all huddled together in the center of the room. They all turned to look at Cat as the big, wooden door slammed shut behind her.

Marcy crossed her arms over her chest, jutting her chin forward. "We were worried you weren't going to make it. You know, after your little lovers' quarrel."

Cat dropped her bag to the floor along the front mirror, which stretched across one full wall in the studio, and took a deep breath. She would not let them get to her. "Here I am."

"You know, if my boyfriend talked to me the way he spoke to you, I'd kick his ass to the curb." Nick flicked his wrist for emphasis. "That shit was cold."

"Ha ha, very funny." With a roll of her eyes designed to let the other dancers know she wasn't amused, Cat bent down to tug up her leg warmers. She'd wear them for the first few minutes of rehearsal, until her calf muscles weren't so tight.

"Seriously, though. She can't dump his ass," Marcy continued with a mischievous twinkle in her eye. "If she weren't fucking the director, she wouldn't have gotten Clara. Instead, she'd be dancing in the corps where she belongs."

Propping her leg up on the bar to stretch, Cat ignored Marcy's last remark. She hoped paying no attention to the commentary would make them stop. Unfortunately, it didn't work out that way.

"Look at her over there." Marcy clicked her tongue. "Dmitri Fedorov shows an interest in the girl and now she thinks she's hot shit."

"To think, you're her understudy." Nick rested his hands on his hips and shook his head. "What an injustice."

In response, Cat merely switched legs and tried to focus on what was important: her dancing and this staging of *The Nutcracker*.

"For someone who chewed me out for being late on the first day, I really would have expected our fearless leader to have gotten here by now." Nick pointed up at the clock. "We should have started five minutes ago."

Even though she wasn't facing the group, Cat could feel Marcy's eyes narrow on her. "He's probably just freshening up from the quickie him and

Little Miss Clara just had in his office."

The three dancers in the center of the room erupted in laughter just as Dmitri walked in. His gaze drifted toward Cat before immediately darting toward the small group trying to contain their mirth.

Apparently, he planned to continue ignoring her.

"What's so funny?" he asked in a deadpan manner, his deep blue eyes expressing nothing.

"Just something that happened during break." Nick hooked his thumb toward Cat. "She wasn't there, so that's why we're the only ones laughing."

"I see," Dmitri responded, sounding disinterested. "Less laughing, more dancing. What do you think?"

"That sounds great, sir." Marcy stepped forward with a saccharine-sweet smile plastered on her face. While Dmitri's outburst hadn't exorcized the dancer of her spiteful ways, it had at least taught her to be careful of who she decided to gossip in front of. Now that Dmitri had entered the room, she'd stopped smirking at Cat and started to stretch, just like she should have been doing the entire time.

Meanwhile, Cat sneaked a glance over at Dmitri as he walked over to the trusty folding chair he'd been using She noticed that his limp seemed more pronounced than it normally was, and she wondered if that had anything to do with the way he'd pounced on her earlier. He'd left his cane behind his desk when he'd made his move. Though she'd been focused on trying to protect her place in the company and her relationship to the new director, she couldn't help but notice when he walked without it.

Nick lightly jogged ahead of Dmitri and opened the folding chair for him. Instead of issuing a verbal thank you, Dmitri merely dipped his head toward the dancer before taking his seat. As he walked away, Nick flashed Cat a truly hateful sneer, knowing that Dmitri wouldn't be able to see it from where he sat.

Watching Marcy and Nick act like kiss-asses while they accused Dmitri of secretly sleeping with his leading lady made Cat sick. It was no secret that Lillian and Cat had not seen eye-to-eye on many things, but at least they were both up-front about their feelings toward each other. After almost every cast listing got posted, Cat made her way to the director's office to see why she'd been relegated to the periphery. Her discontent was just as well-known as Lillian's distaste for the small dancer's style.

Once the pianist sauntered in and Dmitri had finished berating her for her lateness, the group began their rehearsal. The dancers learned the choreography together, the understudies shadowing the two leads as they all got the steps down via Dmitri's vocal instruction. After, they took turns performing what they'd learned, each couple would have time to sip water and work out any kinks they might have before going at it again.

Dmitri tried to coach the dancers through a complicated two-handed promenade turn. The move typically required a lot of coordination between partners, but the way Dmitri expected them to twist and move their arms complicated things further. The female was to remain in an attitude position en pointe while the male circled around her, ensuring the different transitions blended together seamlessly, all while the female spun on her toe. When no one had gotten it quite right, Dmitri slammed the butt of his cane to the floor and stood.

"Cat and Nick." He hobbled toward the center of the room, waving the two dancers over to join him. "I'll demonstrate."

He pointed at Cat, still avoiding her gaze. "Sous-sus." After Cat assumed a picture-perfect sous-sus, pressed up onto her toes with her ankles crossed, Dmitri handed Nick his cane. "Hold this."

Cat had to bite back a smile as Nick took the polished piece of dark wood and stepped back.

She didn't need to glance up at the mirror to know Dmitri was behind her, ready to start. The heat radiated off his body, signaling his presence, just as it did in his office. Cat stiffened, anticipating the touch of his hands to hers and hoping she wouldn't falter because of it.

"Arms in position."

Cat lifted her arms, raising one overhead and positioning the other out to the side. She inhaled sharply as Dmitri's fingers touched hers, too busy trying to focus on the task at hand to worry if the other dancers in the room heard her. Together, they executed a gorgeous promenade, complete with all the seamless transitions Dmitri envisioned and demanded. Cat impressed herself with her ability to perform the maneuver without any error, considering she could hardly breathe due to Dmitri's distracting proximity. Typically, partner work was just that: work. She'd never felt an attraction to any dancer she'd worked with and things never got awkward.

But one promenade turn with Dmitri left her body feeling charged, exactly like it had earlier after he'd kissed her and then unceremoniously kicked her out of his office.

Dmitri turned and addressed the others. "That is how it should be done. Any questions?"

"Can I run to the bathroom really quickly?" When Dmitri and the rest of the group looked at her in confusion, Cat shrugged. "Too much water, I guess."

Dancers didn't typically take restroom breaks, but Cat didn't care just then. She didn't even have to use the bathroom. If she had to spend the better part of the next hour with Dmitri, she needed to splash some cold water on her face to help quell whatever bodily reaction she was having to his touch.

"Go," he said with a wave of his hand, his gaze lingering on hers for a few beats, his eyes narrowing with interest, before he turned and addressed the other dancers.

Cat scurried out of the studio, grateful for the impromptu break.

Dmitri could have demonstrated the promenade with Marcy, but he'd chosen her. He also could have told her to wait to use the bathroom, but he hadn't.

Both instances gave Cat hope their professional relationship wasn't destroyed.

Now she just had to get used to knowing what it felt like to kiss Dmitri and knowing she could never let herself do it again.

Lisa Hahn

CHAPTER TEN

With one bud plugged into his ear, Dmitri listened to the final waltz of *The Nutcracker* at his desk. He swayed to the swooning and sweeping music, dreaming up choreography he'd teach to his dancers later that day. He restarted the song every thirty seconds, jotting down ideas for the beginning in a lined notebook every time one came to him. When rehearsals started, he hoped to have a decent chunk of choreography ready to impart.

Dmitri paused the music when a knock sounded at his door, frustrated by the interruption. He'd planned to come up with most of the new choreography the day before, but he'd been too distracted by reminisces of his kiss with Cat to get anything done. It wasn't a problem he'd had before, and he didn't know what to do about it. In the past, his relationships with women had been transient. He'd tire of one and quickly move on to the next with no emotional baggage to speak of.

But things were different now that he'd met Catherine Brown.

"Come in," Dmitri called out begrudgingly, sitting back into his cushy vinyl chair.

The door cracked open and Simon poked his head in. "Is this a good time?"

Dmitri glanced over at the paused media player on his computer screen and crossed his arms over his chest. "It's as good a time as any."

The dancers were in the middle of their daily technique class, which was taught by a former member of the Miami Ballet, so the two men were not likely to be interrupted. At least, that was what Dmitri had hoped when he'd sat down to choreograph.

"Perfect." Simon entered the room and shut the door behind him, a sign he wanted to talk in private. They hadn't yet discussed the incident from yesterday, in which Simon had unexpectedly been summoned from his office to run rehearsal. Certainly, he had to have a few questions and concerns.

Simon sat in a narrow wooden chair facing Dmitri's desk, tossing the tail of his trademark silk scarf over his shoulder as he settled in. "How are things going in your rehearsals?"

"Good," Dmitri answered plainly. He despised small talk. Both men knew where this conversation was heading, and Dmitri wished Simon would cut out the bullshit and ask the difficult questions straight away. "I suppose you want to know what happened yesterday."

Simon crossed his legs, looking more comfortable now that Dmitri had addressed the elephant in the room. "I am curious, yes. It's not every day I get called out of my office to run a rehearsal I hadn't planned to participate in. I'd also like to know if there are problems among our performers. I've been working with these people for years. Perhaps I could provide some insight on how best to deal with them."

Dmitri eyed his assistant director, annoyed by the insinuation Simon might be better suited to dealing with the dancers than he was. After all, Dmitri had just been a dancer at one of the prestigious companies the world. He knew exactly how their minds worked.

"During the first week of rehearsals, I noticed some of the cast acting unkindly toward Catherine. Yesterday, during a break, I saw Marcy and Phoebe whispering among themselves. Whatever they said angered Cat enough for her to respond. I jumped in before an altercation broke out."

"And you ended up bringing Cat back here?" Simon motioned around him to the drab, undecorated office. It was very different from the cluttered, personal shrine Simon worked in.

"Yes. I asked Marcy to share what she'd whispered to Phoebe, and Cat jumped in to say it wasn't necessary. She blatantly challenged my authority, and I could not let that stand."

"Really?" Simon's tired green eyes widened in surprise. Producing a ballet was difficult work, and Simon felt the pressure to help the company succeed just as much as Dmitri did. The fifty-year-old assistant director had been staying late after rehearsal to contact donors and possible advertisers, leaving sometime after dark every day. "Maybe she didn't think you needed to jump to her defense. Cat's fiercely driven. She's had no problem speaking up for herself the past few years."

"Cat needs to focus on her work as Clara, not the petty cattiness that is taking place." Dmitri sat up straighter, perching his elbows on the edge of his desk. "Furthermore, I don't want the company to think I will tolerate such displays of disrespect."

"Cattiness and pettiness have gone hand-in-hand with our discipline for generations. You must have experienced that at ABT."

"Sure. Never toward me, of course." Even though Dmitri was the son of two accomplished dancers, the New York City ballet community viewed him as a prodigy by the time he'd hit adolescence. He'd never encountered anyone who didn't think he deserved all the roles he'd been given. Most considered themselves fortunate to share the stage with him. "Even so, the dancers I worked with were wise to wait until the director wasn't around to make such remarks."

Simon nodded in agreement. "I can understand that. Not only are you their new director, but you're Dmitri Fedorov. They should be worshipping the ground you walk on. I think it will all come in time. Right now, everyone's still getting used to you being here."

"Perhaps." Dmitri rested his chin on his balled-up fists. While he enjoyed the recognition of his past accomplishments, Dmitri knew the man he was back then was much different than the one sitting at that antique desk. Sometimes he thought it wasn't fair for him to take credit for the efforts of his old self.

"So," Simon continued, "what happened when you spoke with Cat?"

Looking over Simon's shoulder, Dmitri glanced at the door just as the scene from the day before replayed in his mind.

He had to clear his throat before answering, suddenly very aware of the way his palms were sweating at the memory of pressing Cat up against that door and taking what he'd wanted from her. "She said it would never happen again."

"Perfect." Simon switched the cross of his legs. "On to the next matter of business. I received a call from the publicity director at ABT yesterday. They'd like for you and three dancers to visit this weekend."

Dmitri's eyes widened. "Really? For what purpose?"

No matter what the reason, Dmitri assumed his parents had something to do with the unexpected invitation. ABT did not typically reach out to small companies.

"As a former and incredibly illustrious member of their ranks, the company is interested in your current work. They're inviting your dancers to attend their Saturday morning class in hopes we can work out some sort of collaboration. They send a few dancers each season to us for special guest appearances, and depending upon what they see in class, they may be willing to work with some of our members for a guest spot or two."

Stunned, Dmitri ran a hand through his hair and slumped back against his chair. The entire situation was highly out of the ordinary. He wondered if it was a ploy from his parents to lure him back, or if the offer was borne from genuine interest from the community he used to be a part of.

"We have to do this," Simon continued as he shifted closer to the edge of his seat and placed both his feet on the floor. "It would be great exposure for the company if everything works out. If not, it's a chance for three of our stronger dancers to take class with some of the best performers out there today. Certainly, they can learn something from an opportunity like that."

Dmitri made a steeple with his fingers and pressed them to his lips. "Can you go in my stead?"

Simon shook his head. "Your presence was specifically requested."

As much as Dmitri didn't want to return to the city and the company he'd left behind, he knew he didn't have a choice if he truly wanted to succeed at Bretton Falls. Putting on must-see productions was his number-one priority, but he also recognized how important publicity and building relationships were. His tenure with the company wouldn't be considered a success if he didn't bolster its reputation and draw the nation's most talented dancers to their auditions.

He sighed. "What is the plan, then?"

Simon smiled, clearly glad Dmitri hadn't given him too difficult a time on the matter. "A car will take you and the three dancers of your choice to the city Friday night to meet with the assistant artistic director and the artistic administrator for dinner. You'll all attend the company technique class Saturday morning with the dancers. Then it's over." He made a wiping motion with hands. "It's as easy as that."

"Easy." Dmitri repeated the word, laughing to himself over its use. Simon wouldn't have any idea just how trying this trip would be. Not only would he be involuntarily returning to the city and studio that reminded him of everything he'd lost, he'd be there with Cat. He didn't have a choice. He had to choose her as one of the three to come along. She was his Clara, and the best female dancer they had.

"Who do you think you'll bring?" Simon asked, like he'd read Dmitri's mind. "Cat and Nick are the obvious choices, since they're *The Nutcracker* leads."

"Cat, Nick, and Phoebe," Dmitri responded without hesitation. One could have argued, and Dmitri feared Simon might, that Marcy belonged in the group in place of one of the others, but Dmitri refused to consider her after the comment she'd made about him the other day. Dancers shouldn't speak ill of their director publicly if they weren't ready for it to affect their career. Plus, he couldn't fathom traveling with both Cat and Marcy. The tension between the two was palpable during rehearsals, and it would only get worse after they'd been stuffed in a car together for close to four hours.

"Clara, The Prince, and The Sugar Plum Fairy. Perfect." Simon brought his hands to the arms of chair, poised like he was getting ready to stand. "Is there anything else we need to talk about?"

Cat's face, her pink lips swollen from kissing him, flashed into Dmitri's mind for a split second, a reminder of the secret they shared.

"No."

"Okay, then." Simon stood, shoving his hands into the pockets of his dark-wash jeans. "I'll email you the travel information for this weekend."

He turned toward the door and waved over his shoulder. "See you in rehearsal."

As soon as the door shut behind him, Dmitri buried his face in his hands. Between Cat's frequent intrusions in his thought process and his anxiety over his impending return to the company he'd abandoned, Dmitri was unlikely to get any choreography completed that morning.

Lisa Hahn

CHAPTER ELEVEN

Cat's mouth spread into a wide, genuine smile when Simon waltzed into the Land of Sweets. Reaching behind herself, she pushed open the door into the kitchen.

"Simon's here!"

After alerting the rest of the Brown clan to the older man's presence, Cat greeted him. "I haven't seen you around here in a while."

He kissed her cheek before resting his hands on her shoulders and giving them an affectionate squeeze.

"I've been busy. We were without a director for a while, remember? Then we hired Dmitri Fedorov and now my phone won't stop ringing. Everyone wants to know what he's doing in Bretton Falls."

Cat playfully rolled her eyes. "Touché."

Grace burst through the kitchen door first, followed closely by Elise and Louise. The fifteen-year-old barreled toward Simon with her long, brunette ponytail waving behind her. She collided into him with a thud, throwing her arms around his waist. Cat had smartly moved out of the way when she saw her little sister coming.

"Hello, Grace." Simon smiled and patted the girl on the back.

While Grace wasn't on track to become a professional dancer, she did take a few classes a week at Bretton Falls Ballet School. In fact, all three Brown sisters had taken beginner ballet classes as children. Elise, however, knew early on that something as serious and strict as ballet wasn't her cup of tea. She'd asked Louise if she could quit a few weeks before her sixth birthday.

Nonetheless, she viewed Simon as an honorary member of the Brown extended family, just like her sisters did.

Once Grace had released him, Elise held up her hand for a high-five. "What's up, Uncle Simon?"

He slapped his palm to hers, an action that made Cat giggle a little to herself. She was certain Elise was the only person ever to get Simon to give a high-five.

"Work, work, and work." Simon tipped his head in gratitude as Louise handed him a cup of coffee with a splash of milk, just how he liked it. "Thank you for this. I need it."

"Cat tells us rehearsals have been going well," Louise said, wiping her hands on her chocolate-splotched apron.

Simon cast a knowing glance in Cat's direction, hinting he knew that wasn't entirely the case. After all, he had been called in to run a rehearsal the previous day because she'd infuriated the director so much that he'd needed to deal with her in private.

Simon would never bring the incident up in front of Louise. Although he had no idea what had happened once Dmitri got her alone, he knew Cat was a professional and he treated her as such.

"Dmitri's doing a lovely job with the company. You'll be impressed when you see what he's thrown together."

"We can't wait." Louise placed a hand on Cat's shoulder. "Especially since my beautiful daughter is dancing the lead role."

"I'll let you all in on a little secret," Simon said confidentially as he leaned in close to the Brown women, "she's going to be the best damn Clara you've ever seen."

Cat beamed. "I've been working really hard." Simon's opinion meant a lot to her, and he knew it.

And she had. Despite the copious amounts of gossip she'd encountered during rehearsals, she'd been able to keep a clear head and focus on her job. However, that didn't mean she'd been able to keep Dmitri off her mind. Her mouth watered and her palms got sweaty every time he was within three feet of her.

"It's really cool that she gets to go into the city this weekend." Elise crossed her arms over her chest and pouted, sticking out her bottom lip. "I'm so jealous. I've been begging for *someone* to take me to the Museum of Modern Art for *weeks*!"

"We'll go soon, honey. You know both me and your sister have been too busy." Louise kissed the top of her daughter's head. Elise instantly recoiled.

"Gross, Mom." She brushed off the top of her head as her upper lip curled. With that, the temperamental teen sulked off toward the kitchen. "I have art history homework to finish." She waved over her shoulder, changing her tone a little. "Catch ya later, Simon."

He returned her wave with a sweeping arc of his arm. The man couldn't help but look like a dancer in nearly everything he did. "It was a pleasure seeing you, Elise."

Louise shook her head as the high-schooler pushed through the door. "Well, the trip to New York should be fun. It'll be a good opportunity for Cat to practice with some of the best dancers in the country before *The Nutcracker.*"

"Indeed." Simon cast Cat a knowing glance.

Placing a hand on Grace's back, Louise began leading her to the kitchen. "We'll leave you to it, then. You must have bundles of things to discuss, what with Cat's demanding new role." She looked to Simon. "Can I get you anything to eat?"

"Just two of those ungodly delicious dark chocolate truffles of yours to go with my coffee." He held up the cup like he'd just given a toast and then took a sip.

"Coming right up." Louise dashed behind the counter while Cat and Simon settled down at their usual corner table. When Louise returned, she placed a small, white ceramic plate with two truffles on the table. Their rich chocolatey scent made Cat's stomach grumble. She would kill to eat a dozen truffles, but costume fittings were next week. She'd be mortified if she couldn't fit into the outfits Phoebe and Marcy had worn in years past, especially since she was at least five inches shorter than both of them, with a much narrower frame.

Simon took a bite of a truffle, closing his eyes as he savored the melt-in-your-mouth chocolate.

Looking up at Cat, he asked, "So, do you want to tell me what happened Monday during rehearsal?"

Her cheeks heated immediately. Not only did she not like disappointing Simon, she feared he might press her for too many details.

"I challenged Dmitri and I shouldn't have." She tucked a piece of hair that had come loose from her long braid behind her ear. "I apologized, and everything is okay now."

Simon eyed her curiously. "That's pretty much what he said." He rested his forearms on the table and leaned in closer. "Why didn't you want Marcy to repeat what she'd said?"

Cat swallowed hard, mentally paring down the story to a half-truth. "I've been getting a lot of flak from everyone because Dmitri treats me like a teacher's pet."

Simon popped the rest of the truffle in his mouth and nodded with a knowing grin. "They're just upset they aren't the teacher's little pets anymore." He reached across the table and placed a hand over one of Cat's. "You can't let them get to you. Girls like Marcy and Phoebe are why most people think ballerinas walk around with sticks up their asses."

Cat snorted a laugh, unaccustomed to hear Simon say something so vulgar.

He raised an eyebrow. "Well, it's true." Lifting his hand off hers, he adjusted his scarf. "Dmitri's taken a liking to you and for a good reason. You're one of the best damn dancers we've got, and it's about time the artistic director recognizes that."

"Thanks, Simon." Cat smiled and sat up straighter in her chair, unaware she'd even been slumping. It was a bad habit she fell into whenever she was uncomfortable, and now she had no reason to feel anything but confident. A pep talk from Simon always seemed to be just what she needed.

"No problem." He waved a finger at her. "But if something like this happens again I want to hear about it from you first."

"Yes, sir." She traced an X over her heart with her pointer finger. "I promise."

"You're a good girl, Cat." He shook his head, looking amused. "Listen to me, calling you girl. Sometimes I forget it's been seventeen years since we met."

"It took me seventeen years to get my first leading role." Cat propped her elbow up on the table and rested her chin in her hand. "How long did it take you?"

Simon gazed up at the ceiling, his face wrinkling as he did the math in his head. "About twelve years."

"Damn." Cat slapped her palm down on the table playfully. "You have me beat."

He laughed. "Well, I didn't have an unfair bitch of a director."

Giggling, and surprised again by his language, Cat reached across the table to gently shove Simon. "What's gotten into you? The Simon I know doesn't swear. You're beginning to sound like the rest of us."

Simon blew out a heavy breath and shook his head. "Lack of sleep."

The bell atop the front door sounded, and Cat froze in her seat when she saw Dmitri walk in.

He had on the same well-fitted jeans and black plaid shirt he'd had on at the studio, so she assumed he'd come right from work, like Simon had. His sleeves were rolled up to the elbows, exposing his lean, powerful forearms...the same arms that had her pinned to his office door the day before.

Cat realized she must have been staring when Simon followed her gaze and glanced over his table.

"Dmitri." Sounding surprised, Simon stood and faced him. "I wasn't expecting to see you this evening." He glanced at Cat before addressing Dmitri again. "Have you been to the Land of Sweets before?"

"Once," Dmitri answered simply, peeking over his shoulder and looking like he wanted to bolt.

"Well, I assume you came here to see Cat, then." He popped his second truffle in his mouth and flashed her a questioning glance. Though Simon frequently visited the shop, it was unusual for the director and the assistant director to see the dancers outside of the studio. It helped the people in charge to maintain their authority. "I was just getting ready to go. I'll let you two be."

Cat stood when Simon did. "You don't have to go."

After what happened the last time she'd been alone with Dmitri, she didn't trust herself to be in that situation again. When she closed her eyes, she could still feel his soft, hot lips on hers.

"Yes, well, Sandra is waiting." Sandra was Simon's adorable little Pomeranian. When the company wasn't in hectic rehearsal mode, he'd sometimes bring her to the studio with him so all the dancers could fawn over her.

"Tell her I said hello," Cat called out as Simon started to the door.

"Will do." He stopped to shake hands with Dmitri. "Catherine's here to work. Don't keep her too long. I've dominated enough of her time, I'm sure."

Dmitri gave a single nod as Simon made his way out the door. Then, he turned his attention to Cat. She felt her throat go dry at his blatant perusal of her body, his gaze scanning her from head to toe. It felt different when he watched her during rehearsal; it was his job to look at her then. Now, as she stood there in jeans and a zip-up hoodie, she couldn't help but notice the animalistic quality in his ocean blue irises. He still wanted her just as much as she wanted him. She was sure of it.

But she also hoped he was smart enough not to act on his feelings. With the trip to New York approaching, it was more important than ever they maintain a professional relationship. She was nervous that the temptation to abandon decorum would heighten when they were in the city, away from Bretton Falls and the rest of the company.

Dmitri is my boss. Dmitri is my boss. Dmitri is my boss.

She swept her arm toward the table she and Simon had just been sharing. "Do you want to sit?" she croaked, wishing she had a bottle of water nearby to alleviate the dryness in her throat.

Wordlessly, Dmitri approached her. She slowly sank into her seat, feeling trapped in his stare. Even if she wanted to get away, which she didn't, she felt certain Dmitri had her in some sort of trance that rendered her powerless against his brooding, quiet demeanor. Bracing his weight with his cane, Dmitri sat down as Cat pushed Simon's empty plate off to the side.

"So," she started, drawing out the word, "what brings you over here tonight?"

Dmitri rested his cane against the edge of the table. "I wanted to talk about what happened yesterday."

"Oh." Cat was at a loss for words. She'd hoped that Dmitri would never broach the subject and two of them would go on pretending they hadn't shared the most earth-shattering, knee-weakening kiss in the history of kisses.

"I would like to apologize." Dmitri cleared his throat and shut his eyes momentarily, clearly uncomfortable with apologizing. Cat wondered if, over the past few years, he ever had to say he was sorry for anything. "My actions were wholly inappropriate, both in and out of the rehearsal."

"Okay." Cat shifted in her chair, crossing and uncrossing her legs as she tried to get remotely comfortable. "Uh, thanks." Ready to change the subject, she tipped her chin toward the display cases over his shoulder. "Would you like something? Maybe another macaron? I can package it up for you to go."

As much as Cat didn't want him to leave, she knew it was for the best. The sexual tension between them was so thick she had a feeling it was only a matter of time before one of them crossed the line…or at least she knew she might.

A smile tugged at one corner of Dmitri's mouth. "Ah, you've discovered the real reason I'm back here."

A tingly feeling spread throughout Cat's chest, and she was unable to bite back a smile of her own. Dmitri was being playful. It was a side of him she had never seen before. In fact, after what a hardass he'd been, she assumed he simply did not have a sense of humor.

"Which flavor would you like? Wait. Let me guess." She tapped her pointer finger on her lip. "Red velvet."

Dmitri held up two fingers. "I'll take a couple of those to go." He patted his stomach. "I need the sugar to keep me energized while I plan the last bits of choreography."

Cat drummed her hands on the table and stood. "Coming right up." As she went to walk away, her ankle got caught on the leg of her chair, which sent her reeling forward. Cat grabbed for the lip of the table, managing to support her weight on it long enough to delay her inevitable crash landing. Closing her eyes and bracing herself, Cat prepared to hit the ground.

She hadn't expected Dmitri to break her fall. Not with his bad knee and his predilection for being a jerk most of the time. Yet there she lay in his strong, capable arms as he knelt to the floor beneath her. Instinctively, she moved to sit up and scramble away, knowing the way Dmitri held her was inappropriate, given their relationship and the misstep the day before. But he overpowered Cat, pulling her into his chest when she tried to get away.

"Jesus, Cat. Are you all right?" His clipped tone gave off the impression of genuine concern.

"I'm fine." Realizing her weight rested on his bad knee, she shifted to the black and white checkered tile floor, wiggling out of his grasp. "How about you? Is your knee hurt?"

"Don't worry about me. I'm a broken-down old man." He cupped his hands on either side of her face. "But you can't get hurt. Not my Clara."

Dmitri used his thumbs to trace comforting, soothing arches over her cheekbones. Unconsciously, she leaned into one of his hands, enjoying the way it felt to be touched by him.

"I'm fine," she repeated, but this time her voice was nothing more than a faint whisper. Dmitri's unexpected tenderness had taken the breath right out of her. "I promise."

His startled expression warped into something far more grave as he stroked her hair. No one was hurt and both parties could get up, but neither did, choosing instead to exist in that transient moment where they could sit on the floor of the Land of Sweets and be close with one another.

Cat noticed his gaze drop to her mouth and she licked her lips, hoping he'd see it as a sign she wanted him to kiss her again. She shouldn't have done it. She knew that. But it was impossible to be that close to Dmitri, to breathe the citrusy scent of his cologne, without wanting him in every possible way she could have him. Since they were in a public place, her mother's store, more specifically, she'd have to settle for another kiss.

Dmitri wrapped his hand around the back of Cat's neck and pulled her toward him. Her eyelids fluttered just as a bright, blinding light came through the storefront windows. Pulling away and shielding her eyes with her hand, Cat saw an SUV pulling into one of the parking spots out front.

Instantly, Dmitri released his hold on her. He gripped the edge of the table, grunting and looking unsteady as he tried to get up.

Noticing this, Cat climbed to her feet and pressed a hand to his back. "Do you need some help?"

"No, I don't need any help," Dmitri spat back at her over his shoulder as he finally got both of his feet on the ground. Balancing on his good leg, he bent and flexed his hurt knee a few times. "Besides, it looks like you have a customer."

Cat wondered if Dmitri's knee was sore from the dive he must have taken to catch her, or the sheer strain of having to get up from the ground. Either way, it was her fault he was hurt. To make matters worse, they'd nearly kissed again. And this time, Cat thought she might have been the one to initiate it.

She started to the counter, hoping to make a sort of peace offering. "Let me get your macarons."

"Maybe next time," he said, before grabbing his cane and limping out the door.

Lisa Hahn

CHAPTER TWELVE

The drive into New York was the most uncomfortable trip of Cat's life. Simon had arranged for a driver to take everyone together in one car, meaning she would be crammed into the vehicle with two people who hated her and one she couldn't stop thinking about. Dmitri sat up front, to take advantage of the leg room afforded there so he could stretch out his bad knee, leaving Cat wedged in the back between Phoebe and Nick, both of whom had deemed the middle seat too uncomfortable to sit in.

When they got to the hotel, Cat didn't waste any time checking in. She hurriedly made her way up to the eighth floor. She immediately collapsed on the king-sized bed in her room, feeling emotionally exhausted from the past three and a half hours.

Cat was relaxing on the pillowy mattress and soft blankets when her phone buzzed from inside her purse. She rolled onto her belly to reach for it and smiled at the sight of Abby's name.

"Hey, Ab." She sounded tired and had to stifle a yawn with the back of her hand. Despite the trip to New York, Dmitri had insisted she, Nick, Phoebe get in a full day of rehearsals. She was glad to put in the work, but it had left her feeling drained.

"How was the car ride?" Abby drew out her words, curious and eager for gossip.

"Fine." Cat rested her chin on one of her forearms. "Pretty quiet, actually. After what happened on Monday, I think Phoebe and Nick were too afraid to talk to Dmitri. No one wants to set him off."

"That's good."

"Kind of. I guess they figured ballet would be the safest topic of conversation, so they reminisced a little about some of our old productions. Nick didn't miss an opportunity to make a dig at me, though. He kept asking what role I'd had in every ballet they talked about, even though he knew full well I was relegated to the background for most of them."

"What a jerk." Abby spat out the words.

Cat couldn't help but smile. "You're a good friend, Abby. I really appreciate the support."

Abby shrugged. "Just doing my job as a best friend."

"I better get used to it though, I guess," Cat continued, "because we're going to be spending more time than I'd like to together while we're here. We're meeting with a few people from ABT for dinner tonight, then tomorrow we have the class in the morning and then the drive home."

"Look at the bright side. You'll get to dance in front people at ABT who might see everything in you that Dmitri does and Lillian never did. Maybe they'll invite you to do a guest performance or maybe they'll send one of their best male dancers up to us, specifically to partner you."

"That's what I love about you, Abby, your eternal optimism!" Cat usually thought positively, but she needed Abby around for the rough spots when she occasionally lost sight of things. Even if it would unheard of for ABT to invite her to perform with them, it was one of the many opportunities that could come from this exposure.

"You're right." Cat glanced over at the clock. She had a little less than thirty minutes to get ready and meet everyone in the lobby. "Wish you were here. You deserve this just as much as I do."

"My time will come. Just like yours has."

Cat sat up, pulling her fingers through her hair. They got ensnared in a nasty tangle she'd need a comb to get out. She'd left her house in such a hurry earlier, she hadn't gotten to dry her hair before she met the group back at the studio. "Listen, I have to run and get ready for this dinner."

"You'll be great. Text me later and let me know how it goes. Love you."

"Love you, too."

Cat ended the call and tossed her phone on the pillows, wishing for a second she was back home making skirts and leotards like any normal Saturday. Then she remembered what Abby had just said and that made her even more determined to make this work.

Dmitri was giving her a second chance. If it weren't for him, she'd probably have danced her entire career in the corps of a minor company most people had never heard of. If she ruined this opportunity, she'd be an idiot.

Twenty-five minutes later, Cat was in the lobby. Her long hair cascaded down her back in natural waves, hitting just above her waist. With ballet and her work at the shop, she rarely got an opportunity to wear it down, even though it was how she liked it best. The emerald green lace dress she wore hugged her slender body, highlighting her slight curves. Abby had ransacked Cat's closet the night before, looking for the perfect dress for the occasion and swore this one would do the job. The short hem and tight fit added a bit of sex appeal, while the high neckline and long sleeves were the perfect accents for the demure ballerina. According to Abby, paired with stylish nude pumps, the dress would garner attention for all the right reasons. Cat wouldn't look too uptight, but she also wouldn't look like she was headed out to one of the many nightclubs in New York City.

While Cat had been leaning toward a less eye-catching black A-line number, she ultimately went with Abby's suggestion, in hopes it would attract some positive attention from Dmitri. Though things between them had returned to normal during rehearsal, she couldn't help but feel a coldness from him. He still summoned her often after their run-throughs to relay his suggestions, but she noticed he had a hard time meeting her eyes when he did so.

She believed pursuing any sort of relationship with him would be wrong, but she found herself missing the way her entire body tingled when she felt his gaze linger on her a few seconds more than would be considered appropriate. Certainly, a body-hugging dress would garner a few stolen glances in her direction. When they returned to Bretton Falls, she could go back to being the straight-laced ballerina who would make the perfect Clara.

Cat had been pacing the ruby-carpeted lobby when she heard the elevator ding, signaling the arrival of someone she hoped would be Dmitri. To her disappointment, Phoebe and Nick stepped out, looking every bit as regal and refined as they did on stage. Nick had on a pair of flawlessly fitted black slacks and a crisp white shirt, while Phoebe had donned a salmon-hued dress that flattered her fair complexion and fiery red hair.

"Well, well, well," Nick said when he spotted her. "Little Catherine Brown sure cleans up well."

It would have been appropriate for Cat to express gratitude, but she was so thrown off by Nick's compliment that she was stunned into silence.

He laced his arm with Phoebe's and steered her toward one of the gold-framed mirrors lining the walls. "Not as well as us, though."

There it is, Cat thought. The dig she had been expecting.

Phoebe nodded in agreement as she smoothed a hand over her hair, which was twisted up in her perpetually perfect ballerina's bun.

Cat bit her tongue while she watched Nick and Phoebe's display of narcissism.

"You look lovely," whispered Dmitri into her left ear as he passed behind her, his voice low.

Cat jumped, surprised by his presence and the tickle of his breath against her ear. She pressed a hand to her pounding heart as he stopped to stand at her right side. "You scared me. I didn't hear the elevator arrive."

He tapped his cane on the floor a couple of times, finally drawing Nick and Phoebe's attention. "Walking around with one of these means I'm usually given a room on the ground floor."

Nick tugged at his cuffs when he noticed Dmitri. "You look well tonig—"

Dmitri held up a hand to stop him. "Save your flattery for the people we'll be dining with. I'm sure they'll appreciate it far more than I do." Tugging up the sleeve of his dark gray, untucked button-up, Dmitri checked his watch. "We have ten minutes to walk the two blocks over there. We should go."

Nick rushed ahead to open the big, glass doors leading to the street, nearly knocking Phoebe out of the way in the process. "Are you sure you're okay to walk all that way, sir?"

Dmitri pushed passed him without bothering to stop and answer. "Do I look like an invalid to you?"

"No, sir," Nick responded dejectedly, holding the door for Phoebe to pass through but releasing it when Cat approached the threshold. With gritted teeth, she caught the door and pushed it open. She knew remarking about Nick's rudeness would rile Dmitri, and she didn't need him stepping in to defend her again. It would just rev up the rumors Marcy was already spreading.

"Who are we meeting with?" Phoebe asked as she tugged a snow-white jacket over her shoulders. When the sun set, the temperature dipped below fifty degrees. Since ballet dancers had a lower body fat percentage than most, they tended to feel low temperatures acutely. Cat pulled on the black pea coat she'd had slung over her arm.

"The assistant artistic director and the artistic administrator," Dmitri answered succinctly without glancing over his shoulder at her.

The group walked the short distance toward the restaurant in silence. Dmitri led the way, which meant the three dancers following him had no choice but to maintain his rather slow pace. Cat felt her heart tug as she watched Dmitri's uneven gait. She noticed his limp had been more pronounced all week and suspected it had something to do with the dive he'd taken to break her fall on Tuesday.

He walked with his head held at a downward slant, his confidence mingling with his desire to avoid interaction with the people he passed. He stalked around the studio in between rehearsal sessions the same way. Dancers, pianists, and administrative workers alike all stepped aside when they saw Dmitri coming, dropping their conversations to silently nod their heads in acknowledgement to their director.

Cat noticed Dmitri had a similar effect on the streets on New York. People didn't veer to the side when he approached because he walked with a cane; it was because he had a silent way of commanding everyone's respect.

Rosie's restaurant had a royal blue awning spanning its storefront, the color bright and vibrant. Several black wrought iron tables speckled the outdoor seated area in front of the establishment, and the group wound around them. As they approached the door, Nick slipped past Cat, nearly elbowing her in the side. He went to reach for the brass doorknob when Dmitri growled and slapped his hand away. "If you don't stop treating me like a goddamn cripple, I'm never casting you in one of my ballets again. Do you understand me?"

Nick nodded and took a step back, cowering like a puppy who'd just been scolded. "Sorry, sir. It won't happen again."

Dmitri swung open the door, ready to let Cat and Phoebe pass through as he began to address Nick. "I trust it won—"

His cutting reply dropped off so abruptly, Cat craned her head to see what had startled him from inside the restaurant.

Lisa Hahn

CHAPTER THIRTEEN

Dmitri's jaw tightened. A subdued hiss between his teeth replaced the litany of obscenities he wanted to unload upon seeing his parents standing between the two people he'd been informed would be attending this dinner. Knowing they'd find out about his trip from people within ABT, he'd phoned them earlier that week to schedule a visit. They'd agreed to meet for brunch on Saturday afternoon after the company class his dancers took that morning, which his mother was teaching.

Yet, there Ivan and Constance Fedorov stood before him, beaming at their son.

"Dmitri." Constance stretched her arms out toward him. He stood in the doorway, still reeling from the surprise of seeing his father and her there. Undeterred, Constance made her way over to him. "I'm glad you're here. A mother shouldn't have to go this long without seeing her son." She pressed her hands to his cheeks, kissing him on each side of his face before stepping back to study him. "I don't know if I like you with a beard."

He jerked his head away as she ran her fingertips over the facial hair he'd grown since relocating. "I like my beard."

"I like it too." Ivan moved forward in one fluid, graceful step. "You look good, son." Ivan's Russian accent had waned after living in the States for almost forty years, but his country of origin was still very much evident in the way he spoke. Dmitri softened a little at the sound of his father's voice, feeling at home because of it.

"What's the hold-up?" Nick's irritating, high-pitched complaining pulled Dmitri back to the current moment. He greeted Anna Greenwich, the assistant artistic director, and Paul Brindley, the artistic administrator. After shaking hands and brushing off remarks about how good it was to see him back in the city, Dmitri stepped aside to introduce his dancers, who were clamoring for space by the door in the cramped foyer.

"Let me introduce all of you to three of Bretton Falls Ballet's best dancers. This is Catherine Brown." He placed a hand to the small of her back, urging her forward an inch so she could dutifully shake everyone's hands like a good ambassador. Cat's spine went ramrod straight at his gentle shove, and Dmitri had to force himself to retract his hand. If he could have it his way, he'd stay plastered to Cat's side the entire dinner, making sure long-nosed string beans like Paul Brindley didn't look her up and down like she was a sports car, not a respected and talented woman. Instead, he swept his hand toward Phoebe and Nick. They both stood by with ready smiles, looking eager to meet everyone. "Phoebe Braxton and Nick Briggs."

Dmitri stood off to the side as all the handshaking and cheek-kissing took place around him. With everyone preoccupied, he took the opportunity to press his weight into the left side of his body and stretch out his right knee. It had been killing him all week. He'd chickened out before he kissed Cat again, and now the pain in his knee mocked him for not even benefiting from throwing himself down to break her fall. Dmitri knew she would have been fine if she'd hit the floor. Probably just a little embarrassed. But he'd been desperate for an opportunity to touch her again and seized the one he had.

Before his conscience kicked in.

The bow-tied host led the group to a table in a nook toward the back of the restaurant for privacy. Dmitri followed Cat, listening while Paul Brindley yapped her ear off about what being an artistic administrator entailed. She nodded along as he spoke, her lips parting occasionally like she wanted to interject but Paul rattled on and never gave her the opportunity.

A small fire crackled beside their table, warming up the area. Dmitri quickly skirted around the edge of the group while they all tried to figure out who should sit where, and pulled out a chair.

"Cat." He touched her shoulder to get her attention. She excused herself from her conversation with Paul, interrupting him midsentence, to face Dmitri. He motioned to the chair. "Perhaps you'd like to sit by the fire. It's much warmer here."

A smile crept up on her lips as she met his eyes. "Thanks. That would be perfect."

Cat began removing her coat, but Dmitri quickly rested his cane against the table and moved to help her. "Allow me."

Obliging him, she dropped her hands from the lapel and nodded. Dmitri let his fingers graze her arms as he removed the coat and he carefully placed it on the back of Cat's chair.

Cat sat, looking at Dmitri through her long, fluttering eyelashes. "I didn't know you had it in you to be such a gentleman." She'd said it in a low, sexy whisper so only he could hear.

"Is that so?" He settled down in the seat beside her, sucking his bottom lip in between his teeth to stop himself from snarling when Paul took the chair directly across from her.

"Cat," Paul said, bumping one of his bony knees into the table as he tried to cross his long, gangly legs. "How long have you been with Bretton Falls Ballet?"

"This is my seventh season," she responded with a polite smile, her demeanor noticeably cooler than it had been seconds ago when she'd been talking to Dmitri.

The touch of a hand on Dmitri's shoulder stole his attention away. His mother pressed her full weight into him as she lowered herself into the next chair. A lengthy and celebrated career as a principal with ABT had left Constance's body in shambles. She'd danced well into her forties, which only a small percentage of women did.

"I'm so happy to see you." She huffed as her backside finally reached the chair. "Damn arthritis," she said under her breath.

"While I am happy to see you, I didn't think you'd be joining us tonight." Though he'd been vexed, of late, with his parents' insistence he return to New York, he was glad to see them, especially since seeing him seemed to make them so happy. Dmitri had spent his life trying to please his parents, working to live up to their expectations. It gratified him to see that despite his injury and his refusal to do things their way anymore, he still had the ability to make them smile. For a few months, when he'd been deep in his depression over the loss of his career, he feared that might not ever happen again.

"I wanted to surprise you." She, grinned like she had all those times he'd spotted her in the wings when he was on stage. "Did you think you could come home and leave after just one measly brunch with your mother?"

Ivan, who was now seated on the other side of Constance, leaned forward over the silverware and expertly folded napkins to interject. "I told her to call you." He made a slicing gesture in the air with the blade of his hand. "She would not hear it."

Dmitri felt one corner of his mouth tug upward. "Well, I'm glad we're all here."

Their waiter came to read off the specials and take everyone's drink orders. Cat requested a glass of water with lemon, but at the poking and prodding of the rest of the table, she eventually asked for a glass of chardonnay as well. As Dmitri suspected she would, Cat had barely touched the wine throughout the meal. She had an important morning, and she would not risk it. Judging by her small size, she'd be tipsy before she even drained the glass.

He paid special attention to Cat throughout the meal, appreciating the delicate, ladylike way she ate her food and the charming, flawless smile she wore while listening to someone else talk. She'd been the star of the evening, while Phoebe and Nick clamored for opportunities to speak. Dmitri wondered if her ease of conversation came with serving customers at Land of Sweets, or being the offspring of Louise Brown. Though he'd only met her mother for a minute, he could tell she was as outgoing and friendly as he was closed off and reserved.

Dmitri couldn't help but feel proud as he watched her charm Paul, Anna, and his parents. While he liked to think anyone who took control of Bretton Falls Ballet would have instantly recognized it was a tragedy Cat had been held back, he could not have known for sure. He had been happy to give her an opportunity to shine, and happier to see she'd taken it.

As he sat back in awe of the talented, lovely, gorgeous woman beside him, he'd never wanted her more.

Her dress didn't help matters. The wrap skirts she wore during rehearsals covered more skin than that green lace did. It had taken everything in his power not to drag her back to his room when he'd walked out into the lobby earlier and seen her standing there.

After the dinner course was cleared, Paul ordered a fruit platter and coffee for everyone. The more time Dmitri spent around that man, the more he found himself disliking him. Even little things, like the bushiness of his eyebrows, ticked Dmitri off.

"So, Cat," Paul began as the waiter strode away, "when was the last time you were in Manhattan?"

He'd been talking to her all night, asking asinine questions he didn't truly care to get the answers to. Paul just wanted Cat's attention, and he'd been working himself into a fit all night to get it.

"Hmm." She glanced at the ceiling as she considered the question. "It's probably been five or six years."

"That long, huh?" Paul seemed genuinely surprised. Like Dmitri's parents, he couldn't imagine an existence outside of the bustling city. Dmitri used to think like that too, but Bretton Falls had started to grow on him. In this new phase of his life, he'd learned to enjoy the quiet.

"My family owns a business back home and it can be difficult to get away."

"I guess I can use that same excuse to explain away why I never leave the city." Paul chuckled, sitting back in his chair. "ABT is my life, and ABT is here."

Cat smiled at him. The glow from the fire hit her perfectly, making it seem as if she wore a halo of fuzzy, warm light. She tucked her hair behind her ear, revealing the most beautiful profile Dmitri had ever seen: sculpted, round cheekbones; a small, yet elegant nose; lush, kissable lips. Her eyes shone, their evergreen color enhanced by the green lace.

Dmitri felt a warm pressure in his chest he'd never experienced before, even though he was well acquainted with various forms of beauty, from the world-class ballets he'd seen to the knockouts he used to take home after a performance.

Overwhelmed with emotion and furious with Paul for flirting with her, Dmitri felt overcome with an urge to punch the jackass from his chair. Since he couldn't, he did the one other thing he could think to do.

Discreetly, he slid his hand onto her chair and grasped Cat's slender thigh. A quick intake of air showed her surprise at his bold action, but Cat played it off by coughing and no one seemed to notice. While she continued to feign interest in Paul's boring rhetoric about how New York was the best city in the world, Dmitri's fingers curled into her leg, kneading her flesh and silently claiming her as his own. Though he desperately wanted to slip his hand under the hemline of her dress, he kept his hand in a much more decent location, should they get caught.

And they could not get caught.

The conversation switched gears when Paul and the two elder Federovs went on in enthusiastic detail about ABT's planned productions for the upcoming season. While they talked, Dmitri danced his fingers toward the inside of Cat's thigh. She jumped slightly as he tickled her.

Reaching under the table, Cat caught his hand and pinned it down with her own. "What are you doing?" she asked, her voice low and her expression calm. "You're going to get us in trouble."

Dmitri flashed her a smile and sat back in his chair, acting casual. "I only get caught if I want to get caught."

If Cat knew the innumerable legions of ABT dancers he'd fooled around with backstage, she'd be stunned. Many people gossiped about Dmitri's dalliances over the years, but he could be discreet if he needed to be.

He tugged his hand loose from her grasp, entwined their fingers, and rested their joined hands on her thigh. "Better?"

Cat pulled her bottom lip between her teeth, looking like she was fighting a smile. He imagined she was completely caught up in their attraction, just like he was. Acting on his feelings could destroy their careers but not acting on them could wreak havoc on his mental health, which was already in an unstable state. Before she could answer, the waiter swept over and reached between them to place a tray loaded with honeydew, cantaloupe, and berries in the center of the table.

"That looks lovely," Constance remarked, elbowing her son in the side, oblivious to the way he'd been swooning over the pretty girl beside him, his hand still tangled with hers. "Wouldn't you agree, Dmitri? Will you serve me some?"

Reluctantly, Dmitri flexed his fingers and pulled his hand from Cat's. He'd dished out fruit for his mother before resting his hand, palm up, back on her thigh. As she grabbed for her fork with her right hand, Cat carefully placed her left one back in his, where it remained for the rest of the time they sat at the table.

After the check was paid, everyone filtered out onto the sidewalk to say their goodbyes. While the group politely wished one another a good night, Dmitri draped an arm over Constance's narrow shoulders and pulled her off to the side.

"Can you do me a favor?" He wrapped his arms around her, giving his mother the hug he knew she wanted, and spoke quietly into her ear.

She squeezed him tightly. "Anything for you, my Dmitri."

"Pay attention to Cat tomorrow. I think she would fit in at ABT and I want to see her audition for next season."

Constance pulled away, stealing a quick glance at the girl. "How old is she?"

"Twenty-four." Constance parted her lips to respond, but Dmitri stopped her with a raised palm. "I know she is older, but you'll understand why I asked when you see her train tomorrow."

Constance smiled, cupping her son's cheek in her hand. "I'll take a look and let you know at brunch."

"Thank you, Mom." Dmitri nearly smiled before restraining his excitement. He didn't want to raise any suspicion from Constance about his complicated relationship with Cat.

A dancer as beautiful as Cat deserved to be seen by a broader audience. She should be performing in world-class productions in front of six-figure-a-year patrons, not selling candy part-time at her mom's shop.

Constance motioned for Dmitri to crouch down so she could kiss his cheek. "See you in the morning."

Once the group parted ways, Dmitri headed back to the hotel with Cat, Nick, and Phoebe in tow. Much like on the walk to the restaurant, everyone stayed quiet. Dmitri preferred it that way. He'd endured enough small talk over the course of their dinner.

Less than a block from the hotel, Nick stopped in the middle of the sidewalk and groaned. When Dmitri looked back at him, Nick threw his head back and dragged his hands over his face.

"What's wrong?" Phoebe asked.

He dropped his arms and patted his pockets. "I must have left my phone at the restaurant. I'm going to have to go back for it."

"I'll go with you." Phoebe pulled her jacket tighter across her chest. "I'm not really tired yet, and I'm enjoying the fresh air." She managed to get the last word out before her teeth chattered.

"See you in the morning, then. We'll meet in the lobby at eight-fifteen," Dmitri said matter-of-factly before turning and continuing in the direction of the hotel.

Cat was at his side after a few hurried steps. "You know they're going out, right?" She looked over her shoulder at Phoebe and Nick as they retreated. "They didn't even have the courtesy to walk all the way to the hotel with us and hide out in their rooms for a few minutes first." Her upper lip curled, and Dmitri wanted to bite it. She was cute when she was upset. "Instead, they came up with that pathetic excuse."

"I don't mind." Dmitri walked briskly, ignoring the sting in his knee. "It'll just make things easier."

One of her brows raised. "What do you mean?"

When they reached the hotel, Dmitri swung open the door, meeting Cat's eye as she passed through. He said nothing in response to her question. Words weren't Dmitri's forte. Actions were.

Cat looked adorable, standing in the lobby with her forehead wrinkled and her pretty, pink lips pursed. She was confused, which meant she probably expected him to act as if they hadn't just been holding hands and exchanging stolen glances for the past two hours, just like he'd acted at work all week like he hadn't kissed her. He laced his fingers with hers and started to lead her in the direction of his hotel room.

"Dmitri." She said his name softly, looking over her shoulder at the elevator as they passed it. "What are we doing?"

Instead of answering, he squeezed her hand as they turned the corner into the ruby carpet-lined hallway. His room was close, only three doors down. Eager to get inside, Dmitri unlocked the door and tossed his cane inside with such force it hit the back wall. He wrapped an arm around Cat's waist. She stumbled into him, her eyes wide like a doe's, and pressed her hands into his chest, her fingers fanning out over the hard planes of muscle.

"You're still so strong," she whispered, kneading into his flesh.

Dmitri wished he could sweep her up and carry her into the room, but while his upper body strength was more than sufficient to lift Cat's tiny frame with ease, his knee would be in sad shape after. Instead, he held her close and pulled her inside with him, kicking the door shut once they were in.

Immediately, Dmitri shoved Cat into the brocade papered wall, his lips seeking out hers. She arched her long, graceful neck and met him halfway. Their warm mouths collided. Dmitri braced his weight against the wall with one forearm angled over Cat's head, not wanting to lose his balance because of the instability in his knee. He wrapped his free hand in her long hair, enjoying the deep, purring sound Cat made every time he gave it a gentle tug. Meanwhile, her hands traversed his side, occasionally drifting toward his back. She'd reached under his thick coat, so he could feel her fingernails raking over his shirt. The quiet, crunchy sound of the fabric made something deep down in his stomach clench.

With his hand still tangled in her hair, Dmitri tugged Cat's head back and bared her neck to his mouth. He kissed her in meandering, haphazard patterns, nibbling her skin in places where she felt particularly soft. Cat writhed against him in response, her hands gliding over him with more force than before.

"Let's go to the bed." Dmitri spun her around, and his erection pressed into her back as he steered her toward the king-sized mattress. He brushed some clothes to the floor before throwing the blankets back. Cat went to climb on, but Dmitri pressed his hands to her taut stomach, keeping her glued to the front of him.

"I like feeling you against me," he whispered before nibbling her earlobe. She arched her back and moaned in response. The breathy sound kicked Dmitri's libido into high gear. He released her and began removing his coat. He was about to instruct Cat to do the same, but she quickly followed suit without instruction, tugging off her pea coat while simultaneously toeing off her heels. Dmitri smirked, noting how anxious she seemed. For a girl who had been playing coy in the hall, she moved quickly.

Cat's coat hadn't even hit the floor before Dmitri was on her again, his hands fanning out over her cheeks as he maneuvered her back onto the bed. They kissed wildly as they shifted position, forgoing finesse to fulfill their baser instincts. Their bodies tangled together so perfectly, the beauty of their synchronicity rivaled the world's most stunning pas de deux.

Dmitri wished he could have leaned over and kissed Cat in the middle of dinner, rather than secretly holding her hand under the table. He wanted everyone to know how fiercely he cared for the girl. It was a feeling unlike anything he'd experienced before, which made it especially hard to control. It was why he leading her back to his bed instead of insisting she get a good night sleep to prepare for what could end up being the most important class in her ballet career.

When the backs of Cat's thighs bumped the mattress, she sat back onto it. Dmitri followed her descent to the bed, pushing her back so he could cover her body with his. His knee stung with the pressure he put on it, but Dmitri was nearly oblivious to the pain. If it meant he got to be with Cat, he'd endure the discomfort.

Cat was worth it, even if this were the only night he ever spent with her. Chances were, after the adrenaline had worn off and he faced the decision to bring her back to his room in the light of day, he might end up regretting what he'd done. Not because he didn't want Cat, but because being with her had the potential to destroy their careers. He'd be the gruff and cold-natured director who slept with his dancers and practiced nepotism, and Cat would be the dancer who had to sleep her way into to a decent role. Neither scenario was true, but that didn't mean everyone wouldn't see it that way. Dancers tended to have a flair for the dramatic.

Dmitri rolled off Cat and flopped onto his back. Angry about having to force himself to stop, he slammed his fist down on the mattress. Cat sat up immediately, her gaze shooting toward his leg.

"Is everything okay? Is your knee hurt?"

"It's fine." He bent and straightened his leg, testing it out. As expected, there was soreness, but he'd be able to walk to the studio the next morning without a problem.

"Oh, okay." Cat self-consciously tucked a strand of hair behind her ear and looked around the room. "Do you want me to go?"

Her soft voice betrayed her waning confidence. It was the first time he'd ever heard her sound less than sure of herself.

"No." Dmitri wrapped his fingers around her wrist and pulled Cat back down to him so she was tucked into his side, her head resting on his chest. "If I wasn't such a selfish son-of-a-bitch, I'd make you leave."

She dragged a fingertip along his chin, tracing his jawline. "But I want to stay, so you can't be selfish."

"I am." He pulled her tighter even though he knew he should be letting her go. "Anything that happens between us has the potential to disrupt the trajectory of your career. I can't have that on my conscience."

Not when he cared so deeply for her. But he couldn't admit that. Not then. Not when being in her presence made him feel so vulnerable. He was liable to promise her the world.

"It doesn't have to be that way." Cat dropped a hand to his chest, her palm resting over his heart. "No one has to know."

"You don't get it." Dmitri squeezed his eyes shut, cupping his hand over hers. "My feelings for you have already affected my work. I never would have interrupted that argument between you and Marcy if I didn't feel this overpowering need to protect you. I've been giving you preferential treatment from the start."

"So what?" she asked incredulously. "Lillian always had her favorites, and she made it way more obvious than you do. Besides, you just spend extra time with me because I'm your lead, and an unexperienced one at that."

"That's not why."

Dmitri wished he could flip Cat on her back and show her how much he wanted her, but his knee already stung and sudden movements could throw off his stability. Instead, he sat up and gave it to her straight.

"I've wanted you from the moment I saw you when I was watching the tape from last season."

She stayed silent for a few beats, and Dmitri wondered if she could have been surprised. He couldn't keep his eyes off her during rehearsal. There could be twenty people dancing, and she would be the only one he'd watch.

She sighed. "I don't want to leave."

"You can stay." Dmitri swung his legs off the edge of the bed and stood. "But only to sleep."

Cat glanced at her dress. "This is going to be pretty uncomfortable to sleep in."

Dmitri unzipped his suitcase and tossed her a t-shirt. "You can wear this."

Cat caught the tee. "Thanks."

They took turns changing and using the bathroom. Since Dmitri had gone first, he was already in bed when Cat walked out of the bathroom. Dmitri had to look away, unsure if he could stop himself from having his way with her if he kept staring. The white fabric of his t-shirt hit just low enough to cover her panties, though he felt certain the bottom curve of her derriere was likely exposed. As much as he wanted to find out if that was true, Dmitri kept his wits about him. Sleeping beside her without trying anything would be difficult enough; if he caught a glimpse of Cat's gorgeous ass, he wouldn't be able to help himself.

"Hey." A slight smile tugged at the corners of her lips in that adorable way only Cat could manage. When she danced, Dmitri thought she might be the most beautiful person on the planet. When he'd seen her in the tight dress and makeup, he felt even more convinced that it was true. Now, as she stood there half-dressed with all her makeup scrubbed off, he was sure of it.

"Come here." Fully aware of his rapidly beating heart, he threw the covers aside. With a quiet smile, Cat walked to the bed and got in. Before she settled, Dmitri snaked an arm around her waist and pulled her into his side. Together they sank down to rest amongst the pillows. Cat nuzzled into the crook of Dmitri's neck, and he detected the minty scent of his toothpaste on her breath; she must have swirled some in her mouth. He felt the crotch of his boxer briefs tighten and it made him wish he'd brought pajama pants to sleep in. The aroma of his toothpaste continued to waft off her, combined with the fragrance of his laundry detergent and a bit of his woodsy cologne. Unintentionally, he'd marked her with his scent.

"This feels nice." Cat wrapped one of her slender legs around his. "If only I were tired."

Dmitri glanced over at the bedside clock. It was ten.

"You should get some rest. Tomorrow is important."

"I know." She reached across his body to play with the ends of his hair. "But class isn't until nine-thirty. Maybe we could talk for a little first."

Panic seized Dmitri's chest. *Talk?* He couldn't remember ever having engaged an attractive woman in conversation just for the sake of it. Dmitri was a man of few words, and he typically used those few words to entice a woman into bed with him. Since Cat was already there, he wasn't sure what else to say. They had ballet in common, but it seemed unimaginative and dull to discuss work in bed.

"What do you want to talk about?"

"I don't know. Anything, really." She shrugged. "I just want to get to know you a little better."

"What would you like to know?" Dmitri asked the question warily, not sure if he'd ultimately feel comfortable answering her. Ever since the accident, he'd been unwilling to talk about himself—his feelings, his health, his knee—even with the people he cared about, like his parents. Could he open up to a pretty, young ballerina with a sweet disposition, a strong work ethic, and a killer smile?

"What's your favorite color?"

Easy enough. "Blue."

She excitedly tapped his chest. "Mine, too. What's your favorite ballet?"

"*Don Quixote*. Yours?"

"If you asked me a week ago, I would have told you *A Midsummer Night's Dream*. Now it might be *The Nutcracker*, though."

"You like being Clara."

"I love being Clara."

The two continued to talk, asking and answering questions about trivial matters like their favorite foods and movies, to topics with slightly more depth, like stories from their childhoods. Dmitri felt completely at ease with Cat, telling her things he hadn't thought about in years. He realized he'd been smiling and laughing more than usual, even more then he had before the accident.

Eventually, the questions and stories had longer gaps in between, as Cat and Dmitri drifted off to sleep, wrapped in each other's arms.

Lisa Hahn

CHAPTER FOURTEEN

The next morning, Cat felt like she was living a dream. As soon as she woke, she blinked her eyes repeatedly, convinced the man asleep beside her was only a figment of her imagination and not the most beautiful male dancer she'd ever laid eyes on. He looked more handsome when he slept than he did during his waking hours, when the hard, masculine lines of his face were made harsher by his permanent scowl and his propensity for brooding. The memory of him kicking her out of his office almost two weeks before was still fresh in her mind, and she feared what would happen when he woke up. She rolled over onto her back, shifting out of his arms as she considered making a break for it.

Her subtle movements caused Dmitri to stir beside her.

"Good morning," he rasped, his voice scratchy from sleep and his eyes still closed.

She relaxed, realizing he hadn't woken up riddled with regret. "Good morning."

"What time is it?" Dmitri rubbed his hands over his face and yawned.

Cat looked over at the clock. "It's almost six-thirty."

"Early," Dmitri croaked before turning to face her, the corners of his eyes soft with sleep.

The group was scheduled to meet in the lobby at eight forty-five, so they still had plenty of time to get ready. Cat wanted to eat a light breakfast and shower so she didn't smell like her director's cologne during class.

"I should probably get going." She sat up and shimmied her hips so she could tug Dmitri's shirt down to cover herself. "You know, in case Nick and Phoebe come down early to grab breakfast or something."

Dmitri sat up alongside her and tucked her hair behind her ear. "What will you do for the next few hours?"

Cat leaned into him and rested her head on his shoulder, unable to resist being close to him. "Shower, stretch. You know, the usual morning stuff."

"Too bad you can't stay." Dmitri pressed a kiss to her head that made her chest swell with warmth and hope. Even after everything Dmitri had said the night before, she'd thought that when the sun rose, they'd go back to their tiring dynamic. Now, after how affectionate and kind Dmitri was being, she hoped they might have a chance…as long as they kept whatever was going on between them quiet.

Cat got up and walked over to the bureau to retrieve her dress, aware her ass was hanging out beneath the bottom of the T-shirt Dmitri had given her. She thought about pulling the shirt down at the sides to protect her modesty, but then thought better of it. So what if he saw a sliver of her ass? Though she had been disappointed when Dmitri had cooled things down between them the night before, she'd also been relieved. Cat had never had sex with someone without getting to know them, and she feared having sex with Dmitri might have left her feeling used.

Instead, she'd had one of the best evenings of her life. Dmitri had opened up to her in ways she'd felt certain he wasn't capable of. He'd laughed, shared stories, and listened thoughtfully to every word that had come out of her mouth.

If she hadn't been smitten with him before, she was now.

She glanced over at Dmitri as she grabbed her dress, wondering where she should change. Last night, they'd both disrobed separately in the bathroom, which she would feel more comfortable with, but she didn't want him to think she was a prude. Cat knew from the rumors she'd heard over the years that Dmitri never struggled to find women who were willing to give him whatever he wanted, and she worried he'd lose interest if she acted like the woman of limited experience she was. Ballet and work at the candy shop didn't leave her much time for going out on dates.

Dmitri rolled out of bed and padded over. He stopped behind her and wrapped his arms around her waist. When Cat checked out their reflection in the mirror, she couldn't help but giggle at the way Dmitri's hair stuck out at crazy angles.

"Are you laughing at me?" he asked, sounding amused rather than offended.

Cat pinched her thumb and forefinger together. "Just a little."

He leaned in and kissed her cheek. "I'm going to fix my hair in the bathroom so you can have some privacy to change."

Cat beamed at his sensitivity. "Thanks."

By the time Dmitri left the bathroom, Cat had changed, then collected her coat and handbag from where she'd tossed them onto the floor. After, she picked up his cane too.

He stood on the threshold, bracing his hands on either side of the doorway. "I guess I'll see you in a little bit."

"That you will." She handed him his cane. "I'm worried you already hurt yourself last night."

Dmitri reached out like he was about to take the cane, but instead he wrapped his large hand around her much smaller one and tugged her body into his. Their mouths crashed together. Cat parted her lips, her tongue tangling with his.

"I'll see you shortly." He nipped at her lips one more time before opening the door to the hallway.

"See you soon." Cat was aware her whiny, high-pitched farewell made her sound like a lovesick schoolgirl, but she hardly cared. She suspected Dmitri felt the same.

When the door closed behind her, Cat cautiously proceeded down the hallway. She peeked out into the lobby, placing one foot in front of the other so slowly it probably looked like she was avoiding potential land mines. Certain the coast was clear, she dashed into the nearby stairwell, figuring that would be the best way to avoid Nick and Phoebe if they happened to be up and about that early.

After she was safely in her room, Cat stripped out of her dress to take a shower. She thought about Dmitri the entire time the warm water spilled over her, remembering the time they'd shared and wondering what he was doing at that moment. When she stepped out, toweled off, and started to blow dry her hair so she could twist it up into a bun, Cat realized she should be focusing on ballet. She'd be taking a class with ABT company dancers, a rare honor that did not get doled out often. After dedicating most of her life to her craft, Cat should have had eagle-eye focus. Instead, every time she tried to think about dance, thoughts of Dmitri ended up flooding her mind. It didn't help that Dmitri was such a big part of her career now. If it weren't for him, she probably wouldn't have been cast as Clara that year and she would not have been in New York at that very second, preparing for a privilege she'd assumed she would never get: dancing with ABT. Even if it was only for one class.

Cat was running a comb through her still damp hair when she heard a knock at her door. Warily, she knotted her towel tighter around her chest and went to peek through the eye hole, wondering who it could be. It seemed unlikely either Phoebe or Nick would stop by to see her, and since she'd had to quietly slip out of Dmitri's room earlier, she doubted he would risk traveling up to the third floor to see her.

To her surprise, a male hotel employee wearing an all-white outfit stood outside with a tray in hand.

Cat cracked the door open so he couldn't see her partial state of undress. "Sorry. There must be some sort of mistake. I didn't order room service."

The man glanced at the order slip. "Cat Brown, room 332? Is that you?"

She pursed her lips. "It is, but I'm sure I didn't order anything."

"The order was called in for you by another guest."

"Oh." Cat cautiously took the tray, wondering if Nick was playing a prank on her. Likely, she'd lift the lid and find something abhorrent underneath. "Thanks. Hold on a second." She scurried to the dresser, put down the tray, and pulled a few singles from her wallet, all while still holding up her towel. "Here you go." She handed him the cash and flashed a polite smile before shutting the door. Reluctantly, Cat opened the tray, pleasantly surprised to find a plate of egg whites and fresh fruit. A cup of coffee sat beside it.

"Dmitri," she said to herself with a smile, realizing he had to be responsible for the healthy fare.

After she ate her breakfast while daydreaming about the handsome ex-dancer she'd just spent the night with, Cat changed into a basic, black camisole leotard and a baby blue wrap skirt, both of which she'd made herself, and a pair of pink tights. Since she'd be a guest in the class, she didn't want to wear anything too flashy. Hopefully, her dancing would be all she needed to stand out.

After, with little else to do, Cat flipped through the channels on the TV before settling on a morning show to watch while she stretched. When it was time to go, she threw on a pair of heather gray sweatpants and a black wrap sweater to keep her warm on the walk over. Then, she twisted her hair up into a neat bun and grabbed her pea coat before making her way to the elevator, dance bag in tow. Inside, she had everything she might need for the class: ballet slippers, pointe shoes, cushioning for her toes, rosin, bandages, legwarmers, and a water bottle.

When she stepped into the lobby, everyone else was already there. Dmitri had returned to his typical, stoic self. The softness in his face earlier that morning had been replaced by the familiar scowl and hard lines she was used to seeing at the studio. Nick and Phoebe stood around him, looking polished and ready for the class. It would be a big day for them, too.

She caught Dmitri's eye as she approached the group, faltering a bit when his gaze remained cold and impassive.

She offered a tentative wave. "Good morning."

"Good. You're here. Now we can go." Dmitri motioned to the exit, and despite his frequent direction not to give him any sort of special treatment because he walked with a cane, Nick rushed ahead to open the door for him.

"Here you go, sir. Let me help you with this." Nick looked pleased with himself, though his expression dropped when Dmitri passed by with a huff and a shake of his head.

Cat lagged behind the rest of the group as they traversed the sidewalk, feeling dejected. She knew Dmitri couldn't acknowledge their newfound closeness in front of other company members, but she also hadn't expected him to treat her with such indifference. After his lukewarm greeting, he didn't speak a word to her the entire walk to the studio. Phoebe and Nick chatted among themselves, amplifying how ostracized she felt.

When the ABT studio was in sight, Dmitri stopped at a crosswalk a block away from the building. "We'll cross here."

Nick pointed to the lit-up signal, alerting them to the fact that they could continue in the direction they were already going and cross right in front of the studio.

"We're going this way," Dmitri said through gritted teeth.

While Phoebe and Nick exchanged confused looks, Cat glanced at Dmitri and noticed a pronounced twitching in his free hand. Something was making him nervous. He'd seemed perfectly at ease before they'd parted that morning, which made his current state all the more baffling. Perhaps he was nervous to return to ABT, or he could have been worried his dancers would not live up to the expectations his old company would have. He had a lot riding on his tenure at Bretton Falls Ballet. People assumed that with him in charge, the company would flourish. Today would be the first time anyone outside of Bretton Falls would be able to judge how he was doing.

Cat felt compelled to comfort him, to wrap her arms around his waist and tell him everything would be okay. But she couldn't. Not while Phoebe and Nick were standing right there and not while anyone from ABT might be around.

Her heart stung. She and Dmitri weren't even a couple, and already she felt the strain of hiding their relationship. But she had to stay focused. This morning was about ballet. She could worry about everything Dmitri as soon as she stepped back out onto the sidewalk.

The group entered the ABT building and ascended a steep and narrow staircase to the third floor. There they were greeted by Constance Fedorov, who doted over her resistant son before kissing each of his dancers on the cheek.

"It was lovely meeting all of you yesterday," the small woman said with a friendly smile.

Cat could hear the tinkling of piano keys and the muffled voices of the dancers conversing as they warmed up. As soon as she stepped into the studio, Cat had to fight back a gasp. Large floor-to-ceiling windows lined the far wall, showcasing the hustle and bustle outside. The pure white walls looked as if they'd just been painted yesterday, and rows of wooden barres lined the room. The breathtaking sight was quite different than the humble digs at Bretton Falls. Several of the dancers halted their conversations to check out the three strangers entering their realm. Cat held her chin up, acting like she belonged. She set her bag down near an empty space along the left wall and was surprised when Phoebe and Nick followed.

Cat realized they probably felt insecure in their new environment. Phoebe and Nick weren't the top dogs at ABT. In fact, they were far from it. There were renowned dancers all over the room. Cat would have felt intimidated if it weren't for Dmitri's presence in her life. He saw promise in her, and he was one of the greatest dancers the world of ballet had ever known.

When Dmitri entered the room, a rush of people clamored to say hello. Cat's hackles rose at the sight of several pretty, lithe women taking turns greeting him, many doing so with enthusiastic hugs and flirtatious remarks about his newly grown-out hair and beard. She was especially upset with the friendly way he seemed to smile at each of them. As far as Cat had known, a smile from Dmitri was as rare as a white peacock. She frowned as she pulled on her leg warmers, watching the fuss he caused on the other side of the room and noticing that his gaze didn't once drift in her direction.

Rather than letting herself feel bad about the situation, Cat channeled her frustration into her dancing. When Constance called for the start of class, everyone dutifully found a spot at the barre. Cat held her head high and squeezed between two of the women she'd noticed doting over Dmitri, determined to outshine both. She didn't know either of them and assumed they were newer members of the corps, based upon their youthful looks and the shameless way they'd flirted with Dmitri. Every time she started to wonder if he'd slept with either of them, Cat gritted her teeth and focused in on the basic barre exercises Constance had instructed them to perform. She felt like her technique was as close to flawless as it had ever been.

Though some of the combinations Constance came up with were complex, the rest of the class was a breeze. In fact, Cat executed the allegro—an exciting, fast sequence—so well, Constance had her demonstrate it for the rest of the class. After she'd finished, Cat glanced over at Phoebe and Nick, who both practically had steam coming out of their ears. They'd stuck together for most of the class, standing by each other at the barre and relegating themselves to the last row during the center floor portion.

When Cat went to find her place back amid the dancers, Constance patted her on the back. "*Brava*, young lady. I can see why my son picked you to be his Clara this year."

Cat thanked Constance, trying not to look over at Dmitri. Her feelings toward him were confusing, and she couldn't let that bleed into her stellar showing at ABT. Instead, she zeroed in on how exciting it was to finally live up to her potential.

She had auditioned at ABT twice in the past, both times occurring at the beginning of her career. Even though Cat had felt she was just as talented, if not more talented, than every other dancer in the room, she'd never landed a spot in the company. It had been disheartening after her first round of auditions that only Bretton Falls Ballet had wanted her. When she went out to auditions again the following year, her confidence had been shattered and it showed in her dancing. It took a couple of years for Cat to realize she'd just been a victim of bad luck the first time around. She now believed that if she'd just stayed focused and determined while she prepared for auditions the following year, she might have landed a coveted spot at a larger company.

After reverence, the dancers headed over to their bags to decompress after a challenging class. On the way there, Nick bumped into Cat and brushed by her, muttering "show off" under his breath while Phoebe flashed a look of disdain over her shoulder. Cat smiled, knowing they were jealous. When Cat finished packing up her belongings, she met Dmitri, Constance, Phoebe, and Nick by the door.

Constance greeted her with a smile. "Lovely job this morning, Catherine. I'm very excited to see how you do in *The Nutcracker*. From what I understand, it's your first lead role."

Phoebe had let that fact slip out before the appetizer course had been served the night before. She was listing her favorite and least favorite parts to dance and cited Clara at the bottom of the list. She'd claimed not to mind letting Cat step in so she could try her hand as the Sugar Plum Fairy, a role she'd coveted since childhood.

"You're coming to see our production?" Nick's eyes bulged out of his head. Admittedly, Cat was also surprised to hear the legendary Constance Fedorov would venture into the wilds of upstate New York to see what would likely seem like a second-rate production, compared to all the glitz and glamour of ABT's *Nutcracker*. Louise had journeyed into the city with Cat at Christmas to see the holiday classic, and the aspiring little ballerina hadn't stopped gushing for days about the opulence of it all. In fact, that production and the effect it had on her daughter was the sole reason Louise had ultimately decided to name her shop the Land of Sweets.

Constance wrapped an arm around Dmitri's waist and beamed like the proud mother she was. "I wouldn't miss it for the world."

Dmitri squirmed at her praise, eventually wiggling free from her hold. "I take it you three can find your way back to the hotel by yourselves? I'll meet you in the lobby at one. Our car will be waiting outside then."

With that, Dmitri departed and headed down the hall, leaving the group to say an awkward goodbye to Constance on their own.

Nick and Phoebe casually and effectively blocked Cat off from the older woman, angling their bodies to make sure they thanked her for allowing them to take part in her class before Cat got a chance to. Nick even went so far as to knock Cat with his bag as he went in to kiss Constance on the cheek.

After her two company mates exited through the door and headed toward the stairs, presumably leaving her behind, Cat extended a hand to Constance.

"Thank you for having us today." She glanced around at her surroundings, taking them in one more time as she committed the studio to memory. "It was truly a dream come true to take one of your classes."

"The pleasure was all mine." Constance cupped Cat's hand in both of her own before pulling her in a little closer to whisper, "I'm looking forward to seeing you back here this spring."

Cat smiled, knowing that meant that not only would she be invited to audition, but that Constance Fedorov would be on her side. Uncontrollable glee bubbled up inside of her as she dashed down the studio's stairs, eager to call Abby and her mom with the good news.

CHAPTER FIFTEEN

Ivan stood when he saw Dmitri approaching their table, swiftly pulling out an empty chair. "It's good to see you again, son. Your mother told me things went well this morning."

Begrudgingly, Dmitri settled into the chair while wishing his parents wouldn't make such a fuss over his injury. If it weren't for his limp and the cane, his gruff, Russian father would never think to pull out a chair for him. He also suspected they'd requested a table near the entrance so it'd be less trouble for Dmitri to navigate through the busy restaurant. It was something they had made a habit of doing back when he lived in the city, even though Dmitri had made it abundantly clear he did not want to receive special treatment of any kind.

"I have to agree. Things went very well." He propped his cane up against the table and addressed his mother. "What did you think of Catherine Brown?"

"She's marvelous." Constance's face lit up the same way it did every time she watched a truly remarkable dancer or piece of choreography. "The girl has an abundance of talent."

The waitress sidled up to the table. With her bouncing, blond ponytail, blue eyes, and thin physique, she was exactly the kind of girl that would usually catch Dmitri's attention. This time, he was interested to hear his mother's thoughts on Cat and barely even looked at the girl.

"Can I get you something to drink?" she asked him directly. Both his parents already had piping hot mugs of coffee in front of them.

He kept his gaze glued his mom, wanting her to elaborate on her opinion of Cat's talents. "Coffee."

The waitress jotted it down. "Are you guys ready to order?"

"We're going to need a few minutes." Constance smiled at the girl and waved an arm toward Dmitri. "My son hasn't even looked at the menu yet."

"I'll be back in a few, then." The waitress batted her eyelashes at Dmitri before walking away, swaying her hips seductively.

"She's a pretty girl," Ivan observed before bringing his mug to his lips and taking a swig. Like his son, Ivan had a reputation for bedding ballerinas before he ended up in America, where he met Constance and reformed his womanizing ways.

Ignoring his father's remark, Dmitri angled his body toward his mother. "Do you think she would be offered a contract if she auditioned?"

"It's hard to say." Constance shook out her napkin and dropped it in her lap. "She's clearly a talented dancer, but she also isn't getting any younger. How old is she again?"

"Twenty-four."

"Exactly." Constance pursed her lips and looked off over Dmitri's shoulder as she considered Catherine Brown. "Even so, I feel she could be an asset to the company." She pointed to the menu trapped beneath Dmitri's forearms. "Decide what you want to eat so we can order. Your father's hungry."

As if on cue, Ivan's stomach growled. "I haven't eaten anything since dinner."

Dmitri persisted. "So you think she'd have a chance?"

"I would advocate for her, but I couldn't guarantee anything." Constance quirked one eyebrow as she studied the determined look on her son's face. "Why are you so interested in getting this girl in ABT? If she's one of your best dancers, wouldn't you want to keep her in Bretton Falls?"

Dodging the question, Dmitri removed his arms from the table and finally glanced down at his menu. "I remember the omelets here were good."

Ivan crossed his arms over his broad chest. "He's sleeping with her."

Dmitri's face flushed with anger. His parents were not naïve to his penchant for beautiful girls and had often cautioned him against involving himself with other dancers to preserve his public image. None of the other men in the company had their parents watching their every move. It had been infuriating.

"I am not sleeping with her."

"No. It's worse than that." Constance clicked her tongue and shook her head. "He's in love with her."

Dmitri slammed his menu closed. "If you two can't discuss ballet over a pleasant brunch, then I'm leaving."

Dmitri was not in love. He'd never been in love before and was never would be. Love was for fools who had time to waste and emotion to spare. He preferred to pour every ounce of himself into his work, which was why he'd only made time for flings and one-night stands in the past.

Occasionally Dmitri had found himself wondering what it was about Cat

Brown that had him so mesmerized, but he never once considered that he could be falling in love with her. The accusation was preposterous.

Dmitri moved to stand but Ivan reached across the table with one of his abnormally long yet graceful arms, and pushed his son back down by the shoulder. "Stay."

"This is really something." A devilish smile curled up the corners of Constance's lips as she watched her son's face redden. She looked to her husband, amusement wrinkling the corners of her eyes. "I don't believe our son's ever been in love before."

Dmitri sat back in his chair with a thud and snapped, "If I loved Catherine, which I don't, why would I want her in the city while I'm out in Bretton Falls?"

"Because you can't very well date her openly if you're her artistic director." Constance rattled off her explanation as if it had been clear as day.

Meanwhile, Dmitri felt as if he'd been slapped across the face...a sensation he was all too familiar with. Plenty of jilted women who'd expected more out of him had taken the liberty of giving him a good smack when he'd treated them with less courtesy than they thought they deserved.

Until that moment, Dmitri had been sure his intentions to get Cat into ABT had been purely selfless.

"I'm merely concerned for the trajectory of her career." Dmitri balled his hand into a fist, but stopped himself before slamming it down. Getting angry would only help to prove his mother's point. "She deserves to perform in sold out concert halls, not half-filled community college auditoriums."

"I can put a good word in for her, but her age is obviously going to be a factor." Constance placed a hand over her son's fist. "Perhaps your situation would be better handled if you returned to ABT instead."

Dmitri pulled his hand out from under hers and dropped it in his lap. "I am not coming back here."

It would be impossible for him to return. He'd nearly had a panic attack walking to the studio. His palms were sweating, his heart raced, his breath was short, and his body had trembled as they'd neared the site of his accident. He'd made his dancers cross the street early when his symptoms had become too much to bear. If they'd made it any closer to that ill-fated street corner, Dmitri felt certain his physical reaction would have become obvious, and he couldn't have that. They needed his company to see him as strong and fearless—as the man he'd been before he was broken.

"This is where you belong, son," Ivan rasped in his signature monotone voice. "Your mother and I built a legacy here and it's your responsibility to continue it."

"What about what I want?" Dmitri snarled through his teeth, fighting back the urge to shout. He'd spent his entire life appeasing his parents and exceeding their expectations. Now that his bum knee had thrown a wrench in everyone's plans for his illustrious career, it was time to move on. "I am a grown man and it's time I start deciding what's best for me."

"But you're making emotional decisions and not considering what actually may be best for you." Tears filled Constance's eyes, and Dmitri felt compelled to comfort her.

It always killed him to see his mother cry. But he stayed rooted both in his chair and on his stance on the subject.

"You've changed since your accident. The old Dmitri never would have left his family and his company behind." She dabbed the corners of her eyes with her napkin. "Don't you see that this is where you belong? How can you possibly think being at that no-name company is what's best for you and your career?"

"I knew this would happen. I fucking knew it." Dmitri pushed back from the table and grabbed his cane. "Of course we couldn't spend more than five minutes alone together as a family without you two trying to force your will on me."

"Don't walk away, Dmitri." There was a hint of warning in Ivan's voice. He'd used the same tone when cautioning his son against letting his sexual pursuits interfere with his dancing. "Your mother will be upset."

"I'm upset." Dmitri stood too quickly and winced at the stabbing sensation he felt in his knee. His parents flinched at his apparent pain. Their eyes widened with sympathy despite the argument they'd been having, making it even harder for Dmitri to leave. "I can't stay at this table, and I can't stay in New York." He straightened his shirt sleeves and wrapped his plaid scarf tighter around his neck. "When you come to Bretton Falls, you'll see for yourselves just how important the work I'm doing there is. Until then, I don't want to hear anything else about ABT, the city, or how much what I'm doing affects the two of you. You don't know what it's like to have your career cut short, and you also don't know what it's like to limp around when you should be dancing at your prime." He stabbed two fingers into his chest. "That's my burden and I'm the one who knows the best way to deal with it."

With that, Dmitri tossed a few bills on the table to pay for his parents' breakfast and hobbled toward the door.

CHAPTER SIXTEEN

Cat stood in the women's locker room, tying a new wrap skirt around her waist. She'd made it the night before from a spool of chiffon featuring a kaleidoscope of multi-colored butterflies against a pale blue backdrop. She'd picked up the material weeks before she'd known how time-consuming and exhausting her rehearsal schedule would be and hadn't had the opportunity or the urge to pull out her sewing machine. However, when she'd started working on the skirt Elise commissioned her to make for Violet's birthday, she found that sewing was the perfect distraction from her thoughts of Dmitri. He'd practically ignored her at the ABT class and acted even colder on the drive back upstate, not even so much offering anyone a goodbye after he'd stepped out of their car and grabbed his overnight bag from the trunk. Even though they'd never exchanged numbers, she'd hoped he might call her at some point over the weekend, assuming the artistic director of the company she worked for would have the resources to find her cell number.

But as she should have expected, that never happened. Dmitri was a notorious skirt-chaser, after all. The sensitive, caring man she'd spent the night with in New York was just a character he played, using his stage experience to his advantage. She now realized she meant nothing to him. She'd been nothing more than a warm body to snuggle up to in a lonely hotel room.

Abby stood beside her, putting on a matching skirt. "Do you think it's weird we're wearing the same exact thing?"

"No. My leotard's navy blue and yours is black. But there's a ton of other new skirts in my bag if you wanna swap yours out."

After she finished tying the blue ribbons into a bow at the small of her back, Abby riffled through the overflowing chiffon in Cat's bag. "You weren't joking. Busy night, huh?"

"I had a lot on my mind." Naturally, Cat had called Abby as soon as she got home, relaying the events of the trip to her and intentionally leaving out some of the more intimate details, like how otherworldly good it felt to be pressed up against the length of Dmitri's well-muscled body.

Abby nodded in understanding, knowing better than to discuss her friend's rocky and unusual relationship with their director in public. Instead, she rejoined Cat in front of the mirror and snaked an arm around her shoulders.

"I like that we match. It's a solidarity kind of thing."

Cat smiled. "You're the best, Ab."

With her arms crossed over her chest, Marcy stepped up beside the two best friends, ruining their moment.

"Well, aren't you two cute in your matching butterfly skirts."

Abby broke away from Cat and turned to face Marcy. "Cat made these skirts, and I think they look great."

Marcy let out a deep laugh that made the hair on Cat's arms stand on end.

"I'm surprised Cat has time for anything. Between the stress of learning a lead role and sleeping with the boss, her life has to be pretty hectic."

Abby rolled her eyes and threw her hands onto her hips. "That rumor's getting old. Why don't you come up with a new one?"

Cat, on the other hand, turned away to pull her leg warmers from her bag. It was getting harder to be the better person.

"Well, then why don't we talk about this?" Marcy clapped her hands together and then wrung them out. "Not only did little Miss Catherine Brown seduce the new director into giving her a starring role, but she's also using him for his family's connections at ABT. Sources say she'll audition for them later this year."

Cat's jaw hit her chest, wondering how anyone, even Nick and Phoebe, would have picked up on that possibility. After all, that was what it was: a possibility and nothing more.

"Who told you that?" she demanded, her voice laced with her growing discontent.

"Rumors don't just get created from out of thin air, you know." Marcy proudly lifted her chin. "We all see the way he watches you. It's practically indecent." She looked Cat up and down. "And I have no idea why."

Abby's pale skin started to gain color. "How dare you—"

"I've got this." Cat stepped forward, cutting her off. "I want to be the one that tells this bitch she's way out of line."

Cat's legs trembled beneath her, either because of the intensity of her frustration or the adrenaline boost she was getting from the confrontation.

"I'm out of line?" Marcy scoffed, pressing her hand to her chest. "You're the one fucking our new director, and I'm out of line."

Phoebe rounded the row of lockers behind them in a hurry, looking confused. "What's going on here?"

"What did you tell her?" Cat kept her voice calm, even though she wanted to scream at the top of her lungs and demand to know why they were so insistent on trying to ruin this opportunity for her.

Phoebe pulled her neck back like a turtle retreating into its shell. "What are you talking about? I have no idea what's going on here."

Marcy tipped her chin toward Cat, her upper lip curled. "She's upset because I'm airing her dirty laundry for everyone to see."

"All you're doing is making yourself look like a jealous bitch," Cat shot back, her eyes narrowing to slits.

"Catherine Brown," an older woman's voice chastised. Cat turned around to see Sue, the office secretary, standing beside door, her face pulled tight with anger. "What on earth is going on here?"

Cat cleared her throat, feeling like a bucket of ice water had just been dropped on her. "Nothing."

"Yeah, absolutely nothing." Marcy wore the saccharine-sweet smile she used to trick everyone else into thinking she was nice.

"I certainly hope so." Sue pushed her glasses up higher onto her nose and inspected the group, not looking like she'd bought a word they'd said. Her gaze shot to Cat. "Mr. Fedorov would like to see you before class starts."

"Oh." She went to follow Sue out the door. Between the aftershock of the confrontation and her surprise at being summoned by Dmitri, Cat was in a daze. When she realized she still held her legs warmers in her hand, she turned to toss them in her bag just in time to hear Marcy whisper, "Convenient."

Cat noticed Abby bristle beside her and placed a hand on her shoulder. "Don't let it get to you." She glanced over at Phoebe and Marcy, who both looked relieved that Cat hadn't tried to blame them for starting the argument. "They're not worth it."

With that, she spiked her balled-up leg warmers in her bag and stalked through the door behind Sue, feeling every bit as annoyed as she had a few minutes earlier…except now all her anger was directed toward Dmitri. He knew some of the dancers were giving her a hard time about their supposed relationship, and if he stopped to think about anyone other than himself, he would have realized how bad having Sue fetch her from the locker room must have looked. None of the other dancers had ever stepped foot in his office. Only a select few had ever been asked back there when Lillian was in charge. Typically, only those considered favorites had been invited back to the director's office, unless they headed back there on their own to air a grievance, like Cat often had.

Cat's blood boiled as she stomped along the blue carpet, furious that she'd let Dmitri turn the rumors into reality, refusing to take any of the fault herself. He was the one who'd kissed her that day in his office. He was the one who'd invited her to his hotel room.

Sue stopped beside her desk, which was littered with pictures of her grandchildren and pieces of artwork they'd made her. At that moment, she eyed Cat with the look of a grandmother who'd just caught one of the little ones misbehaving. "Care to tell me what happened in there?"

"It's nothing." Cat passed by her without a second glance and barged into Dmitri's office.

He looked up from his desk with a lazy smile. Seeing him look so comfortably happy made Cat soften for a second, the corners of her lips slowly curling before she remembered what he'd done to her. She slammed the door as her mouth formed a hard line.

"You have a lot of nerve calling me back here."

Dmitri's pleasant expression fell, revealing the subtle frown lines she'd gotten used to seeing. "I owe you—" He paused to grimace, looking like he'd just tasted something sour but was trying not to offend the chef. "I owe you an apology."

Cat stayed close to the door, not trusting herself to get close to Dmitri. Even though she felt like quitting the company right then and there, so she'd never have to see the man again, Cat still had a primal urge to be close to him. Sometimes she wondered what angered her more: his silence over the weekend or her knowing that she'd never get the chance to be in bed with him again.

"An apology?" she asked in a mocking tone. "For what, exactly? Leading me on? Blowing me off? Embarrassing me in front of the girls?"

Dmitri stood, snatched his cane from where it hung on the side of his desk, and approached her. "I embarrassed you in front of the other dancers?"

He sounded confused, which infuriated Cat further.

"Yeah. Just now. How did you think it would go over when you summoned me back here? Everyone knows only the director's little pets get invited back to their office. And you've never asked anyone else back here."

Dmitri sat perched on the front edge of his desk, looking at Cat with a hunger in his eyes so pronounced she started taking small steps backward. "I don't want to ask anyone else back here."

Cat wiped her sweaty palms on her tights, backing against the door. She squirmed, remembering what had happened the last time she'd been in his office. Only this time, she was pinned against that old, wood door by his unrelenting stare instead of his rock-hard body. Cat never knew a man's stare could be powerful enough to render someone immobile, but she also knew Dmitri wielded a power to seduce women that no man could rival.

"I should go," she said, though she made no move to open the door.

"Class starts in a few minutes."

Without muttering a word, Dmitri stood and approached her slowly, with measured steps that made his limp seem even more pronounced. Cat's heart beat a hundred times for each step he took. She wanted to look away, to do anything to break the spell he had over her, but he kept her in place with his unrelenting stare.

"I'm sorry for embarrassing you." He finally spoke when he stopped before her and reached out to brush his knuckles against her cheek. "And I'm sorry for neglecting you this weekend."

Cat inhaled a shaky breath, trying to maintain her self-control. Between his closeness and the spicy scent of his cologne, that was difficult for her to do.

"You're nothing more than a playboy. You use women for one night and then you're done with them."

A seductive smile crept up on his lips, devious and delicious all at once. "I'm not nearly done with you yet."

She quirked up an eyebrow in question. "You don't think so?" Even though she tried to sound strong, Cat's turmoil shone through in her unsteady voice. Frustrated, she reached for the doorknob with all the willpower she could muster.

Dmitri caught her wrist before she could close her fist around it. "Hear me out."

Her gaze narrowed suspiciously. "Do I have a choice?"

Dmitri took a step back and help up his hands—one palm faced her while the other hand clutched his cane. "Always."

Cat swallowed down a whimper that bubbled up in her throat as soon as he moved away. Her fingers tingled with the need to touch him. To quell the urge, Cat fiddled with the edge of her skirt.

"Well, what do you have to say?"

"I missed you this weekend."

"We saw each other on Saturday. Remember? Maybe you don't because you didn't even seem to realize I was there."

Cat knew she sounded spiteful, but she couldn't help herself. After spending all her waking hours on Sunday wishing he would call, she had too much built-up animosity to stifle. Dmitri better have a good excuse—or two—if he wanted her to forget how it felt to be ignored.

"Catherine," Dmitri started, pausing to pull a hand through his hair. The strands fell back into his blue eyes, reminding Cat of how handsomely disheveled he looked when he slept. If only he could look as peaceful as he had on Saturday morning all the time. "You know I couldn't acknowledge what happened between us in front of anyone. It would be a disaster for both of our careers."

"Then what's the point?" Cat crossed her arms over her chest and looked away, fighting back tears. Typically, she didn't cry over men. She'd never felt particularly strongly about any of the ones she'd dated before to get emotional over them. But Dmitri had such a powerful effect on her, she could hardly control any of the reactions she had around him—positive or negative.

"I want you." His voice dropped an octave or two into that low, sexy growl that always made her insides stir. "And you want me, too. To deny these urges would impair our creative processes."

Cat shook her head. "So that's how you plan to rationalize whatever's going on between us?" She motioned between the two of them with a wagging finger. "It's all for the sake of ballet."

"No." Dmitri moved toward her again before tossing his cane to the ground so he could cup her face in his hands. Cat flinched at the contact, not because she didn't want him to touch her but because she wanted it too much. "I want to be with you, and I'm sorry for handling it poorly. I'm not used to—" He paused to pull his bottom lip between his teeth, looking unsure of what he wanted to say. "I've never felt like this about anyone before."

Cat's chest swelled at his admission, but she knew she needed to protect her heart. They hadn't had sex yet and his perceived rejection over the weekend stung much more than she'd have liked.

"How can you feel anything toward me? We hardly even know each other."

He kissed her forehead, his lips lingering and sending a shiver down her spine. "I know enough to have my interest piqued. You're beautiful, smart, and confident. You're a hell of dancer, too." Dmitri kissed the tip of her nose, leaving her breathless with hope he'd move to her lips next. "I know there's more to you than that, and I would really like a chance to learn everything there is to know about Catherine Brown." He nuzzled her nose with his own, his lips so close to hers only a wisp of air could pass between them.

Even though Cat longed to close the scant distance between them, she tipped her chin upward and kept the conversation moving. She couldn't kiss again unless she was sure he wouldn't break her heart.

"I can't be your dirty little secret forever."

"You won't be," he reassured her, his voice dropping to something scarcely louder than a whisper. "We'll figure something out. Just give it some time."

Cat mulled over what he offered her, trying to decide whether it would be enough. Dmitri Fedorov was hers for the taking, so long as she wanted to risk her heart and her career on him.

She rested her shaky hands on his shoulders. "Okay."

He seized her at the waist and pulled her against him. "Okay? Are you sure?"

She nodded. "Kiss me."

Dmitri pressed his lips to hers in an earth-shattering kiss that made her legs go limp. She braced herself on his shoulders, so lost in the moment she didn't even consider the effect making him bear her weight would have on his permanently weak knee. Cat had expected his lips to meet hers in the needy way they had before. She expected the kind of kiss that lacked finesse but made up for it with enough fiery intensity to fulfill the longing she'd felt. But this one was different. It was loaded with a depth of emotion she hadn't felt from Dmitri before and from the rumors of his past, didn't think he was even capable of. That moment confirmed she'd made the right decision in letting him kiss her in the first place.

He cared about her.

She was sure of it.

Cat fisted his flannel shirt in her hands, wanting to hold on to him and drag out the moment of tender sweetness before she had to go back into the studio with everyone else. She'd have to face Marcy, Phoebe, and Nick, knowing there would be some truth in whatever they claimed she'd been doing back in the director's office.

Dmitri dragged his hands down her sides until they rounded her hips and slid beneath the butterfly print that hadn't done much in the way of covering her up. He grabbed hold of her ass with both hands, pulling her against him, their bodies pressed together so tightly Cat could feel his erection throbbing through his jeans. She whimpered at the sensation, glad the small sound had been swallowed by one of Dmitri's kisses. No one could hear them. No one could know what was going on.

Cat pulled away, her hands planted on Dmitri's firm chest as she pushed him back in a fruitless effort to create some space between them. He didn't budge.

"What's wrong?" he asked as he kissed down her neck, never once breaking his rhythm.

Cat let out a hissing exhale as Dmitri's tongue brushed over the dip in her collarbone. "We can't do this here."

"Why not?" He nuzzled into the curve of her neck, his voice muffled by closeness. "It's my office. I can do whatever I want in here."

She dropped her head to the side, allowing him easy access to the tender flesh he'd been kissing, betraying her words. "But I can't go into class with swollen lips. Everyone will know what we were doing."

"Skip class today and stay back here with me." He nibbled at her earlobe. "Please."

The hint of desperation in his voice made it even harder for her to step away, but she did, driven by her desire to excel as Clara. Skipping class wasn't an option.

"I can't. You know that as well as I do."

With a grimace, Dmitri laced his fingers with hers then lifted the tops of her hands to his mouth for a kiss. "Tonight, then."

"Tonight?" His words sounded like a promise—Cat knew there would be no getting him to back down again.

Dmitri released her hand to spin toward his desk. He scribbled something down on a piece of paper.

"What time do you finish at the shop later?"

"Eight."

He folded the piece of paper and handed it to her. "My address. Meet me there as soon as you finish and do your best to be discreet."

Cat stuffed the paper into the hip of her leotard, where it was nicely concealed under her new skirt. "I will. I promise."

That increasingly familiar, seductive smile curled the corners of his mouth. "Tonight, then."

Cat flashed a smile of her own, biting down on her bottom lip to stop it from spreading too wide. "Tonight."

CHAPTER SEVENTEEN

Cat cut the engine with a shaky hand. She peered out the windshield in search of apartment seven, unexpectedly finding the brass number hanging beside a door on the second floor. She pursed her lips as she shut off her headlights, wondering why Dmitri would choose a second-floor apartment when she'd seen the difficulty he had climbing stairs. Then, Cat found herself questioning why he'd even rent an apartment in the first place. With the money he'd made dancing over the years, surely Dmitri could have afforded to rent a house. There were plenty of them available off Main Street. Cat would know. She'd often peruse the classifieds in the local paper, fantasizing about the day she could afford to help her family and get her own place.

She pulled the hood of her pink and chocolate-stained sweatshirt up over her head, thankful for the way her thoughts had started to spiral out of control. She'd much rather be daydreaming about two-bedroom ranches than panicking over what Dmitri would have in store for her once she crossed the threshold into his apartment. Would he have dinner, or would he maul her as soon as he opened the door? Throughout her shift at the shop, Cat kept thinking back to the promise in his sexy voice when he vowed he would wait until that night to do whatever it was he'd planned to do to her in his office.

Not that Cat didn't want to make love with Dmitri, because she did. She wouldn't have gone back to his hotel room in the city if she wasn't interested having sex with him. It was their greatly varied experience levels that had her worried. Cat could count all her sexual partners on one hand, and still have some fingers left over. She hadn't seen any of them in well over a year.

Taking a deep breath, she climbed out of her car and quietly shut the door behind her. Dmitri had asked her to be discreet, and she intended to comply. She didn't know if any of his neighbors were aware the great Dmitri Fedorov lived in their building. If the right person saw her sneaking into his apartment, word about their affair would spread through Bretton Falls like wildfire. It'd be hard to show her face at the studio the next morning, if ever.

Cat slinked between cars in the parking lot, keeping her head down as she made her way to the building. She climbed the stairs softly on her tiptoes, wondering if there was such a thing as being overcautious when one was putting one's career on the line. The thought of risking everything she'd been working for made her falter, but the memory of Dmitri's hot lips on her skin drew her toward his door.

She knocked, rapping her knuckles lightly against the white-painted wood before peeking over both shoulders to make sure no one was around. The coast was still clear as far as she could see.

Dmitri opened the door, looking far more comfortable and content than he normally did. His long hair was knotted at the back of his head, allowing the porchlight to highlight his well-defined cheekbones in a way that made him look like every textbook rendition of a Greek god Cat had ever seen. Dmitri still had on the same clothes he'd had on at the studio: a black and blue striped flannel shirt and a pair of jeans. Except now, he was barefoot.

"Hello, Catherine."

Usually, she didn't care for being called by her first name but she loved the velvety way it sounded rolling off Dmitri's tongue.

"Hi." Cat looked over shoulder again, briefly contemplating whether a dark figure off in the distance was someone from the company spying on them or the shadow of a streetlight, before deciding on the latter. Dmitri stepped aside and led her into the barren, empty living room. Artless white walls enveloped the space. A plaid sofa and one of the largest TVs Cat had ever seen sat across each other on opposite walls, with a rich mahogany coffee table resting between. A comfortable-looking arm chair sat off to the side, while a cluttered desk was pushed up against the far wall. Though the apartment looked lived in, it didn't look like a home. She got the impression Dmitri might not have planned to stay there long, which struck her as odd, considering his drive to ensure he kept his position with Bretton Falls Ballet.

Even though she didn't hear him approach after the door clicked closed, Cat could feel Dmitri's presence around her. Suddenly, every flitting thought she'd had about his apartment vanished. The steady sound of his breath was the only thing she focused on. Somehow, it matched the rhythm of her rapidly beating heart.

Dmitri swept Cat's long ponytail over her right shoulder so he could press a single kiss to the back of her neck. The subtle touch of his lips, and the promise of what was to come, sent shivers down her spine. She closed her eyes, wanting to savor the sensation.

"Come with me." Dmitri hooked his right arm around Cat's waist and led her down a narrow hallway to the left. They passed a few closed doors before turning into the only open one at the end of the hall. Dmitri's bedroom was just as plain and unadorned as his living room. A king-sized bed dominated the space. A burgundy comforter was haphazardly strewn across the mattress while a pile of white-shammed pillows was propped up by the black-painted headboard.

Dmitri steered Cat directly toward the bed, turning her to face him when they stopped beside it. His eyes were filled with the same shameless hunger he'd had earlier that day in his office, and she knew there would be no turning back this time. How could she walk away from a man who looked at her like she was the most gorgeous woman he'd ever seen, when she knew no one was around to catch them?

Without breaking eye contact, Dmitri tossed his cane toward the foot of the bed. It hit the hardwood floor with a crash, ending the silence. The crack of wood on wood had the same effect a gunshot did at the start of the race, as it spurred them into motion. Their mouths met, their bodies collided, and their hands were exploring each other's bodies within a split second. Cat ran her palms over the large muscles in Dmitri's back while his fingers massaged the smaller, tender muscles in her shoulders. She practically melted at his touch, leaning her body into his and nearly forgetting that his knee likely was not stable enough to support her weight.

In response, Dmitri sank to the mattress and pulled Cat down to straddle his hips. She enjoyed the new position, perching on Dmitri's lap and towering over him. She felt powerful as he looked up at her, his eyes hooded with desire. It was moments like these where Cat questioned reality. Was she really with Dmitri Fedorov? Did he really think pursuing a relationship with her was worth risking his career over?

"What are you thinking about?" he asked, brushing his thumb over her lips.

Cat crushed her mouth to his in response, not wanting to air her private thoughts and admit she was in awe of her current situation. She'd rather bask in the moment and enjoy the time she had to explore every square inch of Dmitri's lean body. Their tongues tangled as he deftly unzipped her sweatshirt. Cat shrugged it off before finding the elastic in Dmitri's hair and pulling it out.

Conversely, Dmitri wrapped Cat's ponytail around his hand and tugged on it until her head fell back. He dragged his tongue up the expanse of her long neck. Cat moaned, glad not to have to worry about being overheard. Now that they were safely nestled in Dmitri's apartment, rather than his office, she could let go and enjoy the experience.

When Dmitri released her hair, Cat brought her mouth back to his.

Their speed and intensity increased as they writhed against each other, their movements expressing their eagerness. After two weeks spent fighting her feelings, Cat was spiraling out of control. Her body moved of its own volition. Whimpers escaped with such frequency she had no chance to try and stop them.

She arched her back when Dmitri's fingers skimmed the seam of her T-shirt, silently inviting him to remove it. He did so with a single sweep of his arm. His lips were back on hers before the scrap of white cotton hit the floor. Dmitri unhooked her bra with a flick of his fingers and the lacy, white lingerie quickly joined her shirt on the floor. Only then did he break away, kissing a haphazard trail down Cat's neck and chest to reach her breasts. His tongue swirled around one of her pert nipples. It felt so good, Cat buried her hands in his hair, hoping to hold Dmitri there for a little longer. To her pleasant surprise, he showed no signs of wanting to retreat. Instead, he continued to make delicious circles around her nipples, alternating between the two and giving both equal attention. Cat let her head fall back as Dmitri worked his magic, fisting her hands in his hair to keep herself from falling into the growing pile of her clothes on the floor.

All too soon, Dmitri curled an arm around her waist and urged her head back up. Their lips met instantly, picking up where they left off moments before. Feeling more revved up after Dmitri's sensual worship of her breasts, Cat began unbuttoning his shirt. The adrenaline coursing through her body, combined with the fact that she was not looking at what she was doing, made undressing Dmitri a difficult task, but she was not deterred. She needed to get him naked, to feel him inside her. She couldn't wait anymore.

Dmitri's diminishing self-control exposed itself when he wrestled Cat's hands away. He then tore his shirt open and sent buttons flying all around the room. She shoved the flannel down his arms until the shirt fell to the foot of the bed. She caressed his solid torso, impressed with his muscular definition. For a man who walked with a cane and hadn't danced in over a year, Dmitri was in incredible shape.

His fingers brushed the soft skin on Cat's belly above the waistband of her jeans as he made quick work of popping open the top button. He gently pressed against her stomach, a signal Cat took to mean he wanted her to stand. Picking up where Dmitri left off, Cat unzipped the fly and pushed the denim down her hips before hopping out of the pants ungracefully. Dmitri never would have guessed she was a ballerina if he hadn't already known.

Beside Cat, Dmitri struggled out of his own jeans, wincing when he had to put weight on his right leg to tug the pants down his left. Cat made a motion to help, but Dmitri held out a hand to stop her. "Wait for me up there," he demanded in the strong-toned voice he used to command the entire Bretton Falls Ballet, and pointed up to the pillow.

Cat understood that her offer of help could have emasculating consequences, especially after watching the numerous times Dmitri had berated Nick for holding the door open for him or otherwise offering the boss special treatment, so she did what he told her and settled among the pillows. She liked it when Dmitri took control. It was one of the things she found sexiest about him. Plus, it didn't hurt that she got an excellent view of his body from where she lay. Dmitri's muscled back was on full display, the various planes contracting with each subtle movement he made. She could only begin to imagine how beautiful he must have been performing in person.

Cat's heart skipped a beat when Dmitri tugged down his boxers. He kicked off the lightweight cotton with more ease than he had his jeans, and Cat was glad for it. If he flinched in pain one more time, she might think twice about continuing. She didn't want something that was supposed to feel good to be a source of pain.

All thoughts for Dmitri's well-being flew from her head when he turned to face her, his erection in full view. The long, full shaft bobbed near his taut belly, making Dmitri look so incredibly virile, Cat wondered whether she could handle him.

Her mouth went dry as he approached her, his gaze locked on hers. Though he limped, Dmitri walked with his chest held high, looking every bit as confident as she knew he was. Sexy despite his handicap, he dragged a finger along Cat's leg as he strutted toward his nightstand. There, he pulled out a condom and dropped it beside his alarm clock. Cat jumped when the foil packet hit the wood surface, wanting to rip it open. But in what was becoming typical Dmitri fashion, he had her pinned in place with that intense blue stare, warning her not to reach for the packet too soon.

He climbed onto the bed, planted his hands beside her head, and slowly lowered himself down on top of her. Cat sucked in a heavy breath, feeling the heat of his body descend upon her before they made contact. Dmitri's triceps flexed as he continued to move closer, and Cat couldn't stop herself from tracing the bulging muscle in his right arm. He hissed at her touch and lowered down faster to meet her, sighing when he got there like he couldn't have been away from her for a second longer.

Never in her wildest dreams did Cat ever think she'd find herself in this position: in bed with the hottest man in the ballet world. And, to make the moment even sweeter, he wanted her. Hell, he claimed to have wanted her more than he'd ever wanted anyone else.

Dmitri kissed her cheek, a tender gesture that felt like a hand squeezing her heart.

"You smell sweet." His voice was muffled, his beard scraping her skin as he spoke. "Like chocolate."

Cat dragged a hand over her neck and face. "I was helping Mom out in the back today. Maybe I got something on me." She ran her fingers through her ponytail. "Or in my hair."

Dmitri caught her wrist, kissed each of her knuckles, and laced their fingers together. "I like it." He pressed their joined hands into the pillow beside her, making a deep impression into the feathery down. "It suits you."

Cat wasn't sure if he'd been alluding to her presumable innocence with that remark, but she didn't spend much time worrying over it. Who either of them had slept with before that moment was irrelevant; all that mattered was that they were together. Their lips met again, nipping at each other in quick, playful kisses. Cat knew this brief moment of lightheartedness was nothing more than a calm before their storm.

With his free hand, Dmitri reached over for the condom. He pulled away to quickly rip the packet open with teeth before bringing his mouth back down to hers. He stayed like that for a while longer: open condom in hand and kissing Cat while the heat of his erection seared the skin on her hip.

With a growl, Dmitri finally pulled away and stood to sheath himself. Every muscle in Cat's body clenched. She blew out a heavy breath, hoping to get herself to relax. It had been a while since she'd had sex, and judging from the size of Dmitri's member, the first few thrusts may be uncomfortable. Clenching like she was would only make matters worse.

"Is everything all right?" Dmitri asked, looking down at her as he pumped a hand up and down his length.

"I'm fine." Cat smiled, but her lips twitched with reluctance.

Dmitri raised an eyebrow in question while languidly licking the pad of his thumb like it was a gourmet ice cream cone. Cat wet her lips, watching in anticipation as Dmitri lowered his hand to the apex of her legs and parted her seam with his wet thumb. She hissed as he brushed over her swollen nub and rocked her hips to get him to repeat the motion. She writhed beneath him when he did, feeling moisture pool in her core. All apprehensive thoughts vanished from her head, thanks to a few simple sweeps of Dmitri's thumb.

He continued teasing Cat as he lowered back down to hover over her, holding the weight of his body with a single forearm. Cat wasn't even sure exactly when he'd replaced his thumb with the tip of his member. She'd been too preoccupied with how good his touch felt to notice. Cat dug her fingers into Dmitri's hips, pulling his pelvis closer to her own.

"I can't wait anymore," she cried in a quiet, whiny little voice that probably would have sounded grating if she'd been in the right mindset to care.

With a subtle jerk of his hips, Dmitri pushed inside, stopping only a fraction of the way in and blowing out a choppy breath through his teeth.

After another measured thrust, Dmitri buried himself inside her.

"Are you okay?" he asked, resting his forehead against hers and rocking his hips slightly like he was adjusting to the feel of her.

"Fine." Admittedly, the first few seconds had been quite uncomfortable, her inner tissues burning as Dmitri pushed past. But now that he was in, Cat relaxed around him, accommodating his size.

"Perfect." He lifted his head before grabbing her ankles and hooking them over his lower back. "Hold on."

Cat dug her fingernails into Dmitri's shoulders as he thrust into her with so much force, the headboard slammed into the wall. He continued to move with barely contained animalism, jostling Cat's small frame. Her only past partner had been very polite. She'd had no idea how wild and fun sex could be.

Dmitri knew how to fuse moments of tenderness into his otherwise untamed lovemaking. Every so often, he'd kiss the tip of her nose or caress her cheek with the backs of his fingers. These little nuances told Cat what they were doing was more than just a night of unbridled fun. She meant something to him, and she had a funny feeling his affection for her might run deeper than he let on. Dmitri wasn't the sort of person who talked about their feelings, let alone the intensity of their feelings. Cat didn't mind, though. If he continued to *show* her how he felt, she'd be perfectly content.

As the bed springs squeaked beneath her, sounding like the cries of an animal, Cat felt her release building in the pit of her stomach. She clamped down harder on Dmitri's shoulders and gripped every muscle in her body, preparing for what she knew would be an onslaught of sensation that would have the power to drive her into total madness. As the warm, frantic energy from deep in her belly shot out through the rest of her body, Cat squeezed her eyes shut. She squealed, so overwhelmed by the tremors racking her body she nearly didn't hear a sound.

Though it didn't seem possible to do so before, Dmitri increased his speed for a split second before slowing to a much steadier, even-paced rhythm. Cat opened her eyes to see his face contorted above hers, his neck bulging with straining muscle that barely contained a visible pulse ticking right below his ear. Seeing how beautiful and strong Dmitri looked while orgasm wracked his body made Cat feel her own release even more intensely. She wrapped her arms tightly around his neck, pulling him closer until he rested on top of her. Cat needed Dmitri close to her; she wanted to feel what he was feeling. Their bodies shook and twitched in tandem as muted, blissful moans filled the room. Dmitri made no move to save Cat from bearing his full weight. She was too far gone to be crushed by him. Instead, all she felt was his heat and the erratic beating of his heart.

As their breathing slowed and their orgasms waned, Dmitri rolled off Cat and rested on his back beside her. He reached over and searched for her hand. When he found it, he entwined their fingers and kissed the top of them.

"You're incredible. God, Cat, you're incredible," he muttered in a breathy, nearly incoherent voice.

Coming from Dmitri Fedorov, such praise was surely a compliment of the highest regard. With a satiated grin that bordered on smug, Cat rolled onto her side and rested her head on his chest, counting every inhale and exhale of his heavy breathing.

CHAPTER EIGHTEEN

Twenty minutes had passed since Dmitri's orgasm waned, but his heart rate still hadn't regulated. He pressed a hand to his chest, savoring the wild euphoria that came after sex with the incomparable Catherine Brown. He'd slept with plenty of women before—from demure, inexperienced members of the corps to rowdy, scantily clad women of the NYC club scene, and everything between. And yet Cat surpassed them all.

Finally finding the strength to move, Dmitri rolled to his side and stood. He pressed his right hand to the mattress, testing to see how much weight he could put on his bad knee. He hadn't slept with anyone since the accident and wasn't sure how the act would affect the perpetually tender joint. It was sore, but it wasn't anything Dmitri couldn't deal with. He likely could have avoided additional discomfort if he'd kept his wits about him and taken things easy, but he knew as soon as Cat knocked on his front door that would be impossible. His pulse had begun to race before he'd even let her in.

Dmitri stretched his arms overhead, hoping to work some of the kinks out of his body before Cat came in and pouted in the adorable way she always did when she worried he might have hurt himself. Before heading to the bathroom across the hall to clean herself up, Cat had already asked twice about his knee. Oddly enough, when she made a big deal out of his injury, it didn't bother him. It felt good to know she cared.

He had started to tug back on his boxers when Cat appeared in the doorway with a towel wrapped around her narrow body and a lopsided ponytail she hadn't bothered to fix in the bathroom. Not only did Dmitri like knowing he was the reason Cat looked so disheveled, but he also liked seeing the contrast to the polished, professional ballerina. Not a lot of people got to see the dressed-down version of Cat, and he was glad to be one of the few.

"Hungry?" Dmitri couldn't help but let his lips curl at the corners. He'd never been such a smiley, happy bastard after sex before. Satisfied? Yes. Giddy? No way.

Cat pressed a hand to her belly while the other held the heavy cotton knot by her chest. With the light filtering in from the hallway, he could see the silhouette of her breasts through the thin, white cotton.

"Very."

Dmitri sat back on the bed and patted the spot next to him. Cat padded over, looking down as she walked and being careful not to trip over the sheet. When she sat next to him, Dmitri slung an arm over her shoulders and pulled her against him. Cat giggled in response.

"We can order pizza."

"Pizza!" Cat exclaimed, pulling away to eye him with a look of surprise. "You know better than most people I can't eat pizza tonight. My costume fitting is tomorrow and our performances start this weekend."

He kissed the side of her head and whispered into her hair, "But you burned extra calories tonight."

Cat playfully batted him away. "You're so bad."

"Okay, okay." Dmitri held up his hands in a gesture of defeat. "Unfortunately, our options are limited until I can take you out on a real date."

Cat let out a heavy sigh and rested her head on Dmitri's shoulder. "Do you think we'll ever be able to go out in public? It seems like we're in an impossible situation."

"Things will change." The ominous tone to Dmitri's voice made Cat lift her head to look at him with both her eyebrows raised.

"And how exactly do you figure that, All-knowing One?"

Dmitri smiled, draping his arm over her shoulders. "Well, you'll be dancing with ABT next season so it'll no longer be a conflict of interest."

Cat shifted away so quickly it was as if she'd been electrocuted. "What do you mean?" She looked at Dmitri, her eyes brimming with barely contained excitement. "Do you know something I don't?"

Dmitri nodded. "My mother was very impressed with you."

"You guys talked about me?"

"A little." Dmitri coyly lifted and lowered one shoulder. "Let's just say you'll be auditioning there this spring, and I have a good feeling that audition will lead to a job. My mother doesn't choose who joins the company, but she does have some say."

Cat's expression fell. "Am I being offered an audition because I'm a good dancer or because I'm sleeping with a head teacher's son?" She crossed her arms over her chest, her mouth forming a hard line.

Her defensive reaction surprised Dmitri. Didn't Cat want to join one of the most renowned companies in the world? Or did she want to sling her mother's candy for the rest of her life?

"ABT wouldn't even entertain the idea of having you join them if you weren't a talented dancer."

"Let's face it. I wouldn't have even been invited to ABT this weekend if it wasn't for you." Cat stood, popping one hip out to the side and keeping her arms crossed. "And, even if by some strange tear in the universe, I got invited to practice with said company, your mother wouldn't have paid any special attention to me if you hadn't asked her to."

Dmitri shot up to face her, and a jolt of pain stung his knee. He would have winced and reached down to massage the joint, but let his growing agitation drown out the pain.

"You nailed that allegro during class all on your own. I didn't ask my mom to have you demonstrate. She did that on her own."

"So what?" Cat spat back. "Dancing a decent allegro doesn't usually lead to company membership. The only reason ABT would even consider me is because of my connection to you."

"Fine." Dmitri threw up his hands. "Dance in the Bretton Falls Ballet corps for the rest of your career."

Cat gasped, pressing a hand to her chest and looking outraged. "Are you threatening me? Are you saying you'll never promote me to soloist or principal if I stay here?"

"I'm not saying that." Dmitri enunciated each of his words slowly, struggling not to raise his voice. He stepped closer to Cat, stabbing a finger in the air. "You deserve better. You deserve to be on the grandest stage in North America, at the Metropolitan Opera House."

"But I didn't earn this opportunity," Cat argued, her face taut with tension. "It's being handed to me. I've worked hard for everything I've ever gotten." She traipsed around the room, tripping over the sheet and gathering up her clothes. "God, Dmitri. We're not even a couple and you're already going behind my back and trying to manage my life."

"I am trying to do you a favor." His voice boomed, filling the room and startling Cat to the point where she dropped the shirt she'd just picked up.

She snatched the tee back up and looked at him. "Well, don't do me any more favors."

With that, she stomped through his bedroom door and down the hallway. Dmitri could hear the rustling of fabric and assumed she was changing in his living room. Deciding to be a gentleman, he hung back in his bedroom and gave Cat an opportunity to make herself more presentable. By the time he'd managed to pull his own jeans back on, a task that was always more difficult when his knee was acting up, Dmitri heard his front door slam shut. He dashed down the hallway, zipping up his fly as he ran uncomfortably, only to find his apartment empty.

Lisa Hahn

CHAPTER NINETEEN

Margaret Fairchild, the ex-ballerina who led the company class on Tuesday and Thursday mornings, clapped her hands together loudly before the dancers left the room.

"Attention, everyone. Attention!" She waved her skinny arms overhead, and a wisp of dry, white hair fell into her eyes. "Costume fittings start today. Clara, the Sugar Plum Fairy, and the Prince are to head over to wardrobe immediately. The rest of the cast can find their fitting appointments posted outside the locker room doors."

Cat sighed, wiping a thin layer of sweat from her brow with the back of her hand. The last thing she wanted to do was spend time with Phoebe and Nick without Abby around for reinforcement. After the blow-up between her and Dmitri the night before, she was liable to become extremely angry at any piece of criticism either of her dissenting company members had for her. Ever since she'd stormed out of Dmitri's apartment, her body had been coursing with adrenaline. She'd barely slept last night after she got home. Her hands hadn't stopped shaking since she'd walked into the studio that morning in anticipation of having to see Dmitri again. At least she could be comforted by the fact he couldn't confront her at the studio where someone might hear. Cat had half-expected him to call her into his office again that morning and was secretly hurt when he didn't. Dmitri must not have cared for her as much he'd said he did.

To avoid the gossip mill that was the locker room, Cat plopped down on the studio floor and began untying her pointe shoes. Abby settled down across from her and started doing the same.

"Have fun at your fitting," Abby said sarcastically.

"Yeah, nothing takes the fun out of a costume fitting than having to go with those two."

Abby leaned forward, bracing her weight on her elbows. "Think Dmitri will be there?" she whispered.

Too furious to go home right away when she'd left Dmitri's apartment the night before, Cat had pulled off into an empty parking lot to call Abby. She'd given her best friend a rundown of the argument, preferring to keep the events from earlier in the evening to herself. Of course Abby had known what exactly Cat had gone over there to do, but neither girl was the type to go into detail about sexual exploits.

Cat shuddered, mortified at the thought of facing him for the first time since the night before, while Nick and Phoebe were in the same room. "I hope not."

Abby shrugged. "Lillian used to go sometimes."

"Yeah." Once her pointe shoes were off, Cat stretched her legs out and wiggled her toes. "And Dmitri's a pretty hands-on director. He wants to be involved in everything."

Abby waggled her eyebrows. "Very hands-on."

Cat swatted her with a pink leg warmer. "Not funny."

Now that it seemed clear things between her and Dmitri could never work out, Cat wished she hadn't slept with him. No career-minded ballerina made the mistake of bedding her director. She only hoped Dmitri didn't hold the things she'd said against her professionally, though she'd meant every word that had come out of her mouth. She didn't want, nor did she need, his help. If she made it to ABT, she would do so on her own merit.

"Sorry." Abby's mouth twisted to the side as she shoved her pointe shoes into her bag. "I shouldn't be making jokes about that. At least not yet."

"It's okay." Cat pushed to stand and threw her bag over her shoulder. "I'm sure it will all be perfectly funny once I'm sure I didn't ruin my career."

More times than Cat could count, she'd wondered if Dmitri would be petty enough to keep her in the corps when *The Nutcracker* was over. She knew he could be a hard-ass, but she also knew from their secret liaisons he had a soft side...or at least she thought he did. Part of her thought the gentle, tender-hearted man she'd seen in private was a character Dmitri played to get women in bed.

"You'll be fine." Abby stood up beside Cat and patted her shoulder. "You're one of the best dancers here, and you have the potential to be a real locker room leader, unlike Phoebe, Nick, and Marcy, whose reign of terror needs to end."

Cat blew out a heavy breath. "I hope you're right."

"I am." Abby gave her a little push toward the door. "Good luck."

"Thanks," Cat said, hesitating for a second before walking out to the hall. She traversed the royal blue carpet until she reached the stairwell. The costume department was housed on the second floor. Their expansive workspace always reminded Cat of a warehouse, though it was more welcoming and much more colorful. Bolts of fabric lined the top of one wall above a row of sewing machines. Rolling wardrobes were scattered across the room, storing costumes from past performances. Bretton Falls Ballet held on to everything in hopes it could be reused or repurposed for a different production. Their budget was tight, and they made sure to do the best with what they had. Every time Cat made her way upstairs, she found herself envious of the women who worked there. None of them seemed catty or competitive with one another. Their bodies didn't ache from head to toe every day when they left the building. Their creative, supportive relationship with one another seemed to foster the beautiful costumes they created.

Cat smiled when she entered the room, giddy at the thought of all the unused fabric and excess thread. There were so many possibilities there, so many different looks that needed to be pieced together.

Blanche, the senior seamstress, knelt at Nick's feet as she hemmed the billowy white top he'd wear as Prince. Phoebe stood before a clothing rack with two interns as all three of them pushed and pulled different costumes in search of the pink and purple Sugar Plum Fairy outfit used in years past. Luckily, their elusive director was nowhere to be seen. The buzzing of a sewing machine filled the room before Margo, the new assistant seamstress, pushed the garment she was working on aside and waved Cat over.

"What's up, girl? Come here and we'll get started."

Cat liked Margo. She'd started at the company during the previous season, and the two women had hit it off. Margo had gone out with Cat and Abby a few times for their weekly Saturday girls' night, but recently, she'd been too busy to hang out with them. Between her full-time job at the studio and her full-time course load at the local SUNY campus, the poor girl had been worn thin.

Cat rubbed her palms together. "What do you have for me?"

"This." Margo jumped from her chair and pulled the long, white shift all the Claras in years past had worn off the rack. It looked like the kind of nightgown only little girls and old ladies would wear. It was white, relatively shapeless, and totally unlike the gorgeous tutus worn for most other lead roles. The illusion of a waistline would be created with baby blue bow tied around her midsection. Cat had seen it many times before, but she couldn't help but be disappointed at the sight of the drab, old costume.

Margo pursed her lips and studied the dress she held. "It kind of sucks, huh?"

Glancing over her shoulder, Cat made sure Blanche was not in earshot when she answered. Certainly the gray-haired, bespectacled veteran of the company had been the one who'd made the unflattering number. The dancer playing Clara had worn it every year since Cat could remember, dating back to before she'd joined the company.

"It's not my favorite costume, that's for sure."

Margo handed her the hanger before tucking a lock of bright pink hair behind her ear. "Go try it on and we'll see if there's anything we can do to jazz it up for you."

With her bright green eyes and unflappable smile, Margo looked hopeful. She'd already updated quite a few old costumes from previous seasons, displaying what an asset she was to the small company.

Knowing she was in good hands, Cat went behind a curtained-off area in the corner of the room to change into the dress. She'd always thought it strange the costume room had a designated changing area since all the company members had no qualms about dressing and undressing in front of each other. When someone had a quick change between scenes, it was normal for them to switch costumes in the wings with other dancers and stagehands going about their business around them.

Once she was dressed, Cat pushed back the curtain and stumbled at the sight of Dmitri. He looked over at the sound of the curtain screeching open. Blanche was chewing his ear off about something.

"That's atrocious," he spat, interrupting Blanche mid-sentence.

"Excuse me?" She pushed her blue-framed, cat-eyed glasses farther up on her nose to examine Cat a little more clearly. "You don't like it."

At the sound of the poorly concealed snickering over her shoulder, Cat turned to find Margo gathering up the blue ribbon that went with the dress and laughing into her shoulder.

Cat would probably find Dmitri's not-so-subtle criticism of Blanche's work funny, if she hadn't just had him inside her the night before. As she approached the mirror where Dmitri and Blanche stood, Cat pressed her lips firmly together. She didn't know how to act in front of Dmitri now that their relationship had reached brand new heights of complication.

Cat stepped onto the platform in front of the tri-fold mirror where Blanche and Margo did all their fittings, careful not to meet Dmitri's eyes as she passed him. She held out her arms and checked out her reflection. She looked like a ghost. An exceptionally frumpy ghost, if such a thing even existed. Even with some alterations and the sash tied around her waist, Cat feared she'd look as though she were wearing a bedsheet...much like she had been the night before at Dmitri's apartment.

She cautioned a glance in his direction, choosing instead to sneak a peek at his reflection instead of the man himself. He stroked his chin with one hand, his brow furrowed and his eyes squinting as he studied the frock. He was just as displeased as she was.

"And you said Clara's been wearing this for the past eight years?" he asked with blatant disbelief in his voice.

"Maybe even longer." Blanche pinched the white fabric and held it out before letting it fall back into place. "Obviously it needs to be taken in a little."

"Right…" Dmitri's voice trailed off as he looked over his shoulder at Phoebe and the interns still riffling through costume racks to find the Sugar Plum Fairy tutu. "Blanche, why don't you go help Phoebe and the others? They look like they're having a terrible time."

"Oh." Blanche looked taken aback, her eyes blinking wildly. She always did the costume fittings for the leads and soloists, letting Margo help her only with the corps. And though Dmitri was technically her boss, the artistic director rarely, if ever, came upstairs and told the head seamstress what to do. "Okay then. I'll help them and be right back."

Dmitri watched Blanche walk away, waiting until she was out of earshot to ask Margo, "What the fuck can you do to make it so Clara doesn't look like a virginal prude?"

Cat's face flushed at his word choice, wondering if Dmitri was thinking about the night before and how very unlike a prude and a virgin she'd been. Luckily for her, Dmitri and Margo were too busy eyeing the monstrosity hanging off her body to have noticed.

Margo tapped her lips with her pointer finger, backing up a step to view the dress from a different angle. "We can bring the hem up a few inches."

"Of course. The damn thing is just about at her ankles," Dmitri said. "What else?" Since Phoebe and Marcy were both much taller than Cat, the dress would have to be re-hemmed no matter what.

Margo fingered the round neck collar. "Maybe we can cut some of this away and give her a sweetheart neckline. I can add in some white lace to make it…" Margo paused, pursing her lips as she looked for the right word. "Prettier." Her voice rose, making it sound more like she was asking a question instead of making an emphatic statement about how she planned to beautify the atrocious costume.

Dmitri shook his head, his gaze still glued to the shapeless frock. "Is starting from scratch an option?"

"Unfortunately, no." Margo grabbed both ends of the cloth measuring tape she perpetually had hanging from her neck whenever she was at work. "With all the alterations we have to do on the other costumes, there's no way we would have time to design, construct, and fit a brand new dress. With the time constraints we're under, we're both already going to be working overtime this week."

Cat spoke up. "Maybe I could help." Margo and Dmitri both looked at her curiously.

"How so?" Dmitri asked, addressing her directly or the first time since she'd come out of the makeshift dressing room. A light sheen of sweat that hadn't been there earlier coated her brow as her throat went dry. Trying to work with Dmitri after what happened would be harder than she'd originally thought.

"Cat makes all of her own leos and tights," Margo chimed in, sounding hopeful Cat might have an idea that would please their boss. "She does a really good job."

Dmitri met her gaze in the mirror and lifted an eyebrow. "Is this true?"

Cat nodded. "I've never made anything more complicated than that, but I think with Margo's help I might be able to put together something that looks a whole lot better than this." She pulled the dress out to the side, demonstrating just how big and unflattering it was.

Margo bounced up and down on her toes, brimming with excitement. "What do you have in mind?"

Cat pointed to a nearby desk strewn with loose paper to be used either for sketching or taking down measurements. Blanche was notoriously unorganized, but she always surprised everyone by getting their costumes to fit them perfectly. A cup of pencils sat in the corner, making Cat's fingers twitch. She had the perfect idea.

"May I?" she asked.

Margo swept her arm out. "Be my guest."

Cat realized she should have checked with Dmitri to make sure he'd even entertain the idea of a dancer designing and constructing her own costume, but she didn't want to give him a chance to say no. Once he saw what she had in mind, she knew he'd be on board with her idea.

To make things even sweeter, the dressmaking process would be so time-consuming, she wouldn't have time to think of what could have been between them.

She hopped off the platform, landing beside the desk, and grabbed a pencil. She pulled a piece of paper toward over and started a rough sketch of the costume she'd envisioned: a babydoll dress with a skirt and bell sleeves made with flowing, white chiffon. Lace adornments would be added to the hems, and tiny rhinestones would be glued to the bodice so that Cat sparkled under the spotlights.

"Wow." Margo nodded approvingly, watching over Cat's shoulder as she put the finishing touches on the sketch. Dmitri held off, standing back by the mirror and watching intently as she drew. She could *feel* his eyes on her the entire time.

He didn't walk over until she'd dropped the pencil back into its cup.

"Let me see what you came up with." Dmitri held out his hand expectantly with that demanding, authoritative allure she'd come to loathe and love in equal measure.

Cat hesitated before placing the paper in his hand, irritated by the command. She knew it was how Dmitri spoke to almost everyone, but she resented it anyway.

His expression remained blank as he looked over the sketch, studying it for nearly two minutes before looking up from the paper.

"Do you think the two of you can pull this off?" Dmitri's gaze shot directly to Margo, bypassing Cat and irking her further.

Margo beamed, seemingly excited by the challenge. "It'll be tough but we can do it. If we don't have the right fabric laying around, I'll run out and grab it this afternoon." She looked to Cat. "Maybe you and I can get started on it tonight."

A smile spread across Cat's face, replacing the scowl that Dmitri had caused.

"I'm in."

"Cool." Margo flinched at the distinctive sound of Blanche's nitpicking as she chastised one of the interns for pulling out a wardrobe for an entirely different ballet. "We just need to clear everything with Blanche."

"No need," Dmitri said, matter-of-factly. "I'll inform her of the new plans."

"Ohhh-kayyy." Margo drew out the word and looked to Cat. Gossip must take an exceedingly long time to travel upstairs because Margo looked surprised by Dmitri's brazenness.

Cat, on the other hand, knew it was one of the many things that made him unbearably sexy.

To avoid facing her lingering attraction to Dmitri, Cat reminded herself to focus on *The Nutcracker*. She had a dress to make and a lead role to master and less than a week to do it all.

She looked to Margo. "Text me when you leave here later. I'm pretty sure mom will let me leave the shop early tonight to work on this."

Cat felt bad about bailing early on her shift, but she knew her mom would understand. If everything went well with *The Nutcracker*, Cat would likely not take the management position her mother was holding for her at the new shop. However, she'd be able to offer financial assistance that her mom could put back into the businesses or she could use it for Grace and Elise's educations.

Margo pumped a fist in the air. "Bring some dark chocolate salted caramels and I'm there."

"Can you search for the white fabric now?" Dmitri gave Margo a pointed look. "I'd like to talk to Catherine for a moment."

Margo's brow furrowed briefly before she pasted on a grin and saluted Dmitri, a silly gesture Cat knew their boss would fail to see the humor in. "Aye, aye, captain." She smiled at Cat with a glimmer in her eye that communicated her desire to know why the director had taken such a strong interest in her friend. After all, it was entirely unheard of for a dancer to make her own costume. Cat knew she would have some explaining to do later and hoped a dozen salted caramels would be enough to buy Margo's silence.

"See you later," Margo chirped, wiggling her fingers in farewell.

"Bye." Cat's gaze followed Margo's retreat over to the bolts of fabric lining the wall, unwilling to meet Dmitri's stare.

"Cat." He spoke quietly so only she would be able to hear him.

She shut her eyes, holding back unshed tears. "Is this about work?"

A few beats passed before he responded softly. "No."

Dmitri is my boss.

"Then I don't want to hear it." As soon as the words left her mouth, Cat scampered off to the dressing room, not bothering to look over her shoulder to see Dmitri's reaction. She knew he wouldn't be pleased with her stomping away from him again.

CHAPTER TWENTY

Dmitri slammed his office door shut with such force, it shook in the hinges. He stormed over to his desk, resenting the limp that slowed him down, and tossed his cane to the floor when he got there. He picked up the stapler, one of the few items he kept on his clutter-free desk, and hurled it at the wall. It hit with a crash, denting the plaster before dropping to the ground with a loud thud. He didn't care about the attention the noise would draw to his outburst. He'd conditioned everyone there to expect his horrid moods daily, so it didn't matter how many things he threw or how many holes he put in the boring, beige walls.

All he cared about was Catherine Brown.

Why did she have to be so stubborn? Her impending invitation to audition at ABT was not the result of nepotism; instead, it was borne from her undeniable talent. Sure, she might not have been invited to ABT the previous weekend if it had not been for Dmitri's prior association with the company, but the same went for Phoebe and Nick and he didn't have any personal interest in advancing either of their careers. It was just the way things worked sometimes in their industry.

Left to try to decipher Cat's bull-headedness on his own, Dmitri surmised that she was not used to receiving support from within the company. Simon's mentorship had kept her going during the seemingly dark years while Lillian was in charge, but Simon had been powerless with such a short-sighted person running the company. In the twenty-first century, dancers came in a variety of sizes. Lillian had been a fool to write off a talented dancer simply because she was short.

Dmitri slammed his fist down on his desk, cursing himself for falling for Cat. He planted both palms on his desk, hunching over his workspace and seething with anger directed at both himself and Cat. He knew he should be at rehearsals, but he'd be of no use to anyone in his current state.

Luckily, Dmitri hadn't locked himself in for any one rehearsal that week. He had the dancers working in small groups with the company teachers, allowing him to bounce around among different studios and the costume department with ease. *The Nutcracker* had been thrown together with such little preparation, Dmitri knew there'd be no telling where he'd need to be during the final few days before their first show.

At the sound of a gentle knock on his door, Dmitri looked over his shoulder with a growl.

"What do you want?"

The door cracked open and Sue poked her head in.

"Did I say you could come in?" Dmitri's voice dripped with venom, making the older woman jump.

"No. Sorry." She retreated and began to shut the door.

"What did you want?" he asked just before the door clicked in place.

Sue pushed open the door a few inches. "I heard all of the commotion in here and thought I'd check to make sure everything was okay."

Dmitri spun to face her, a devilish grin pulling up on corner of his mouth as he held his arms out to the side. "Does everything look fine?"

Sue scanned the room, her brown eyes growing wide beneath her glasses as she spotted the dent in the wall.

"Don't worry about it." Dmitri spit out the casual phrase like a command before making a shooing motion with her hand. "You can leave now."

"Actually, Mr. Fedorov, I have to talk to you about something."

Dmitri raised an eyebrow at her boldness. Once she saw for herself how sour his mood was, he'd fully expected Sue to tuck her tail between her legs and retreat. Instead, she took a cautious step into the room. The powdery scent of her perfume hit his nose, angering him further. Now he'd have to air out his office to rid it of the strong smell.

Dmitri sat back and crossed his arms over his chest. "What?" he asked, sounding wholly uninterested.

"Well, I…" Sue entered the room and quietly shut the door behind her. "I'd rather we talk in private."

Dmitri motioned to the closed door. "We're in private. Talk."

"As the office secretary, I think it's my duty to let you know about the rumors circulating the studio about you and one of the dancers." Sue looked him directly in the eye as she talked, reminding Dmitri of the way his mom would question him when she already knew what he'd done wrong and was trying to get him to admit it himself.

He looked away, not wanting to give Sue any information. His mom was always able to tell when he was lying and he didn't want to risk the nosy secretary being able to do the same.

"There will always be rumors. They don't concern me."

"That's the thing." Sue came farther into the room, putting herself back into his line of sight. "I'm not so sure these are rumors."

Dmitri snapped his head up to look at her. "Are you accusing me of something?"

Sue held up her hands defensively. "Not at all. I just want to make sure you know what you're doing."

Dmitri pushed off his desk and limped over to where Sue stood, getting close enough to intimidate but staying far enough away so that he didn't choke on the scent of her perfume. "Do you know who I am?"

"I do, Mr. Fedorov, but—"

"I'm Dmitri Fedorov. My mother is the great Constance Fedorov. She is a wonderful woman who did a tremendous job raising me. I don't need another mom." He pointed to the closed door. "Leave."

Sue flinched before continuing. "Catherine Brown is a talented girl, and I'd hate to see an ill-thought-out dalliance ruin her reputation here."

While Dmitri wanted to berate the older woman for disobeying him, he respected her persistence. They were both worried for Cat's future. Consumed with his burgeoning affection for the girl, he decided hear Sue out so he would know what exactly everyone else thought they were seeing.

"What makes you think I'm sleeping with her?"

Sue lifted her chin, seeming proud of herself for getting him to listen. "I've heard the rumors in the hallway and thought nothing of them. You came to the company and shook things up. Everyone was so used to Lillian that naturally there would be a few dissenters in the ranks, especially the dancers that she'd marked as her favorites."

Dmitri rolled his wrist. "Let's hurry this along."

"Well, I first realized there might be some truth to the rumors when I went to fetch Cat from the locker room for you and overheard a spat between her and Marcy Gray. I only caught the tail end of it, but it sure sounded like Marcy was accusing the girl of sleeping with you. Cat seemed pretty riled up after." Sue pointed to her glasses. "Then I started paying attention."

Dmitri scoffed. "What does that mean?"

"That girl went into your office angry as a hornet and came out smiling ear to ear, for one. I had to run two messages to you later that day while rehearsals were going on. You didn't even turn at the sound of the door opening. It was like you only had eyes for her."

"I was watching my dancers," Dmitri growled. He turned and walked to the window behind his desk. "Get out of my office."

"Sorry to have bothered you." Sue's sincere tone left Dmitri unaffected, too dumbfounded by her gall to care about her feelings.

When he heard the door shut behind him, Dmitri pressed his hands against the window sill to shift his weight and relieve the pressure on his injured knee. He shouldn't have stood so long without his cane, but it had never crossed his mind to fetch it after Sue confronted him. The pain lessened as soon as he took some of the weight off it. His bum knee was far from being his biggest problem.

Dmitri looked out into the barren woods and pondered what he was going to do about Cat.

CHAPTER TWENTY-ONE

Pieces of Cat's *Nutcracker* costume sat on the Browns' kitchen table. Cat and Margo had spent most of the evening working on the design, breaking only for a quick dinner delivered by Abby. They'd gotten as far as making a pattern and cutting the fabric before deciding to call it a night.

Margo rubbed her hands together. "Now I'm going to have some of those caramels."

Cat chuckled and pointed to the small, pink candy box on the counter beside the coffeemaker. "Go ahead." She gathered the pieces of chiffon and spandex off the table.

In a chair pulled back against the refrigerator, Abby still poked at her salad. "That dress is going to look gorgeous on stage."

Cat carefully arranged the fabric in the box. "I hope so."

"You know, people in rehearsal were already taking guesses as to why you're allowed to design your own costume." Abby tossed her salad into the nearby trash can and then sat back in her chair. "I'm sure you can imagine the kinds of the things they were saying."

"Things like 'Cat Brown is so talented. Not only is she the lead in our show but she's also making her own costume.'" Margo paused to lick a smear of chocolate off her thumb. "They all probably hate you now, huh?"

Cat pushed the box off to the side and took her seat at the table. "Not for the reasons you'd think."

Margo perked up. "Oh my god. I can't believe I forgot to ask. What is going on between you and that stone-cold fox of a director? This has something to do with him, doesn't it?"

"Everyone thinks I'm sleeping with him."

"You're not, so it doesn't matter. The dude clearly has the hots for you, though." Margo shrugged and popped another caramel into her mouth.

"But I *am* sleeping with him." Cat began picking at the random split ends in her hair. "At least, I was. Or I have. Once."

"It's so much more than just that," Abby chimed in as she joined the other two women at the table, dragging her chair over. "I'm pretty sure Cat's in love with him."

"Abby!" Cat pushed her chair back from the table, looking astounded. "I am not in love with him."

"It certainly seems like it. He's practically all you ever talk about, and you two have been hot and cold ever since he moved here."

Margo watched the back-and-forth between the two best friends like she was engrossed in the world's most entertaining tennis match, chomping on caramels as she looked on.

"You've never even seen us together," Cat argued.

"I've seen you in rehearsal, and it's so obvious you two are in love with each other." Abby rubbed her fingertips together. "I can feel it in the air."

"You're crazy." Cat waved Abby off and sat back in her chair, crossing one leg over the other.

"But maybe she's not that crazy." Margo leaned forward on her forearms, interjecting herself into the conversation. "I definitely noticed something between you guys this morning."

"You noticed the lingering awkwardness from last night." Cat made a slashing motion with her hands. "But things are over now."

"Why?" Margo's brows pulled together as she looked at Cat like she was crazy. "Dmitri's hot as hell and everyone's been saying he's a much better director than Lillian ever was. He's a little abrasive, but otherwise he seems like a real catch." She popped another caramel in her mouth.

Cat shook her head. "That's all part of the problem." She began to count off her issues. "For one, he's my director. My boss. Secondly, you're right, he is abrasive. He's difficult to deal with on all fronts. Thirdly, he thinks I'll upend my entire life for the sole purpose of being with him."

Margo's mouth pulled to the side. "But he's hot."

"Which makes it even harder to ignore my feelings for him every time I see him in the studio."

"Sounds like you've gotten yourself into a no-win situation." Margo pushed the box of candy down the table to Cat. "Have one of these. You need it."

Ordinarily Cat wouldn't think twice about turning down candy, with a performance looming in the future, but Margo was right. Maybe the sweetness would overpower the sour taste she had in her mouth after her night with Dmitri. She plucked one from the box before sliding it across the table to Abby, who shrugged and took a caramel out for herself before returning the box to Margo.

"Now, do you mind me asking how exactly Dmitri tried to upend your life?" Margo asked, wiping her fingers on a paper napkin.

"He used his connections with ABT to get me an audition there. Well, technically I haven't gotten the official invitation yet, but it's been made clear its incoming. *And*," Cat dragged out the word to put emphasis on how bad she thought Dmitri's offenses were, "he all but promised me his mom would do whatever she could to make sure I would be asked to join."

"Cat, isn't that your dream? To dance with a company like ABT?" Margo asked, sounding surprised by her friend's reaction.

Feeling slightly defensive, Cat crossed her arms over chest. "Yeah, but I wanted to get there on my own."

"You know," Abby pipped in, wagging a finger in the air like an idea had just come to her. "As talented as you are, the chances of you getting into ABT on your own would be slim to none because of your age. You need outside help for opportunities like these."

Margo snapped her head to look at Abby. "Ouch, girl. What happened to you being the supportive best friend?"

Abby held up her hands defensively. "I am, but we can't tiptoe around the issues here. *The Nutcracker* starts in a few days, and Cat needs to be on her game." She planted her hands on the table and looked to her friend. "Dmitri thinks you're a good dancer. He made you the lead in his first ballet with the company based on the way he saw you dance, hidden in Lillian's corps. And you know full well Simon spent years begging Lillian to give you a chance. Would you turn down a soloist's role from her because you knew Simon had a hand in helping you get it?"

Cat's mouth pulled off to the side while she considered Abby's point. It all made sense, but there was a small caveat she'd forgotten.

"Dmitri came right out and told me he wanted me to work for ABT so he and I could be together. How could I be so sure he'd want me to audition over there if he didn't have a personal stake in the matter? I mean, he's told me that I'm his best female dancer. If he honestly believes that, wouldn't it make more sense for him to keep me here?"

Margo propped an elbow up onto the table and tapped a finger to her lips. "Both of you make intriguing points." She reached over and slapped Cat on the back. "You've got yourself in a really shitty situation here."

Cat rolled her eyes. "Tell me about it."

"Let's look at the bright side." Abby lifted and lowered one shoulder, flashing a subtle smile. "You're the lead in a ballet."

Margo hooked her thumb toward the box. "And your costume is going to be freakin' gorgeous."

"Let's focus on that for the next few days, then we'll worry about Dmitri and ABT." Abby stuck out her hand for Cat to shake.

Cat hesitated, knowing how hard it would be to push her complicated feelings for Dmitri to the side. Ultimately, she knew what she had to do.

She stuck her hand in Abby's and gave it a firm shake. "Deal."

CHAPTER TWENTY-TWO

After a long, tedious ascent up the stairs to the costume room, Dmitri made his way directly over to Margo who was hunched over a sewing machine. He'd visited the pink-haired girl that morning, hoping to get a sneak peek of the costume she informed him they'd spent most of the previous night working on.

Margo had been firm in her instance Dmitri wait to see the costume until it was completed, claiming it would look even more beautiful when Cat had it on, but he tried to throw his weight as director around anyway. Margo, it seemed, was the only person other than Cat who wasn't intimidated by him.

Now, hours after he'd visited her earlier that morning, Dmitri was done waiting. He needed to see the costume.

"Well," he said as he came up behind Margo's workstation, startling her mid-stitch.

Margo glanced at him before turning her attention back to the crooked stitch she'd just put into the Marzipan tutu. "I guess I'll fix this later."

"Where is it?"

Margo pointed to the curtain housing the makeshift dressing room. "She's putting it on. Why don't you go wait over there and I'll let her know you're here?"

With a nod, Dmitri started toward the trifold mirror. He'd seen Cat during rehearsals earlier but had avoided talking to her. As much as he'd wanted to confront Cat and explain that he thought she deserved to be in ABT just as much as every celebrated dancer who'd ever graced their halls, he knew she needed to focus on her current role. He would come clean after opening night, in hopes a stellar, crowd-pleasing performance would make Cat more likely to hear him out.

When she came out from behind the curtain, Dmitri's breath caught in his throat. She looked beautiful and vibrant in the flowing, white chiffon. Cat was exactly as he'd pictured her when he watched the tapes from the previous season and chose her as his *Nutcracker* lead. Clearly dancing was not Cat's only talent; the girl had an eye for design most people went to school for years to hone. She'd captured his vision without his having to explain it to her. All she had to go on was the choreography she'd been dancing. From the bright grin on her face, Dmitri could tell she knew she nailed it.

Cat avoided eye contact with Dmitri as she stepped up onto the podium in front of the mirror. Margo stood behind her, fussing with the dress and trimming loose threads she hadn't yet gotten the chance to clean up.

"So, what do you think?" Margo asked, looking up at Dmitri as she snipped a frayed edge on the skirt.

"It's perfect," Dmitri said, surprised by the softness and sincerity in his own voice.

Margo looked up at him, scissors poised to take off another thread. "You're not being sarcastic, are you?"

"He's not," Cat interjected. Ignoring Margo behind her, she held out her skirt and did a spin much like she'd done as a little girl when she played dress-up in her mom's dressy clothes. "He couldn't be. This dress is perfect." She looked down at her friend and offered a hand to help her up. "And it's all thanks to you."

Margo accepted Cat's hand before pushing to stand. "No way, girl. The concept was all yours. I just helped with the construction."

"I've never made a dress before. I needed you."

Margo smiled and turned to Dmitri. "You really think it's perfect, huh?"

Dmitri nodded once. "I do."

"What is this?" Blanche came up behind them, her glasses pushed up her nose. "The dress I never commissioned?"

"The girls did a wonderful job, don't you think?" Dmitri's initial instinct was to threaten Blanche's job security if she ever spoke to him with such blatant disrespect again. Then he realized he would infuriate the old bat more if he showered Cat and Margo with praise. "They put a lot of time into the costume, and it shows."

Like he'd hoped, Blanche's face tightened with fury. She smoothed a hand over her gray hair, twisted behind her head and held in place with a pencil, looking flustered. "Mr. Fedorov, can I please speak with you?" She glared, at either Cat or the costume, he wasn't sure. "Alone."

Dmitri turned to face her head-on and rested his hands on top of his cane. "What do you have to say, Blanche? Do you think I should have used the godawful dress you made over twenty years ago? Would you have been willing to make a new dress from scratch if I'd asked you?" He motioned to Cat, who had since hopped off the podium to stand with Margo. They were both doing a poor job of pretending not to listen to him berate the head seamstress. "Do you think you could have made a better costume than this one?"

Blanche threw her hands up, looking flustered. "I would have gladly made you a new dress if you'd given me enough time to get the work done."

"Cat and Margo made a new dress in a day." Dmitri narrowed his gaze, knowing it would intimidate her. "Why couldn't you do that?"

"I've been doing all the alterations." Blanche's voice rose, drawing the attention of the interns and other dancers in the room. "It's a shame, really. The head seamstress being relegated to the busy work."

"The head seamstress should be willing to do what is asked of her, even if it means putting in extra work. We all know it gets busy around the studio when a show is about to premiere." Dmitri kept his tone cool and even, antagonizing her further by not getting upset.

"This is outrageous." Blanche pointed to the door. "If you can't have a civil conversation with me, then I'm going down to tell Simon about the miserable job you're doing with this company."

A flicker of anger ignited in Dmitri. "You think I'm doing a terrible job with this company? Do you think it matters what you think?"

"I wish you would just follow the procedures Lillian put in place. She gave the seamstresses several weeks to prepare for a performance. She never came up here and told me how my department should be run. And she never gave anyone preferential treatment."

"You're kidding me, right?" Dmitri chuckled. "Lillian's tenure was rife with nepotism and antiquated views that hindered the company's development."

"If that is true, which I highly doubt, at least Lillian didn't make her favoritism as obvious as yours."

In two steps, Dmitri stood in front of Blanche. He seethed, clenching his jaw to keep his temper at bay.

"I suggest you stop there, Blanche."

"Why? It's all the dancers wanted to talk about when they were up here yesterday." She lifted her chin, more defiant than agitated now. "You have a favorite dancer and everyone knows it." Stopping to glance around the room for support, Blanche subtly nodded to Marcy, who had undoubtedly given Blanche much of her information. As far as Dmitri knew, Marcy was the source of the rumors being spread about him and Cat. "Honestly, you let a dancer with no experience design and construct her own dress. And you assign my assistant the task of helping her. It's short-sighted and irresponsible. Think about the well-being of the company Lillian handed down to you. The one she tended to with the doting affection of a mother. You think you can come in here and throw around your reputation to get exactly what you want."

By the time she'd finished her tirade, Dmitri shook with rage. He wanted nothing more than to verbally tear Blanche apart before dismissing her from her duties, but he knew he had to be professional in this situation. He couldn't have other people believing what she'd said about him.

"Get out," he said slowly and crisply, watching her flinch at the hard consonant at the end of each word. "You're done here."

She blinked wildly as she looked around the room again for support. Now that her actions had gotten her fired, she found none, not even from Marcy. She turned back to Dmitri, her mouth agape. "But I've worked here for thirty years."

Dmitri tossed his cane to the floor and flipped the flimsy work desk beside him, unable to contain fury Blanche had awakened in him. "I said get out." His thunderous voice echoed in the room.

"Blanche, let's go get your things." Margo wrapped her arm around her former boss' shoulder and led her to the stairs. "I think everyone needs a minute to cool off."

Everyone in the room watched in silence as the two seamstresses headed to the staircase, the collective gaze turning back to Dmitri once they descended the steps. Dmitri looked over the twelve people gawking at him, knowing they were all waiting to see what he would do next.

For the first time since he'd referenced her early in the argument, Dmitri turned to Cat, fearing the reaction she'd have to the older woman's public questioning of their relationship. He knew checking on her while everyone still watched him would all but validate the accusations being thrown their way, but Dmitri didn't care. Cat was a good woman with a heart of gold; she didn't deserve to have her personal life be a part of public controversy.

Tear tracks streaked her face, leaving mascara stains beneath her angry eyes. "I quit," she announced loudly enough for the whole room to hear even though she spoke directly to Dmitri.

"Don't do that," he pleaded. "We both know you don't want to do that."

"Mom is opening a new candy store, and I can be the manager there if I want." Her hands balled into fists at her sides, and Dmitri knew Cat already regretted what she was about to do. "I will fulfill my *Nutcracker* duties and then I'm retiring."

With that, she spun on her heels and hurried down the stairs. Dmitri didn't know where she planned to go in her costume, but he was depending on Margo being there to calm her down. He was too keyed up to trust himself to say anything to her that wouldn't make matters worse.

Instead, he addressed the room.

"If anyone here thinks that I'm resting on my laurels as a world-renowned danseur, you're wrong. I've been living and breathing this

Nutcracker since I discovered I'd be Lillian's successor. If I'm critical or harsh, it's because this show, this company, and this discipline mean everything to me. I want Bretton Falls Ballet to grow and expand. I want people all over the state of New York and the country talking about the fucking good work we're doing here, and I will do whatever it takes to get us there. Understood?"

A few people nodded, but most stood still as statues.

With his pulse still racing, Dmitri headed to the stairs to put another hole into his office wall.

Lisa Hahn

CHAPTER TWENTY-THREE

Opening night was less than twenty-four hours away, and the costume department was running behind on their alterations. With the dismissal of the head seamstress, Dmitri had expected as much. All the lead and soloist outfits had been altered, but there were several members of the corps that wouldn't get to try on their costumes until right before show time. Simon had stepped in and called a few mothers of the students in their school to see who knew how to work a sewing machine and had a few hours to spare.

Unfortunately, one of those mothers was Louise Brown.

Dmitri avoided the woman every time he ventured up to the costume department to check their progress, opting to speak briefly with Margo before retreating to his office. Dmitri didn't know how much Louise knew, but judging by her willingness to pitch in last-minute, he assumed she hadn't heard much. Nonetheless, he figured it was safer to avoid her than to try to talk to her.

Avoidance would be much more difficult the following night, when Louise hosted the company's after party at the Land of Sweets. Typically, they had a small get-together backstage after the first show of the season, but Simon had wanted to put together something a little grander to thank Dmitri for his hard work and to celebrate Cat's first performance as a leading lady. Dmitri would have preferred skipping the hoopla, but Simon persisted. Dmitri assumed Simon must have been the only person in the entire company who hadn't heard the rumors circulating about the questionable nature of Cat and Dmitri's relationship, or else he would have known the after party would likely be an uncomfortable event.

Though no one else had the gall to confront Dmitri after Blanche's blow-up the day before, he knew everybody in the bloody building had heard about the older woman's accusations, Cat's retirement announcement, and Dmitri's subsequent tantrum. Everyone, including the building's janitorial staff, who typically remained untouched by the gossip constantly filtering around, looked at Dmitri a little differently when he passed them in the hall—like they knew a dirty secret about him.

Luckily, years of sleeping with members of ABT while performing with the company helped to prepare him for situations such as these.

Dmitri was blown away by how much he missed Cat and how difficult it had been to stay away from her. Since she seemed so comfortable with her role, Dmitri decided it would be best if he did not attend any of her rehearsals. He wanted to see her practice, to be there for her as a good director should, but he knew his presence would likely do more harm than good. He could only hope a little space would help her see how great she was and how little her success had to do with him.

Other than that, Dmitri had no idea how to change Cat's mind about retirement. Her career was blossoming. She was dancing better than ever and she was in favor with some of the top people in ABT. She shouldn't be retiring; she should be rejoicing that all her hard work over the years had finally paid off.

It was Dmitri's fault Cat wasn't enjoying her newfound success like she should. He should have stayed away and let her embrace the opportunity. Maybe then, she would audition for ABT without feeling like she'd been gifted the invitation. Maybe then, she could stay in Bretton Falls and not worry about the other dancers crying nepotism when she got promoted to soloist. Dmitri knew he had to fix this mess for Cat. He just hadn't figured out how yet. He'd been so busy with last-minute preparation for the show, he'd barely had a chance to sit down and think of anything.

Dmitri sat at his desk, his vision blurring as he looked over the show program one more time. It had already been a twelve-hour work day, and he knew he wouldn't head home for another few hours. He pressed his fingers to his temples, blinking a few times before trying to look at the program again. He'd already read through the first page several times and hadn't been able to process the information, thoughts of Cat and other tasks that needed to get done distracting him.

The scent of garlic and melted cheese pulled Dmitri's attention from the screen. His stomach rumbled at the aroma, reminding him he hadn't had anything other than a dozen cups of black coffee and a few convenience-store doughnuts all day. Drawn by hope of hot pizza, Dmitri grabbed his cane and headed over to his office door. He opened it and saw a teen girl with purple streaks in her hair heading toward the stairs with a stack of pizzas in her hands.

"Excuse me," he called after the girl, hoping to grab her attention before she disappeared with the food. When she stopped to look at him, he hobbled over to her. "Are you delivering those?"

"No." She hitched her head back to the entrance. "But someone else did. I'm bringing these up to the costume department."

As soon as Dmitri stepped into the lit hallway, the girl's eyes brightened with recognition.

"You're Dmitri Fedorov, aren't you?"

He nodded. "I am." The girl looked familiar, but he knew there was no way they'd met before. Dmitri typically left before the students at the school started to come in for evening classes. Plus, with her purple hair and worn out Rolling Stones tee, this girl didn't seem like the ballet type.

"Great. I hoped I'd run into you tonight." The girl pushed past him into the open front office and put the pizzas down on Sue's desk, completely unbothered by the neat piles of paper she'd disturbed. "We need to talk."

Dmitri pursed his lips and leaned back against the wall. "And you are?"

"Elise Brown, Cat's sister."

Dmitri nodded and stood a little straighter. Now he understood why the girl seemed so familiar to him. Her pretty face and self-assured demeanor were identical to her sister's. He had no idea what she might want to talk to him about, though. He didn't think Cat would share her sexual exploits with her teenage sister.

"I would love to talk, but I have a lot of work to do. I have a premiere tomorrow evening." He pushed off the wall and started toward his office. "You know that, though. Your sister's the star of the show."

Elise stepped in his path and cut to the chase. "Why is Cat retiring?"

Dmitri veered to his right to continue, but Elise stepped to the side and blocked him again.

He sighed, not wanting to have this conversation. "I don't know. Maybe you should ask her yourself."

"I did." Elise crossed her arms over her chest, eying Dmitri suspiciously. "She said it's the right time for her to hang up her pointe shoes, but I don't believe her."

"What makes you think she would have told me something different?" Dmitri kept his tone even, trying his best to seem disinterested in the conversation. He hoped a few short, broad responses would make her give up and leave him alone. He didn't owe her any explanations.

"I know something was going on between the two of you."

Dmitri swallowed hard, feeling uncomfortable. "There is nothing going on between Cat and me."

It was one thing to be accused of messing around with Cat by the adults that worked at the studio. But being confronted by her teenage sister, a girl who truly cared for Cat and questioned her decisions, made Dmitri feel guilty. Guilt, however, was not an emotion Dmitri typically experienced, so the only way he knew to express himself was to get angry.

He met Elise's gaze and lifted his chin. "I suggest you move aside or you will be the sole person responsible for whatever issues arise during tomorrow's show because you kept the director away from his work with your pointless questions."

Instead of doing as he asked, Elise took a step toward him, getting so close the toes of their sneakers nearly touched. "You'll be the sole person responsible for tomorrow's show being lackluster if you don't tell me what's going on. Cat's heart isn't in this, and that's literally never happened before. Even when she didn't get callbacks for any of her auditions and had to work under Lillian for years." A tear rolled down the girl's cheek and she quickly brushed it away, trying to look the part of the tough, unflappable sister she played. "Something's wrong and I need your help to fix it. Cat doesn't want to retire. She wants to dance. She's always wanted to dance."

At Elise's show of emotion, Dmitri felt a tug at his heart. Not only had he driven Cat into retirement, but he'd caused distress within her family. While he didn't know the Browns well, they seemed like a nice lot. Simon thought highly of the family, and Dmitri knew the close relationship spoke volumes about how much the Browns had encouraged Cat in her career.

His body felt heavy with remorse, while the fiery attraction he had for Cat still burned deep in his being.

He had to fix what he'd done. He just needed to figure out how.

Hesitantly, Dmitri lifted a hand and placed it on the girl's shoulder. His instincts told him to pull away, drop his hand, and pretend he never offered a consolatory gesture. Instead, driven by his budding love for Cat, he ground his teeth together and forced himself to follow through.

"I'm sorry that Cat wants to retire, but I promise that I will do everything in my power to make her change her mind."

It wasn't a confession of guilt, but Dmitri hoped it would appease the girl and give her a little hope that her sister would return to her normal, ballet-loving self.

Awkwardly, he dropped his hand back to his side. Before the girl could question him further and ask for specific information on just how he planned to right his wrong, he looked to the pizza boxes. "You girls can't eat all of that, can you?"

By the way Elise mashed her lips together, Dmitri could tell she was trying—and failing—to suppress a smile.

"I can eat four slices on my own, but I don't know about everyone else. They've all probably worked up an appetite."

"You wouldn't mind if I stole some for myself then, would you?" He motioned to the stack of flimsy paper plates wedged between the coffeemaker and the microwave on the westward wall.

Elise snatched up the pizzas, rounded Sue's desk and headed toward the stairs. "You can come join us if you want to eat our pizza. Plus, I know Margo wanted to talk to you."

Dmitri grinned. Elise was a little firecracker, just like her older sister. It was an aspect of Cat's personality he already missed, and it had been a little over a day since they'd last spoken. Spurred on by the lingering scent of pizza, Dmitri trudged up the stairs, hoping to grab a few slices and check in with Margo before Louise spotted him. The last thing he needed was to be confronted by another Brown woman. Dmitri thought he could be tough in an argument, but Elise and Cat had already taught him that his intimidation techniques might not be as foolproof as he'd once thought.

By the time he reached the top of the stairs, the women had already gathered around a long folding table and dug into the pizza. When Elise saw him, she ran over with a plated slice in hand.

"Here you go." She handed him the food before dipping her hands into the pockets of her black jeans. "I hope you'll keep what we talked about in mind."

"I haven't stopped thinking about a way to change Cat's mind since she made her announcement yesterday."

Elise smiled smugly. "Good."

Margo joined the group, draping an arm over Elise's shoulders. "She's a good kid, right?"

Dmitri nodded. "Seems like it."

"Elise had never sewn a stitch before tonight, and she's already working faster than everyone else." Margo dropped her arm to playfully elbow the teen in the ribs. "She and her sister are natural talents, I suppose."

Elise pushed her away, seeming equal parts annoyed by the praise as she was pleased with it. "Stop it, will you?"

"Go get some pizza while I talk to the big, bad director, okay?" Margo raised an eyebrow, looking unsure about whether the girl would comply.

"Okay." Elise turned, took a few steps, and then stopped to respond. "And he isn't so scary. He just likes to think he is."

Margo laughed, covering her mouth with her hand when everyone in the room looked.

"She's really got your number, huh?"

Dmitri grunted in response before biting into his pizza. He closed his eyes as he chewed, enjoying the fresh, warm slice. After he swallowed, he dabbed his mouth with the napkin Elise had tucked under his plate and turned his attention to Margo.

"You wanted to see me?"

Margo beamed, looking proud of herself. "I just wanted to let you know that we'll wrap up in here tonight, so the corps can try on their costumes tomorrow to see if I need to do any last-minute adjustments."

"Wonderful. That should leave plenty of time, yes?" Dmitri asked before taking a big bite of his pizza.

"I think so." Margo gestured over her shoulder at the group of women gathered around the table. "I never could have done any of it without them."

"We edited the program this evening to include a thank you to all involved." Dmitri turned a few inches toward the stairs, eager to get away before Louise noticed him. "If that's all you needed, I have some more work to take care of downstairs." He handed her his plate. "Have Elise put another slice or two on here and bring it down to me."

"Wait." Margo held up a hand, signaling him to stop. She glanced around to make sure no one was listening. "With Blanche gone, I was wondering what was going to happen with the costume department."

"Are you asking if you're to be offered her job?" Dmitri asked with a smirk. He wasn't going to let her tiptoe around the issue. If Margo wanted the job, he wanted her to have the nerve to admit it.

She smiled, dropping the polite act. "So am I head seamstress or not?"

"How busy are you with school?"

"I can scale back my course load if I need to. This job would be my priority."

"Perfect. You start tomorrow. Simon and Sue will meet with you next week to discuss the particulars like salary and benefits."

Margo pumped her fist in the air. "Yes." She held up his plate. "More pizza coming right up."

Even though she'd worked twelve-hour shifts two days in a row, Margo scurried off with a bounce in her step. The new head seamstress was a little presumptuous, but Dmitri knew they'd work well together. Even if Sue hadn't been out of line, she wouldn't have lasted long. Dmitri would had been infuriated by her bullheadedness and undying allegiance to Lillian and likely would have fired her in favor for the spunky, pink-haired assistant.

Dmitri glanced over at the trifold mirror, remembering the uncomfortable moment when Cat, with tears in her beautiful green eyes, announced that she would retire after *The Nutcracker*'s run. His chest burned at the recent memory, and he hoped he could get her to change her mind. At this point, saving Cat's career was infinitely more important to him than trying to resurrect their romance. As difficult as he knew it would be, he would keep their relationship strictly professional if it meant the pint-sized dancer would continue to share her gift with the community. If everything went well with *The Nutcracker*, the Bretton Falls Ballet would be getting more attention and he wanted Cat to be at the center of it. If she chose to audition at ABT, he would be supportive of that decision as well. He just wouldn't contact anyone at the company on her behalf again.

Just then, surrounded by sparkly costumes and fluffy tutus, an idea struck him. He checked his watch. Seven-thirty. Simon would likely still be in his office. Dmitri turned to the stairs, nearly forgetting all about the pizza Elise would bring him and the ache in his heart over Cat's retirement.

"Mr. Fedorov," a woman called. "Please wait."

He turned to see Louise Brown rushing over, a friendly twinkle in her eye that would have put him at ease if he wasn't in a hurry to get downstairs and catch Simon before he left.

"Good evening, Louise." He dipped his head in greeting. "I don't mean to be rude but I'm in a hurry."

"Oh, I won't keep you." She flicked her wrist, waving off his concern. "I just wanted to wish you good luck." She grinned, pressing her hands to her cheeks. "I can't wait to see my girl out there."

"She'll be beautiful, Mrs. Brown. I'm sure of it."

Lisa Hahn

CHAPTER TWENTY-FOUR

Cat stood front and center on Bretton Falls Community Theatre stage, bursting at the seams with emotion. When life had gotten overwhelming the past few weeks, she would shut her eyes and imagine herself dancing a picture-perfect rendition of Clara—a performance to rival Gelsey Kirkland's infamous televised performance of the popular character. That night, the opening night of the show, Cat felt like she'd danced even better than she had in her daydreams. As soon as she stepped on the stage, something clicked inside her. Her nervousness dulled as she floated and skipped about the stage with pure joy in her heart. As the audience stood in honor of her performance, Cat felt a surge of pride. Nothing felt better than accomplishing a goal that did not come easily.

It didn't take long for sadness and regret to overshadow her triumph. There were a few more weeks of *Nutcracker* performances left, but after that, she'd never experience the feeling of being at center stage again. By the time the new year rolled around, Cat would be in Saratoga Springs, putting the finishing touches on her mom's new store.

The enjoyment she got from performing would never be enough to erase all the difficulties she faced back in the studio. She was head-over-heels in love with her controlling and demanding artistic director, and everyone there knew it. She couldn't enter a room without people staring and whispering about her indiscretions. Cat didn't want controversy marring her career. She would much rather bow out before her reputation was completely run into the ground. After all, her little sister was a dancer at the school and her mom owned a prominent business in town. She didn't want her poor decisions to affect them.

Auditioning at ABT wasn't an option, either. While Cat still wished Dmitri hadn't pushed so hard for her to try out, his insistence wasn't the main reason she wished to stay in Bretton Falls. She knew the challenges that would await her in the large, world-renowned company. There would be more dancers like Nick, Phoebe, and Marcy, waiting to break her spirit and spread rumors about her connection to the Fedorov family. The ballet community was small, and she had no doubt the dancers at ABT would hear about the affair by the time she arrived to audition.

Cat would miss Abby and her family when she left. The Brown women were close, and Cat didn't know how she would get along without their constant support. They all would call and visit often, but Cat also knew her the distance would affect treasured relationships.

In the end, Bretton Falls was her home and she didn't want to leave.

The applause revved up when Simon walked onto the stage, carrying a bouquet of two dozen red roses. Cat delicately wiped her tears away with her fingertips, forcing a smile as he approached.

"Hi, Simon." Her voice came out as a scratchy whisper. "Did I do you proud?"

He leaned in to kiss her cheek. "More than you'll ever know."

"Thank you for everything." She sniffled as she accepted the flowers. "I wouldn't be here if it wasn't for you."

"We both know that isn't true. You're a talented woman, Cat." He placed a hand on her shoulder and dropped his voice. "Stop by my office before you head out to the after party. I need to talk to you."

Cat's heart plummeted into her stomach like it was an eight-hundred-pound weight. She had a feeling she knew what he wanted to talk about. He had to be disappointed by the news of her retirement. Simon had been watching Cat dance since she was a little girl. Then he'd acted as her advocate for six years while Lillian seemed hell-bent on hiding her in the corps.

She nodded. "I will."

Simon kissed Cat's cheek one more time, wiggling his fingers and grinning toward the rest of her family. Elise, Grace, and Louise were front and center, standing and clapping just behind the orchestra. Tears streaked Louise's face. She'd put in long hours and invested a lot of money to ensure her daughter danced a lead role, and all her sacrifices had finally come to fruition.

Cat hadn't yet worked up the courage to talk to her mom about the job at the candy shop. She knew Louise never would have even considered offering her the position if she had known her daughter might be promoted or scouted by other companies. Louise would be disappointed to hear the news, especially once Cat's reasons for leaving the company were revealed. It would likely mark the first time in her life Cat had ever disappointed her mother, and she was not looking forward to facing that.

In a daze, Cat followed the other dancers as they exited the stage, avoiding the wing where Dmitri waited to shake hands with his dancers and congratulate them on a job well done. She hoped she could make it through the next few weeks without having to interact with him at all. Abby had promised to act as a buffer, stepping in and pulling Cat away from any situation that involved their director.

In fact, Abby lingered behind Dmitri as Cat approached, ready to provide a distraction if she needed to.

"Oh my god." Abby threw her arms out wide, ready to pounce on Cat with a great big hug. "You were amazing."

Cat smiled genuinely, a feat given her sour mood the past few days. "You were too. Best Arabian I've ever seen."

The two women hugged, Abby so exhilarated and excited, she swayed from side to side, moving Cat with her. "I'm so proud of you," she said, sadness causing her voice to quiver.

She pulled back, holding onto Abby's shoulders. "Don't cry."

Abby tried to blink back her tears, but she couldn't stop her big, blue eyes from welling up. "The thought of you retiring just makes me so sad."

Cat gave Abby's shoulders a reassuring squeeze. "It's for the best. You've seen how hard things have been for me around here."

"It could get better," said Abby, the eternal optimist.

"Maybe." Cat slung an arm around her much taller friend's waist as they started toward the locker room. "But there's still Dmitri. I don't think the two of us could ever work together again."

"I can't believe how messy everything got."

"I know." Cat leaned her head against Abby's shoulder, wishing her decisions didn't have to affect the people around her. "Me too."

The two women made their way into the locker room, where Cat got unexpectedly inundated with praise from other members of the company. The positive attention relieved her nerves and gave her hope that after everything blew over, her family's good reputation in the community would remain intact. As soon as her *Nutcracker* run ended, she'd disappear from the company and no one would remember any of the controversy she'd caused. Even though most of the dancers were congratulatory, Phoebe, Marcy, and Nick ignored Cat, turning their noses up as they walked by. She hadn't expected them to concede she had been a good choice for the role; to do so would damage their pride.

Once Cat had changed into her simple black A-line dress, she parted ways with Abby, promising to catch up with her at the party. She had to drive to the studio to see Simon first. Cat wasn't looking forward to the fatherly speech she knew he would give her on being able to take things in stride to achieve her goals. It was the same thing he'd said every year when Lillian's disapproval left Cat waiting in the wings while less-talented dancers took the stage. This time, though, circumstances were much different. Cat was sure the rumors about her and Dmitri must have reached Simon's ears, and the thought made her face flush. Up until this point, Cat had been nothing but professional at work. She knew Simon would be disappointed she'd thrown away her reputation for a chance to sleep with ballet's hottest bachelor.

Her affair with Dmitri had been far more complicated than everyone knew. It wasn't just about sex. She had genuine, all-consuming feelings for him that even now she had a difficult time suppressing. No one talked about that possibility, though. They preferred the tawdry stories that featured Cat as a villainess who slept with her boss to get ahead.

When she got to the studio, Cat found Simon's door ajar. She rapped lightly with her knuckles and pushed it open when Simon summoned her. He sat behind his desk, toiling at his computer. There was always heaps of work for him to do. He took every chance to knock items off his never-ending to-do list, even if that meant stopping off at the studio after a successful and gratifying opening night performance.

"Cat." He shoved his keyboard aside and turned to face her with an uncharacteristically stony expression. "Thank you for coming by."

"Sure." She walked into the room and sank into one of the chairs facing Simon's desk, feeling uncomfortable. It was likely the only time in her entire life she'd ever dreaded to talking to her mentor. Ballet was his life, and he knew it was hers, too. She knew he wouldn't let her quit without a fight. "What's up?"

"I need to talk to you about that little announcement you made about your impending retirement yesterday."

Cat slid forward in her seat, ready to defend her choice. "I know it seems impulsive, but I'm sure you've heard the rumors about me. Not all of them, but some of them are true, and—"

"I would like to offer you a soloist position within the company, effective immediately," Simon said as a cheeky smile tugged at his mouth and wrinkled the corners of his eyes.

Cat's hands flew up to cover her lips. "What?"

"There's more." Simon sat back in his chair and crossed his ankle over his knee, looking confident in his offer. "Your role as a performer will be limited to a few shows a year. We'd also like to bring you in as the new assistant seamstress. You'll divide your time between the two roles."

Cat jumped to her feet, too surprised to stay seated. Her heart pounded as a rush of different emotions flooded her brain. She'd been working toward a soloist position for years and finally achieving her goal made her heart sing with glee. However, she knew everyone would see the offer as the blatant nepotism it clearly was.

"Did Dmitri have anything to do with this?"

Simon dropped his gaze, seeming uncomfortable and understandably so. To him, Cat was still the little girl with the big dreams he'd met almost two decades ago, not a woman who would soil her reputation for a chance with a dance celebrity.

"It was his idea, but last night we decided I would have the final say in all staffing decisions. And I, for one, would love to have you on board in both capacities."

Cat began to pace the room, worrying her hands together as she walked. "But what will everyone say?"

"What does it matter what everyone says? You're a great dancer and a talented seamstress, Catherine. You proved that tonight when you graced the stage in that gorgeous dress. If people don't think you deserve this, then that's their problem." He leaned forward on his elbows and linked his fingers together. "People will always talk. The gossip about you just happens to be the crème de la crème right now. It will all blow over when there's another juicy story to gab about."

Cat shook her head, wearing out a path in the carpeted floor. "You don't know that."

"But I do." Simon sounded sure, completely at ease in opposition to Cat's all-encompassing anxiety. "These things always work out."

She stopped in front of his desk and settled back into the chair, her eyes soft with worry as they locked on his. "There's one more thing that scares me."

Reading the clear emotion in her expression, Simon sat up straighter. "What is it, Catherine? Let me help you."

"I don't think I can see Dmitri every day at work."

Instead of eyeing her with judgement or disgust, Simon regarded her with the unconditional love of a father. "Why? What happened between you two?" he asked in a warm voice that was laced with concern.

Cat hugged her arms around her waist, comforting herself as she prepared to put into words her shaky and unusual relationship with Dmitri. "He was nice to me. Much nicer than you'd expect, given his usual demeanor. He made me feel special." She shrugged, trying to downplay the effect Dmitri had on her. Just talking about him made her body heat up. "Then he got me an audition to ABT so we could be together and not worry about how our relationship might affect our work. He was practically shipping me off. And to make matters worse, I'd always know I didn't earn the audition."

"So, it's as bad as I thought." Simon sat back in his hair and ran a hand over the stubble on his chin. The little hairs served as proof of just how tired and worn-out the older man must have been. Simon only skipped a morning shave when work was hectic. "He's in love with you."

Cat froze, sure her heart had stopped beating. She'd considered that Dmitri might love her before, but always assumed it was wishful thinking. Simon was good at reading people. If he said Dmitri loved Cat, there was some merit to it. "I don't think—"

Simon held up a hand to stop her. "I've seen the way he looks at you. I noticed it the very first time I stepped foot in rehearsal, but I thought it ended there. I thought Dmitri would be smart enough not to get involved with one of his dancers, but I should have known from his reputation he wouldn't be able to restrain himself." He got up to walk around his desk and sat in the chair beside Cat. "What about you, Catherine? What were you thinking?"

Cat hung her head, feeling foolish. "I tried to stay away from him."

A ripple of laughter passed over Simon's lips. "There are a select few women in this world who are immune to the charms of Dmitri Fedorov. Unfortunately, you're not one of them." He covered Cat's hand with one of his, and the gesture instantly comforted her. Simon wasn't giving her a lecture. Instead, he'd offered her a job and his forgiveness for the mistakes she'd made. "We typically don't discuss your romantic exploits, but I think we're close enough for me to know you wouldn't risk you career for a chance to bed a notorious rake." A subtle smile crept up on his lips. "You love him too, don't you?"

Cat sighed, blowing out a heavy breath that ruffled tassels on her scarf. "I don't know. It doesn't matter. Things are over between us, anyway."

Simon raised an eyebrow, looking unsure. "Why do you think that?"

Cat glanced up at him through her eyelashes. "Well, I've been avoiding him."

"I know, sweetheart." Simon patted her hand with a playful glint in his eye. "Dmitri's had me checking in on you during rehearsals. I had to give him a full report on how you're faring every day. But why have you been ignoring him?"

"Well, he…" Cat let her voice trail off as she tried to figure out exactly why she'd been staying away from Dmitri. Everything had gotten so convoluted so quickly, she felt like her head was spinning. "He pushed for me to audition at ABT. He wanted to ship me out there without even asking me if it was what I wanted."

Simon's brow furrowed. "Isn't it what you want?"

"It is, or at least it was." Cat pursed her lips, wondering how to articulate what had made her so upset. "But I wanted to get there by myself. I wanted ABT to want me because I'm a good dancer, not because someone tried to convince them I'm a good dancer."

"From what I heard, you outshone almost everyone in the ABT class you took, including most of their company members." Simon pointed at her. "You did that all on your own. You got their attention." He sat back in his chair. "There's something else bothering you, isn't there?"

"I don't know if I really want to go to ABT. All my life, I looked forward to leaving Bretton Falls to join an internationally renowned ballet company. Now that I have the opportunity, I don't want to leave my family or Abby." She shrugged. "Life without them just wouldn't be the same, and leaving them isn't a sacrifice I think I want to make."

Simon nodded silently, letting her explanation sink in before he responded. "Those are valid concerns to have. Life in the big city without your family can be scary. Trust me. I've been there. But it could also be incredibly liberating to shed all of your earthly responsibilities and attachments so you can throw yourself into dance."

"Is that what it was like for you?"

"It was. And then when I was ready to retire, I found a small company in a quiet, woodsy town so I could get away from all the hoopla that goes on in the city." Simon glanced out his office window at the rows upon rows of trees behind the building and the moonlight filtering through them. "I prefer a quieter life."

Cat followed his gaze and smiled at the sight. She doubted the moon shone as brightly in the city. "I think I might too."

Simon playfully slapped her on the knee. "What about continuing your career here? With all the attention Dmitri's brought to the company and the contacts he has, we're sure to become more of a force in the American ballet scene. We could use a performer like yourself in our ranks."

Cat was conflicted. While she wanted to continue dancing, she didn't think she could face Dmitri daily. Even if the rumors died down and everyone turned their focus to the next scandal, she felt like they'd end up back where they started: hopelessly attracted to each other but unable to act on their irresistible feelings. It would be a disaster.

"Before you give me an answer, talk to Dmitri." Simon held up a palm when Cat parted her lips to protest. "Trust me. Talk to him and you'll feel better."

Cat nodded once. "I will. I promise."

"Good." Simon stood and opened his arms wide. "Now give me a hug and then head out to your party. You danced beautifully tonight, and you should celebrate."

"Are you coming?" Cat asked, stepping into Simon's fatherly embrace and pressing a cheek to his chest.

"I'll meet you there." Simon patted her back. "And try to have a good time. You deserve it."

"I will." Cat pulled away and forced a grin. She'd been confused before she'd met with Simon. Now that she'd heard his offer, she felt completely lost.

Simon motioned toward his computer. "I need to respond to a few quick emails. Media calls," he said in a sing-song voice.

Cat wiggled her fingers as she backed out his office door. "If you're more than twenty minutes late, my mom will panic and assume you're not coming because she did something to offend you."

Simon settled into his seat before stretching out his arms and wiggling his fingers to prepare to type. "Tell her I'll be there with bells on...as soon as I finish."

"I will." Cat shut the door and bit her bottom lip. *Holy hell.* She hadn't been expecting that to go the way it had. But before she could even begin to sort out how she felt about everything, she heard Dmitri speak from somewhere in the room.

"Did you take the offer?"

CHAPTER TWENTY-FIVE

Cat spun around at the sound of Dmitri's deep, velvety voice, searching the dark office space for his tall frame. It wasn't until he stepped out of the shadowy corner by the copy machine that she finally saw him. He wore the same black shirt and slacks he'd had on at the theatre, looking dapper despite his disheveled hair and beard. It looked like he'd been pulling his hand through the shoulder-length strands all evening, a habit Cat had noticed when something was bothering him.

"Well, did you take job?" he asked again.

Cat pulled her pea coat tight around her torso like it would offer her protection from Dmitri's allure. "I'm thinking about it."

"Fair enough." He jutted out his chin and nodded, looking like he wanted to say more to convince her but knew better than to try. "You were beautiful tonight."

"Thanks." Cat bit her bottom lip, stifling a grin. Even though she still harbored animosity toward Dmitri, she couldn't help but feel a flutter in her chest at his compliment.

He took a few steps farther into the light, still standing a good fifteen feet from Cat, and swept his arm toward his office. "Can we talk?" When Cat looked unsure, he added, "Briefly. I know your family and friends are waiting for you at the party."

"Umm, sure." Cat tentatively started toward Dmitri's office, the hair on her arms rising when she came within a few feet of him. His effect over her never ceased to amaze Cat. It was something she couldn't turn off, and it was exactly why she was afraid to stay at the company. How could she work with the man, when his mere presence heightened the sensitivity of every nerve ending in her body?

Dmitri's computer screen cast a blue glow over the room. Cat assumed he had squeezed a few quick emails into the space of time between the performance and the party, much like Simon had. The audience had been filled with local reporters and media outlets, as well as a few national dance publications and blogs, all eager to see how the great Dmitri Fedorov fared as an artistic director. Judging from the ovation at the end of the show, he'd exceeded expectations. Dmitri likely had journalists from all over clamoring to get a word with him.

When Dmitri shut his office door, Cat wasted no time starting the conversation. "Simon suggested I talk to you before I make up my mind about his offer."

"I think you should take it." Dmitri stayed beside the door, and Cat couldn't help but notice the distance he kept between them.

"It's a difficult decision." Feeling awkward, Cat clutched her hands near her waist, not sure what to do with her arms or how to stand. She wanted to give off the impression of being closed off, even though it seemed unnecessary. Dmitri could hardly meet her gaze.

"It's a once in a lifetime opportunity to pursue both of your passions," Dmitri argued, making it sound like the decision should have been an easy one. His ability to keep his opinions to himself was slowly fading, which irked Cat. Dmitri was an opinionated man, which was part of what made him such a talented artistic director, but it was also part of what made Cat wonder if he'd ever be good boyfriend material.

"I have a few options to consider."

"Bullshit," Dmitri snapped, looking up to meet her gaze. "Slinging chocolates in your mom's shop isn't an option. You're a dancer, goddammit. Not a cashier or a candy maker!"

"What I decide to do with my life is none of your business." Cat pointed a finger at Dmitri in an accusatory fashion. "And, frankly, you're the reason I don't want to work here anymore. But you probably already know that."

"Why?" Dmitri limped toward her, relying heavily on his cane. With *The Nutcracker* beginning and the mess in the costume room, Cat knew he must have been moving around more than usual and aggravating his injury. "Because I believe in you? Because I want the best for you in your career? Because I have the power to get you into positions that will allow you to showcase your talent?"

"Because you think you know what's best for me and you don't." Cat's voice rose as she stepped to meet Dmitri, her pulse racing at his closeness and from the rush of anger she felt at his defense.

"I do know what's best for you, and it's not working for your mom the rest of your life." Dmitri reached out to caress her cheek, stopping midway to ball his hand into a fist and drop it back to his side. It was a smart choice; Cat was prepared to smack his hand away. "You're a dancer, goddammit. You need to dance. I don't care where you do it."

"I can't dance here."

"Why not?" Dmitri asked. He gripped his cane so tightly his knuckles had turned white.

"You know why."

"Say it," Dmitri ordered, his voice smooth and commanding. "I want to hear you say it."

"I...I..." Cat struggled to find the courage to admit what she felt to a man she knew she could never have, not after what they'd already been though and the struggles they'd continue to face. She thought back to her conversation with Simon and his claim that Dmitri loved her. "Oh, hell." She shoved his chest, needing space, but Dmitri dropped his cane and caught both of her wrists in his hands to stop her. "I love you, dammit."

With his hold on her wrists, Dmitri pulled Cat's body into his. Their lips met, and before Cat had a chance to second-guess herself, she returned Dmitri's kiss. Their mouths moved together, conveying the depth of feeling they had for one another.

Dmitri broke away, releasing his hold on Cat and bringing his hands to cup her cheeks before resting his forehead against hers. "I love you, Catherine Brown. I love you more than I've ever loved anyone or anything."

She wrapped her fingers around his forearms, aware of how heavy her breathing was. For someone with cardiovascular capacity to dance a two-act ballet, she should have been surprised how Dmitri could steal her breath away. But she wasn't. Cat had known about the power Dmitri had over her for some time, only then she'd been trying to deny it. Now she knew there was no hope. She loved Dmitri so fiercely her feelings couldn't be ignored.

"How can this possibly work?" Her voice was scratchy, her throat tight with emotion.

Dmitri wrapped his arms around her shoulders. "With your responsibilities as assistant seamstress, you won't be able to dance in every ballet, at least not in a lead role. It will give plenty of other dancers the chance to prove their worth. And it will allow me the opportunity to cast my favorite dancer in whatever roles I think she would do well in, without having to worry about accusations of unfairness among the ranks."

"How can you be so sure?" Cat asked, her voice muffled by his closeness.

"Because I am." Dmitri rubbed soothing circles along her shoulder blades. "And I'm never wrong."

"Overwhelming arrogance aside, how can you be so sure things will work out?"

"Well, I hate to sound like an ass, since you just commented on my arrogance, but people respect me and they'll respect my choices. They have to. I'm the boss around here, and in less than two months I've done more for this company than Lillian had over the course of nearly three decades.

And I'd be a miserable son of a bitch to deal with if I had to see you every day and couldn't touch you." Dmitri leaned in and pressed another kiss to Cat's mouth, dragging his teeth over her bottom lip before pulling away. "Or kiss you. God, I missed kissing you."

"Do you remember what you said when you brought me back to your hotel room?"

Dmitri pressed his lips to the sensitive spot beneath Cat's ear, the one that always made her pulse race. "I don't remember anything I said until after we climbed in bed and committed to sharing a chaste evening together."

Cat glanced over her shoulder toward Dmitri's desk before returning her gaze to his with a mischievous glint in her eye. "You said that if people were going to talk, we might as well give them something to talk about."

A devilish smile spread across Dmitri's face, causing his eyes to wrinkle in the corners. "I'll have to add this very moment to the ever-expanding list of reasons why I love you."

He brought his mouth back to meet Cat's, kissing her with such fervor, her entire body ignited with heat. He dipped his tongue into her mouth, dragging it against hers. At the same time, he lowered his hands to her hips and steered her back toward his desk. When the backs of her thighs bumped the desk, Cat released her hold on Dmitri to hop up onto the cool, wood surface. She quickly wound her legs around his waist, pulling him in close. His hardness pressed against the apex of her legs. She hadn't expected him to become aroused so quickly. She writhed against him, turned on by the man himself as well as the effect she had on him. Though she couldn't be sure of the number, she knew Dmitri must have slept with dozens of women, and still there was something about her that made him go from zero to turned on in no time flat. Knowing that was intoxicating.

Dmitri kissed along her neck as his fingers danced beneath her dress, tickling her sensitive flesh as he searched for the waistband of her black tights. When he found it, he began to tug the tight material down. Cat had to hoist herself up so he could pull them down her hips. He stepped back to remove them from her feet, every touch of his fingers sending tiny bolts of electricity up her calves.

Once her tights were on the floor and Dmitri's lips were back on hers, Cat made quick work of his belt buckle. She left the leather strap hanging limply in its loops, not wanting to sacrifice the few seconds it would take to remove the belt completely. Instead, she unzipped his pants, shoved them down his narrow hips along with a pair of boxer briefs, and freed his erection. She could feel the heat coming off his member as it pressed against her stomach. Cat brought her hand down to stroke Dmitri, swallowing his moans as they kissed.

Cat's feelings had been oscillating for weeks as she tried to figure out what she wanted out of ballet, Dmitri, and life in general. Now, she knew. She wanted to take the job Simon had offered her. She wanted to be with Dmitri. And, right then, she wanted him inside of her with fiery intensity that made it feel like she might explode.

With her reassurance, Dmitri moved without hesitation. He hooked a finger in Cat's panties and tugged them aside before entering her in a single thrust. The motion jostled the desk, sending a plastic cup filled with pens tumbling to the floor. Neither of them noticed. Cat dug into Dmitri's shoulders, preparing herself for the deluge of pleasure she knew would soon overtake her. He shifted in smooth, measured strokes that made Cat see stars.

Dmitri maintained a steady rhythm, managing to change his pace exactly when Cat wanted him to. When she craved calm, tender lovemaking, Dmitri slowed as if he'd read her mind. When she wanted to be a bit wilder, Dmitri drove into her with the reckless abandon she'd ached for.

Before long, Cat felt her release blossom in the center of her being. Warm, luscious waves rolled over her body before a pleasantly overwhelming sensation of euphoria consumed her. She clenched Dmitri's shoulders so fiercely, patches of red began to bloom under her fingertips. His hot, panted breaths caressed her skin, driving her further into oblivion. Dmitri let out a deep, guttural grunt just as his body started to convulse. They came together, sealing the commitment they'd just made. In the face of adversity, Cat had chosen the more difficult road. She wanted to be with Dmitri, she wanted to be a soloist, she wanted to continue to design dancewear, and she was going to have all three, no matter what anyone else had to say about it.

Lisa Hahn

CHAPTER TWENTY-SIX

Cat's lips spread as she looked down to where Dmitri's hand rested on her thigh. A folksy song with a twangy acoustic guitar played quietly over the radio while the heating vents hummed with warm, expelled air. The Land of Sweets was less than a mile away, which meant Cat and Dmitri were mere minutes away from facing their fate as a couple. Cat thought it was a bold move to attend the party together, but Dmitri insisted it would be better for them to go public sooner rather than later. When Cat questioned the idea, Dmitri reminded her that he was older, wiser, and more adept at company politics than she was. Turned on as always by his cocky stubbornness, Cat decided to oblige him. Plus, she couldn't deny how much she wanted to spend time by his side rather than steal glances at him from across the room.

"Are you sure you want to do this?" Cat asked as they pulled into an empty space across the street from the shop.

Dmitri squeezed her hand reassuringly. "I want everyone to know that you're mine."

"What if they riot or something?" Cat worried her bottom lip between her teeth. "You're doing so well as director. I don't want you to lose your job."

"I won't." Dmitri released her hand so he could cut the engine. He unbuckled his seat belt and ran his knuckles across her cheek. "Everything is going to be fine. They'll respect our honesty."

"Okay." Cat released a heavy breath, gently nuzzling his hand, before reaching for the door handle. "Let's do this."

She met Dmitri by the trunk of the car, taking the hand he extended to her while he used the other to hold his cane. Together, they crossed the street.

"I noticed earlier that your limp is more pronounced today," Cat observed, trying to keep any trace of concern from seeping into her voice. She knew Dmitri preferred that those around him ignore his injury.

"It's been a busy few days." He flashed her a secret smile: warm and kind and designed just for her. Cat suspected there were few other people in Bretton Falls that elicited obvious happiness from him. "I'm better now, anyway."

Cat blew him a kiss and his grin grew wider. "Glad I could help."

They stopped in front of the door, and Cat straightened her shoulders in hopes she would portray an air of confidence. If she went into the room worried about what would happen, she knew vultures like Marcy and Nick would pounce on her.

"Ready?" Dmitri asked.

Through the glass storefront, Cat saw her family, friends, and colleagues mingling amid a buffet of food. White twinkle lights wrapped around the silvery garland lining the top of every display case, and a Christmas tree occupied one corner. A sign sitting beside it asked people to donate toys for underprivileged children in the area. Though it was still only November, over a dozen wrapped gifts already sat under the fake Douglas Fir Louise put up every year. As Cat observed the scene, she caught her mother's eye through the sea of party guests. A wide, proud grin spread Louise's face as she put down the tray she had been holding and excitedly waved her daughter in.

Cat reached forward and pulled open the door. "I'm ready."

The tune of "Jingle Bells" met the newly anointed couple as they entered the party. Upon seeing them, many of the guests began to applaud their director and the star of their show. The applause, however, died as the crowd noticed Cat and Dmitri's joined hands. Hushed whispers poorly concealed behind cupped hands replaced the sound of clapping.

A rush of nervousness flooded Cat's body. She looked to her mom, only to see her happy expression had vanished. She looked to Dmitri, ready to retreat to his car and berate him for his fruitless reassurance. She was surprised to find him looking totally relaxed, wearing a look of comfortable ease he almost never showed at work.

He signaled to Elise in the corner, who was begrudgingly playing DJ for the evening. "Cut the music, kiddo."

With a nod, Elise shut off the cheery song. The awkward silence that remained nearly sent a shiver down Cat's back. Dmitri waited a few beats before speaking, leaving everyone in the room wondering what he would say.

"First, I would like to congratulate everyone on a wonderful show these evening. We have about a dozen or so performances of *The Nutcracker* left, and I'm confidant each will be as wonderfully produced and performed as the one today." Tentatively, the attendees clapped, exchanging curious glances with those around them. "Looking past *The Nutcracker*, I have a lot of big plans for us. I'm hoping to expand our performance schedule, which will hopefully lead to an expansion of the entire company. To ensure everything runs smoothly going forward, I want to be up front about something." Dmitri looked to Cat with smiling eyes. He looked so serene, so sure of himself, she felt her own lips turn upward. "Catherine Brown and I are in a relationship. I know some of you may worry about things like favoritism and nepotism creeping into the picture, but I want you to rest assured that will not be a problem. I think after tonight's performance, we can all agree that Catherine deserves whatever roles she might land." Louise and Simon led a more rousing round of applause and everyone joined in, a few dancers in the crowd nodding their heads in understanding. "However, this evening, Simon offered Cat a new position within the company. She's been promoted to a soloist role, and she'll also be pitching in at the costume department. There will still be plenty of work to go around, and I hope that you all trust that I will not fail you. I take my role as artistic director of this company very seriously, and I will work tirelessly to ensure we all achieve the highest levels of success."

From the back corner of the room, Simon raised the clear, plastic cup holding his red wine. "To Dmitri and Cat."

Much to Cat's surprise, everyone in the room raised their cups and repeated the phrase. Elise flipped the music back on, and "Rockin' Around the Christmas Tree" replaced any uncomfortable silence that might have lingered what Dmitri had said. The party guests resumed dancing, chatting, eating, and drinking, like they hadn't just heard a shocking announcement. Cat considered whether her relationship with Dmitri was old news. The rumors had been circulating for so long, everyone probably assumed they were together.

Dmitri pressed a kiss to her forehead. "That went well."

Cat nodded. "I think even Marcy, Phoebe, and Nick raised their glasses to us."

Dmitri barked out a laugh and looked in their direction. As soon as Nick caught his boss's eye, he waved overenthusiastically and flashed a cheesy grin.

"Those three are kiss-asses. They'd applaud and support anything that kept them cemented in their positions as principal dancers. They won't push back again until they think our relationship is a threat to them."

Cat's heart sank. "So I'll still have to deal with their crap in the locker room?"

"If they say a word to you about this, let me know. I'll make it perfectly clear disrespecting and spreading rumors about any company member will not be tolerated. Also, I may leave you off the cast of our next production. It will allow you an opportunity to learn your way around the costume department, and it will give everyone else a chance to focus on whatever scandal is coming up the pike next."

Cat pressed into Dmitri's shoulder in a thankful half-hug. "You've thought of everything."

Dmitri caught her chin with a finger and lifted her gaze to meet his. "Having you means the world to me. There's no way I wouldn't have planned everything out so that we could enjoy each other without dealing with the detractors."

Though she wore heels, Cat was still quite a bit shorter than Dmitri. Now that she and Dmitri could finally indulge their desires, she began to press up unto her toes, spurred on by her boyfriend's very kissable lips, when her mother's voice deterred her from pursuing a very public display of affection.

"Well, if it isn't the happy couple." Louise, dressed in a red sweater set and black slacks, held a plastic cup filled with wine in each hand. Her eyes sparkled with unshed tears of happiness as she passed off both cups to Dmitri. "Do you mind holding these for a sec? I need to hug my daughter."

Dmitri obliged and Louise threw her arms around Cat. "I'm so proud of you, honey," she cooed against Cat's upswept hair. "On all accounts. On your performance, your promotion, and your new relationship." She wagged a finger at Dmitri, keeping Cat wrapped up with one arm. "You better be good to my girl."

Dmitri gave her a single nod. "I promise to treat her like a queen."

Cat pulled away, pursing her lips and offering her mom a sympathetic look. "I'm sorry that my promotion at the company means you'll need to find a manager for your new shop after all."

Louise waved off her daughter's concern with a flick of her wrist. "Please! Don't you worry your pretty little head about it." She cupped Cat's face in her hands. "You and I, we're both living our dreams and getting everything we've worked so hard for." She tipped her chin toward the cups in Dmitri's hands. "That's cause for celebration, not an apology."

Cat accepted the wine from Dmitri and took a tiny sip. She didn't drink often and knew the alcohol would go right to her head if she downed the tart, woodsy nectar too quickly. Her mom was right, though: it was a time for celebration. Not only had Cat finally gotten the promotion she'd been working her tail off for, but she'd also picked up an impossibly hot boyfriend and a position in the costume department that would allow her to further explore her creativity. Life was sweet, and she was thankful.

Dmitri flagged down a server, who handed Louise a cup of wine. "To Catherine's new position and Louise's new store," he said, raising his own beverage.

As soon as the small group brought their glasses to their lips, Constance and Ivan Fedorov appeared from among the other party guests.

"I guess this means ABT can't count on either Dmitri or Catherine joining us next season," Constance remarked, crossing her arms over her chest and looking miffed by the announcement she'd undoubtedly heard her son make.

Lisa Hahn

CHAPTER TWENTY-SEVEN

Dmitri sputtered at the unexpected sound of his mother's voice, sending a few rogue droplets of wine trickling into his beard. "Mom. Dad. I didn't expect to see you here for a couple of weeks." He ran a hand through his hair, fighting to keep his composure in front of his dancers and staff. He'd been sure the difficult part of his evening had passed once he'd convinced Cat to give him and the company a second chance. Now, however, anger bubbled up in the pit of his stomach at the thought of having to face his parents' disappointment.

Dmitri felt instant relief when his mother's cold stare was replaced with a radiant expression of pride. She opened her arms wide and wrapped Dmitri up in a tight hug.

"I'm so proud of you, son. We wouldn't have missed your debut for anything."

With a cane in one hand and a nearly full cup of wine in the other, Dmitri could only kiss his mother's cheek as she squeezed him so tightly it became difficult to breathe. Ivan merely patted his son on the shoulder, in his typical non-affectionate parenting style, and muttered congratulations in his muted Russian accent.

"How lovely." Louise, her cheeks pink from wine, beamed at the scene before her. "As parents, we have a lot to be proud of, don't we?"

Constance released her hold on Dmitri and turned to Louise, a warm look of happiness softening the harsher features of her too-thin face. "You must be Catherine's mother. She's a lovely dancer. As a member of the ballet community, I feel I should thank you for allowing her to pursue her dreams."

Louise handed her wine off to Cat and hugged Constance, who accepted the familiar sign of affection without hesitation. "Call me Louise. We're practically family now."

"Yes, we are," Constance replied. "Honestly, I've never seen Dmitri so smitten before."

Louise pulled away and winked at Cat. "You should have seen the way Cat got all starry-eyed every time she talked about Dmitri. She never mentioned having feelings for him, but a mother always knows."

Dmitri glanced at his girlfriend, noticing red patches blooming on her cheeks. He leaned over and pressed a kiss to her temple, hoping to ease her embarrassment.

"That she does." Constance pressed a hand to Ivan's chest. "Ivan, here, was the one who figured it out. He's a man of few words, but his observations are typically spot-on."

Constance and Louise continued to get acquainted, chatting about ballet and the achievements of their children, getting on like old friends. Ivan stood idly by, stone-faced, interjecting a word or two when one of the women addressed him directly.

Curling his fingers around the soft skin at the nape of her neck, Dmitri pulled Cat close to whisper in her ear. "We should sneak away before we have to listen to them plan our wedding."

Cat giggled into her hand, peeking through her eyelashes to make sure she didn't garner any attention from their parents. When it seemed like the coast was clear, Dmitri and Cat began to take slow, measured steps backward until they bumped into the dancers standing behind them. Dmitri muttered a quick "excuse us," interrupting the two newly appointed corps members as they apologized profusely for being in his way. He noticed the way their eyes flickered toward Cat, sizing her up like she was the standard they'd be judged by as dancers. A feeling of satisfaction flickered in Dmitri's chest, knowing deep down inside that Cat wouldn't face nearly as much animosity from the other company members now that they'd gone public with their relationship. If anything, acting as if they had something to hide would have aroused everyone's suspicion about Cat's rightful place in the company. There would still be people who would view their relationship with a negative slant, but he knew that Cat's immense talent, both as a dancer and a seamstress, would eventually silence them all.

Wanting Cat all to himself, he pulled her into the corner with the Christmas tree, partially concealing them behind it. He clutched her shoulders, pulled her body into his, and rested his chin atop her head.

"I assume you'd like to socialize with your friends for a bit," he said with a regretful sigh.

Over his shoulder, Dmitri saw Margo and Abby laughing together. A plate of appetizers sat on the table between them, and each woman nibbled on the catered fare. Cat hadn't spoken to either of her friends since she'd accepted her new position within the company, and he imagined both wanted to congratulate her.

Much to his surprise, Cat burrowed her head into his chest and murmured, "I'd much rather disappear somewhere with you."

Her fingers curled into the back of Dmitri's shirt, and he felt the crotch of his pants strain. As appealing as disappearing for the evening sounded, Dmitri knew he would lose the favor of her family and friends if they left the party so early.

"Let's mingle for an hour, and then I'm taking you back to my place," he whispered against her forehead before pressing a chaste kiss to her warm skin. "Deal?"

"Deal," she agreed with a hint of disappointment in her voice.

Dmitri spent the next hour circulating around the room, talking politely with all his underlings and occasionally stealing glances to where Cat sat with her friends. Every so often he'd catch her eye, and the two would exchange a knowing look. They'd contained themselves for the sake of the partygoers, but they wouldn't be able to keep their hands off each other once they were back at Dmitri's apartment.

Cat still sat with her friends after an hour had passed. Undeterred by the sea of people separating them, Dmitri traversed through the crowd, aware everyone would make way for their fearless leader. Within seconds, he hovered over their table, his pulse rapidly ticking.

"Catherine." He held out a hand to help her out of her seat. "We should be going."

He knew he was being rude, but this was the best he could manage. Now that he finally had Cat, it was impossible to stand across the room from her as if she didn't exist. Abby and Margo should have considered themselves lucky he didn't just scoop Cat up and haul her over his shoulder.

"Hi, Dmitri." Margo waved, flashing a grin. There was no way she was going to let him ignore her. "Remember me? I'm the seamstress that basically saved your ass this show."

"Good evening, Margo." He nodded to the blonde across the table from her. "Good evening, Abby. If you both don't mind, I'll be taking Cat from you."

"Take her." Margo playfully slapped her friend on the ass. "And have fun, you two."

Abby's face turned the color of a tomato, making her look every bit like the immature girl Lillian had accused her of being. She was, however, an immensely talented dancer, so Dmitri was determined to find a way to use her youthful exuberance and appearance to the company's benefit.

At Margo's teasing, Cat merely rolled her eyes. "I'll talk to you guys later."

After making their final rounds and wishing their families a good night, the couple slipped out unnoticed by the rest of the guests. The sounds of holiday music and celebratory mirth faded behind them as they crossed the street and approached Dmitri's car, hand in hand. For the first time since his accident, Dmitri felt light, like he'd finally been unburdened by all the animosity he'd been carrying around. While he might not ever take the stage again, he had found Cat and she made him even happier than ballet ever had.

They stopped beside the passenger side door of the car, an illuminated streetlight humming overhead. Dmitri rested his hands on Cat's shoulders while she clasped hers at the small of his back.

"You know what the main difference between Clara and me is?" she asked, with a playful lilt in her voice.

Dmitri ran the backs of his fingers along Cat's cheek, savoring the warmth of her skin. "She's fictional and you're not."

"No." Cat batted his hand away with a chuckle. "Clara only gets to enjoy her prince and visit the Land of Sweets in her dreams. I get to enjoy the dancing, the candy, and my prince in real life."

Dmitri touched his lips to hers, knowing that of all the roles he'd held—world-renowned dancer, notorious womanizer, up-and-coming artistic director—being Catherine Brown's boyfriend would be the one he cherished most.

Coming in Fall/Winter of 2017

Cinders

The second installment of The Bretton Falls Ballet series

To find out more about Lisa Hahn and her upcoming releases visit
www.bylisahahn.com

Lisa Hahn

Believe in Me

An excerpt from the contemporary romance novella by Lisa Hahn

CHAPTER ONE

"Damnit." I clenched my hands into fists as several snack bags fell to my feet. I'd just backed into a wire display stuffed with pretzels and sesame sticks while trying to load a tray of ready-to-go hummus wraps into a refrigerator case. Knocking the bags down wouldn't have seemed like a big deal if it hadn't already been such a shitty morning. I'd screwed up the first batch of hummus when I'd forgotten to add the tahini, and I'd sliced open my pointer finger when I was cutting the wraps in half.

And I'd only been at the store for half an hour.

With a heavy exhale, I placed the tray on the deli counter before getting to my knees and collecting the snack bags.

I was mumbling and cursing to myself about my terrible luck when a male voice said, "Here, let me help you."

I gathered a few of the fallen items without bothering to look up. "Oh, I've got it."

A stranger knelt beside me, our fingers brushing as we grabbed for the same bag of pretzels. He stared at me with wide, round eyes. Flecks of gold and green accented the blue orbs, adding to their allure. They were nestled amid his creamy, flawless skin and complemented by a narrow nose and full, totally kissable lips. His blue plaid shirt and khaki pants vaguely concealed what appeared to be a toned and trim physique.

In short, he was drop-dead gorgeous.

And I was openly gawking at him.

"I insist." The corners of his mouth curled up to reveal perfectly white, perfectly straight teeth.

If I wasn't dressed like a total slob and wearing absolutely no makeup, I would have thought my luck had turned around the second this handsome and helpful stranger's fingers touched mine, sending a jolt of electricity up my arm.

But I wasn't interested in dating.

I shrugged, playing it off like I was totally unaffected by him. "If you insist."

"I do." He scooped up the bag and tucked it into the nook of his muscular yet slender arm.

"Well, thanks. I appreciate it." Reaching to pick up some pretzels, I caught a glimpse of myself in the deli case. My waist-length, dirty blond hair was swept into a messy bun, and I had dark circles under my eyes. I'd woken up late and hadn't had time to apply the scant amount of makeup I usually wore.

My gaze shifted back to the stranger, and I found myself wishing I'd dedicated more than two minutes to getting ready that morning.

He inhaled sharply through his nose, drawing my attention back to the situation at hand. I picked up a bag.

"What's in those wraps you were putting out? They smell delicious."

The warmth in his voice sent a shiver down my spine.

"Hummus, tomato, alfalfa sprouts, roasted zucchini, and bell pepper." I rattled off the list of ingredients I'd just stuffed inside a few minutes before, careful not to let my gaze wander back to his as I snatched up a few sesame stick bags.

He stood and piled the bags onto the shelf. "Did you make them?" He looked down at me with a raised eyebrow, his hand paused in mid-air as a bag of pretzels dangled from his fingertips.

He looked at me with untamed interest, like he wanted me and he wasn't afraid to let me know it.

Franklin was a small town, and it definitely had a shortage of attractive men. He was the best-looking guy to hit this town since…him.

"Um, yeah." I knew I sounded like an idiot. My mind was scattered.

He flashed me another sigh-inducing smile. "Then I know what I'll be having for lunch today."

I grabbed the last of the fallen snack bags and tried to focus on my breathing instead of whatever was happening between the two of us.

I had to get back into the kitchen, pronto. If I stayed out here any longer, I'd do something I didn't want to do. I had to curtly thank him for his help, tell him to enjoy his lunch, and then scurry back into the kitchen. I'd put the rest of the wraps away after he paid for his food and left.

I didn't like being a bitch. My mom had raised me and my sister to be kind and friendly to everybody.

But before I could put my plan into action, he'd extended his hand to me. "Here, let me help you up."

When I placed my palm in his, I experienced the same rush of electricity that had invigorated my body the last time my skin grazed his. He hauled me up with so much force my chest crashed against his. Without hesitation, he leaned down and planted his lips on mine. For a split second, I thought about pulling away. But I couldn't even if I wanted to. His firm body pressed against mine, confirming he was built like an athlete underneath his polished and professional outfit. His tongue gently coaxed my mouth open before it swept over mine. He tasted minty and sweet.

My knees felt weak. If he didn't have a strong arm wrapped tightly around my waist, I would have melted to the floor like a snowman on a hot day. I clawed at his shirt, pulling him even closer.

I broke the kiss when the sound of my sister's voice brought me back to my senses.

"Sorry, sorry, sorry," Fawn announced loudly as she burst into the store through the kitchen door in a rush of pale blond hair and gangly limbs. "I was on the phone taking down a catering order. No one came in while I was in the back, did they?" She dashed behind the cash register.

"Um, no." Grabbing the stranger by the wrist, I unwound his arm from my waist. "Well, someone did." I glanced over at him out of the corner of my eye, very aware of the heat in my cheeks.

The sexy bastard looked amused.

For the first time since she'd rushed into the store, Fawn looked over at me. "Did I," she paused, her eyes widening with excitement as she took in my flushed cheeks, guilty expression, and close proximity to an absurdly handsome stranger, "did I interrupt something?"

"No." I turned quickly and grabbed the wraps so I could load them into the refrigerator case.

"She was helping me pick something out for lunch." His hand fell to my shoulder, and my skin instantly heated in the spot where he touched me. "I just moved to Franklin from New York City, and as soon as my colleagues found out that I'm a vegetarian, they told me I had to grab lunch from your deli counter."

"Oh." A bemused smile flashed across Fawn's face as she leaned her elbows on the counter and rested her chin on her hands, eyeing him curiously. "And where do you work?"

"Ogden College."

"Are you a professor?" The interest in her voice piqued.

He nodded. "I teach Early American History classes."

Fawn winked at me as the cute professor swiveled around to grab a pricey Kombucha tea. "So, like the colonies and stuff?"

I shot Fawn a look, silently pleading with her to stop asking him questions. She shook her head and smiled mischievously.

Fawn was going to play matchmaker whether I wanted her to or not.

She and my mom were always trying to fix me up with someone. It would have been dreadfully annoying if they weren't trying to do what they thought was best for me.

I picked up a wrap and shoved it at the professor before he had a chance to answer. "Here. You said you wanted one, right?"

"I did." He took it from me and grinned as if he were completely oblivious to my bitchiness. "Thank you."

Out of the corner of my eye, I spotted Fawn glaring at me, her cute freckled nose all bunched up. Determined to ignore both of them, I turned around and continued piling the wraps into the case.

"I'm Fawn, Fern's sister. What's your name?"

She obviously wasn't going to give up. It took every ounce of restraint I had not to lob a wrap at her.

"Adam. Adam Price. It must be nice that you and your sister get to work together."

"It's actually our store. We run it with our mom." Of course Fawn gave Adam more information than I wanted him to have. I shot her another disapproving look over my shoulder as I headed behind the deli counter with the empty tray, and she intentionally ignored me. "Fern actually runs this place, for the most part. She went to school for business."

"Is that so?" Adam looked over at me. I could have slipped into the back, but I wanted to make sure Fawn didn't say anything too embarrassing.

I'd dropped out of college one semester shy of getting my bachelor's degree, and the three of us ran the shop together. I hated having to explain the situation.

"Yep," I answered dismissively, suddenly aware of the droplets of sweat running down my back.

"Well." Adam dug into his back pocket and pulled out his wallet, drawing my attention to his nicely sculpted rear. "If this wrap tastes as good as it smells, I will definitely be seeing you ladies again."

Fawn took the money he handed her. "We'd both like that."

"It was nice meeting you, Fawn." Adam grabbed his lunch and turned to face me. "And it was nice meeting you, Fern. I look forward to seeing you again." His eyes narrowed on mine, conveying the promise in his words.

I waved, feeling a slight tug on my heart as he walked away, secretly wishing I would see him again soon—if only for the chance to feel his soft lips on mine, just one more time.

"Bye, Professor Adam." Fawn waved as he passed by her on his way to the door.

As soon as it shut behind him, Fawn slapped her hands down on the counter. "Fern, he was cute! And I know that you're into him. Why did you have to be such a bitch?"

I shrugged, opening up the display case to rearrange a plate of vegan brownies. I didn't think Fawn had seen us kissing, and I was glad for it. Then I wouldn't be able to get her off my case. "Because I'm not into him and I wanted him to go."

She threw her hands up in frustration. "You're such a liar!"

"Am not," I argued, slamming the display case closed. "You know that I'm not interested in dating."

She pointed an accusatory finger at me. "You say that, but I saw the way you were looking at Adam when I came in. You're so into him and you know it."

I opened my mouth to make my rebuttal, but I restrained myself when I heard the storefront door chime.

Fawn and I glowered at each other, both of us silently warning the other this was not the end of the argument.

www.ingramcontent.com/pod-product-compliance
Lightning Source LLC
Chambersburg PA
CBHW060422130626
46555CB00005B/2174